W9-CES-378

ALL WILL BE REVEALED

a novel by

ROBERT ANTHONY SIEGEL

ALL WILL BE REVEALED

a novel by

ROBERT ANTHONY SIEGEL

MACADAM CAGE

NEW HANOVER COUNTY
PUBLIC LIBRARY
201 CHESTNUT STREET
WILMINGTON, NC 28401

MacAdam Cage

155 Sansome Street, Suite 550

San Francisco, CA 94104

www.macadamcage.com

Copyright © Robert Anthony Siegel 2007

ALL RIGHTS RESERVED

Library of Congress Cataloging-in-Publication Data

Siegel, Robert Anthony.

  All will be revealed / by Robert Anthony Siegel.

    p. cm.

  ISBN 13: 978-1-59692-205-1 ISBN 10: 1-59692-205-2 (hardcover : alk. paper)

  1. Photographers–Fiction. 2. Pornography–Fiction.

3. Millionaires–Fiction. 4. Women mediums–Fiction. 5. New York

(N.Y.)–Social life and customs–19th century–Fiction. I. Title.

PS3569.I3822A45 2007

813'.54–dc22

                                        2006103267

Book and jacket design by Dorothy Carico Smith.

Printed in the United States of America.

1 2 3 4 5 6 7 8 9 0

Publisher's Note: This is a work of fiction. Names, characters, places, and incidents either are the product of the author's imagination or are used fictitiously. Any resemblance to actual events, locales, or persons, living or dead, is entirely coincidental.

For my wife, Karen, and my father, Stanley:
may his name be inscribed in the Book of Life

For me the noise of Time is not sad: I love bells, clocks, watches—and I recall that, at first, photographic implements were related to the techniques of cabinetmaking and the machinery of precision: cameras, in short, were clocks for seeing....

— Roland Barthes, *Camera Lucida*

PROLOGUE

Verena Swann sat beside her brother-in-law, Leopold Swann, writing with a pencil in a large leather notebook. Head to one side, eyes half-closed, she watched her hand move across the page, leaving behind line after line of small jagged letters—the nearly illegible scrawl of her late husband, Captain Theodore Swann. She had no idea what it said; the deciphering was for later, after the rush of words. All she could think of right now was the pressure on the back of her neck, the tingling in her arm, the motion of her hand. All that mattered was the indescribable feeling of being borrowed, a sensation as strange as her first intimate kiss.

She reached the bottom and Leopold turned the page for her.

At that very moment, Augustus Auerbach guided his wheelchair into the photographic studio behind his Fifth Avenue mansion. As big as a warehouse and built entirely of glass, the studio felt less like a building than a porthole for viewing the sky. Auerbach glanced up at the clouds, then wheeled himself across the floor to the bed at the center. As he did so, his two photographic models removed their dressing gowns and stretched themselves naked on the sheets. His assistant took up position behind the camera.

"Let us begin with a kiss," said Auerbach, and watched as the models fit themselves together like the two halves of a broken cup. None of them could know that a dozen photographs later, despite careful precautions, an accident would occur: a child would be conceived.

Auerbach put his hand to his chin. "A little more passion, please."

Thousands of miles away, a group of men on dogsleds stopped before a canvas tent half-buried in snow. For weeks they had traveled the vast ice plain in search of that tent, till the size of the land and its utter emptiness shrank them to nothing. They had become like ants crawling over the surface of a mirror. Now the sky seemed made of ice, the ice around them made of sky. The sun burned beneath their feet.

One of them dismounted and walked over to the tent, then parted the flaps and crawled inside. After removing his glacier glasses he could make out a footlocker, a backpack, a pair of boots set in a corner, and a snowsuit laid out as if to dry. Eventually, he forced himself to look at the corpse lying on top of the sleeping bag, naked: the earthly remains of Captain Theodore Swann, missing three years and presumed lost.

At the table in her parlor, Mrs. Swann watched her hand move across the page:

You see, my dear, there is nothing other than this turning, round and round again. Everything is connected to everything else, everything moves in a great wheel, and the emptiness at the center is God.

1. THE POWER OF INDUSTRY

A ugustus Auerbach's bedroom was on the other end of the mansion, a full city block from the guest wing, and so he heard nothing of the disturbance he knew must be taking place there. It was Police Inspector Wolfscheim's job to adjudicate any disputes and have the members of the Clean Living League out the back door before dawn, where carriages were waiting to take them away.

Nevertheless, Auerbach could not sleep. He kept brooding on the image of Seton Bittersley, editor in chief of the *World Dispatch Leader* and League president, parading around in petticoats stolen from one of the photographic models. He saw the Reverend Voorhees standing on the table, spraying Judge Montcrief from above with a bottle of champagne, and the judge staggering backward into a pedestal holding a bust of Joseph Niépce, which then broke into pieces on the marble floor.

Auerbach pulled the mink coverlet to his chin. Was it not enough that they invaded his home each month to smash his crystal, steal his silver, and waste his time with stories about dog fighting and bear baiting? They had insulted the founder of photography, a tragic genius forced by old age and infirmity to pass his life's work to the ungrateful, unscrupulous Daguerre—Daguerre, who added a few minor improvements and then stole all the credit.

"Look at them," he had said to Inspector Wolfscheim, who sat beside him at the far end of the table. "Do they act like this in their own homes?"

The inspector had given a sympathetic sigh. He was League secretary, but his only real vice seemed to be a penchant for violence—which was almost forgivable, as it was also a condition of his employment. "You're a good sport, Mr. Auerbach."

"It's not as if I have a choice."

"Nevertheless, not everyone would be so good-natured about it."

Auerbach had taken a sip of tea, and then a bite of toast—all he ever ate on these occasions. "Don't fool yourself, Inspector. I see the way they look at me."

"Pay them no mind, Mr. Auerbach."

"Oh, I don't, not a bit. A hundred years from now, they will all be forgotten, and I will be the one who is remembered, as the man who revolutionized an industry."

The inspector had lifted his glass in a little toast. "And made his friends rich in the process."

"Well then," Auerbach had said, raising his teacup in response, "we might as well get on with it." He began clinking a spoon against his plate for quiet. "Gentlemen! Please! Your attention! I know you are all eager to move on to the next entertainment." Bittersley stopped prancing; the judge looked up from the floor. As usual, they would be following the models to the guest wing. "But before you do, I would like to make a small contribution to your worthy organization." He had removed an envelope from his pocket and handed it to Inspector Wolfscheim: the monthly payment.

Oh, how they had loved him then, throwing their champagne glasses in the fireplace and shouting a tuneless round of "For He's a Jolly Good Fellow." But Auerbach knew that if he ever missed a payment, they would attack like pit dogs: the Reverend Voorhees would preach from the pulpit, Bittersley would write an editorial, his good friend Inspector Wolfscheim would lead the police raid, and Montcrief would give him the maximum sentence.

Auerbach turned over the pillow and assumed a new position. When he was just a boy and had trouble falling asleep, his mother would sit beside his bed, singing to him. She was an actress in the musical theater—much sought after at the time, though forgotten now—and had a voice of strange and subtle beauty, like the flicker of streetlamps on a winter's evening. As she sang, she would run her long fingers over his forehead, slowly circling his face, then his chest, around and around as the thoughts emptied from his head, and her sweet, heavy perfume filled his breathing.

By now, his memory of her had been worn smooth as sea glass, free of everything but the essentials: a silhouette in the candlelight, a voice that was hardly more than a whisper. He had tried many times to recapture the words of the song, the feel of her fingers, their near-magical, soothing power, but after decades of failure had finally given up—and had adopted the position that insomnia was a blessing in disguise. A vast business enterprise depended on his vigilance, and there was always more to do: contracts to sign, invoices to review, letters to compose. So on nights like this, he simply climbed into his wheelchair, placed the lap rug over his legs, then wheeled himself to his office down the hall. Once there, he rang the buzzer for Miss Parish, the live-in typewriter. He timed a minute by the clock on his desk, then rang again, timed another minute, then simply leaned on the buzzer till she appeared in a bathrobe, wild-eyed.

"I'm so sorry, did I wake you?" he asked, taking his finger from the buzzer. "I apologize." The clock on his desk said two thirty-nine.

"Sorry, Mr. A. I got here as soon as I could."

He was too relieved to criticize. The clack of the typewriting machine would soon begin: the wonderful music of productivity, forming line after line of perfect little letters—his official correspondence. He reached into the box on his desk for a cigar. "Julius Caesar slept only three hours a night, Miss Parish." He snipped the cigar end with a pair of golden shears. "They say Napoleon didn't sleep at all."

"He must have had the gentlemen from the League in residence," said Miss Parish, who then took her seat at the little desk beside his, where sat the gigantic typewriting machine. She fed in a sheet of paper and put her fingers on the keys. "Ready, sir."

The letter from his Indian distributor was at the top of a large pile of correspondence. He gave it a quick look and began to dictate. "Ahem. Dear Mr. Gupta, I stand in receipt of your last, dated February 20, 1896."

There it was: the snap-snap-snap of the typewriting machine. He felt his shoulders relax, his chest expand. The clatter of the keys brought him back to himself, reminding him of his role in the world as president and sole proprietor of Rive Gauche Photography. He lit the cigar, blowing billows of smoke into the air.

"We value our relationship with Bombay Photographic Company, but we are unable to ignore the growing arrears. All shipments are hereby held in abeyance till the outstanding balance is paid in full. Warmest regards to Mrs. G. Usual close." With great satisfaction, he then impaled the letter from Mr. Gupta on the foot-long spike that stood on his desk for correspondence awaiting filing. A start had been made.

He snapped another letter from the pile and began to read. It was from a mail-order customer and therefore bore the usual name,

John Smith, and the usual address, a post office box. The contents were also of the usual kind:

> Please help me. I have been a customer for the last two years, and now regularly buy the complete contents of each monthly catalogue. The cost far exceeds my means as a schoolteacher, and I have sold our silver candlesticks and plate. My wife has taken our baby and returned to her mother in St. Louis. I do not know where else to turn, nor how much longer I can last. This can only end in death.

"New letter. Dear Mr. John Smith, I stand in receipt of your communication, dated February 21, 1896. As stated in the fine print on page two of our catalogue, our product is to be used in moderation only, for the purposes of bodily relief and healthful relaxation. We cannot be held liable for misuse. Usual close."

He thrust the epistle from John Smith onto the spike, pushing it down till it lay on top of that from Mr. Gupta. He then pulled a new letter from the pile and began to read—and in that way, as the hours passed, the spike on his desk began to slowly disappear under its burden of papers to be filed. All that paper, the collected lies, threats, charades, frauds, misrepresentations, traps, and seductions of the world beyond his office door, done, finished, taken care of, rebuffed, defeated, *spiked*.

Auerbach swiveled from the desk, rolled over to the window, and pressed a hand to the glass. The letters helped, but they did not *solve*. What he needed was sunlight so translucent that he would be able to see the world as he needed to see it, so luminous that it would make him appear beautiful to the models he posed. He watched as the window filled with a gentle blue iridescence, and felt the yearning grow into an almost unbearable ache. Outside, the garden was gathering the light to itself. He could make out a gazebo, a line of bare trees, and then the garden wall. "Do you like the night, Miss Parish?" he asked.

"I guess I do, Mr. A."

"But nothing gets *done*." He caught himself; it was not like him to waste time on chat. "That's all, Miss Parish. You can go now."

Miss Parish got up and left. Auerbach knew nothing of her life outside the confines of the office—knew only that she appeared, no matter the day or the hour, if he pressed the buzzer long enough. He imagined her life to be simple and contented, the life of a housecat with a little late-night typing thrown in. She did not have to say no to Mr. Gupta, and she did not have to point out the fine print to the ever-reduplicated John Smith. She clearly had no trouble sleeping. Most of all, she did not have to worry about the ultimate meaning of his enterprise, and history's final judgment upon it.

Thinking of himself in world-historical terms was as natural to Auerbach as breathing air. He was undaunted by the stigma attached to his occupation, and believed absolutely in its hidden importance—an importance so great that it could not remain hidden forever. Beyond the walls of his mansion, the world was being shaped by the power of industry. Men like Vanderbilt, Morgan, Carnegie, and Gould were leaving a permanent imprint on the physical face of the nation. Railroads were being laid across the prairies, great suspension bridges constructed over rivers, factories built, canals dug, mines bored, oil wells drilled, telephone lines strung, houses electrified. A telephone sat on Auerbach's desk, and an incandescent lamp burned above his head. There were great humming generators hunched like predators in the dark of his basement.

The physical world was under construction, but what about the mental? In the rush to shape the landscape, the interior life of the nation had been forgotten—had been, in effect, left with Auerbach. Fortunately, he had accepted the task with a sense of high purpose. Whatever bridges were needed to reach our secret desires, whatever canals were necessary for the shipment of our darkest wishes, whatever railroads were required to transport our most powerful cravings—he would build them. He would build the tunnels and corridors, the dungeons and pleasure domes of our yearnings.

The task was enormous, and that was why Auerbach could not afford to sleep the morning away like Miss Parish. There was no time. The clock on his desk said six fifty, and at seven he was due in the studio for a photographic session of the utmost urgency.

2. A NOBLE EXPERIMENT

Auerbach wheeled himself out of the office and down the long terrazzo corridor, past the hanging tapestries and suits of armor, the rows of Greek and Roman busts perched on marble pediments. The domestic staff was out in force for the morning cleaning, a swarm of little maids no older than twelve or thirteen, in black dresses and white aprons, armed with carpet beaters, feather dusters, brushes, buckets, and rags. Like Miss Parish, they subsisted at the edge of his consciousness—pale, pinched faces beneath white lace caps, turning to curtsy as he wheeled past, like heliotropes following the sun. He liked the sight of them, just as he liked the sight of the things they polished and buffed with their rags, the carved and gilt furniture he was too busy to use—had never used. They were the signs of his election.

He turned a corner and drew to a stop before the large double doors leading to his studio, then managed a little awkwardly to let himself inside. Instantly, his eyes were flooded with new-morning light.

Auerbach's studio was a former winter garden, attached to the main body of the mansion: an elongated or pointy dome built of iron ribs and glass. He liked to think of it as a kind of mill or factory in which the power of light was harnessed to create photographs, just as the wind is used to turn a windmill, or the water to drive a waterwheel. But this strictly functional description did not capture the feel of it. The sky was everywhere, like the ocean surrounding a ship, and to glance upward was to risk a strange kind of vertigo—the feeling of falling in. And yet one could not help but look up. The blueness darkened and lightened, greened and grayed. Great massy clouds floated like cities overhead. The effect was inexplicably potent, emotional. A sudden fall in the light made one want to weep for no apparent reason. Many of the models did weep, but then they were in a particularly vulnerable state.

Auerbach stopped to look around, thinking about apertures and lenses. He was used to living with this sort of complexity above his head; he managed by ignoring it. The only thing that concerned him was the light, which on this particular day was perfect for photography: clear, clean, white, brilliant but without the cruelty of summer. "Good," he said, as if praising a subordinate, "excellent," then continued on toward the stage set.

His assistant, Elijah Grapes, sat to one side with the two models, Henry Twersky and Jane Larue. They looked very small as he wheeled toward them, but then people always did in the studio, beneath the ocean of sky. It was only later, in the photographs, naked and an inch tall, that they took on real size.

The three rose like schoolchildren to greet him. Grapes doffed his bowler, Twersky removed his top hat, and Jane did a slight curtsy. "Good morning, Mr. A." Their voices sounded childlike in the vast space beneath the dome.

"Good morning to you all," said Auerbach, coming to a stop. "I hope I find you well." He tucked in his dressing gown and straightened the lap rug over his legs. "The light is splendid, isn't it? Are we ready to begin, Mr. Grapes?"

Elijah Grapes was a perplexing little man. Thirty or sixty? Portuguese? Sicilian? Creole? The only thing Auerbach knew about him was that he had sailed on a whaler, been shipwrecked, and survived two hundred days in an open boat. It seemed completely believable. Thin, stooped, hairless, squinty, he was nevertheless the very opposite of frail. Indeed, he looked disconcertingly hard, like a savage little idol carved from wood. "Everything's ready, Mr. A." He gestured toward the stage set.

"And the camera?" asked Auerbach.

"Bessie," said Grapes.

Auerbach glanced over at her, perched atop her wooden tripod. She was a large, boxy thing with a black hood trailing behind and not one but two lenses at the front, like a pair of eyes. Indeed, her lenses functioned much like eyes, focusing on the same point in space from a small distance apart, and thus producing two ever-so-slightly different images side by side on the negative.

That doubling was called stereography, and it was Rive Gauche's specialty. Printed on a single rectangular card, and viewed through a device called a stereoscope, Bessie's twin images merged into one unified picture of extraordinarily lifelike volume and depth—a chunk of the world enclosed in a simple optical instrument the size of a cigar box.

"Good old Bessie," said Auerbach, with genuine affection. He wished his work were all cameras, chemistry, printing, and optics. But it was impossible to eliminate the human element, and so he turned to Henry Twersky. "Are you ready?"

Henry Twersky looked like a circus lion that had seen better days. He had a large, pale, country face, framed by wiry blond mutton-chops—his mane. His walnut-sized wrist bones peeked out of the cuffs of his frock coat, which pinched at the shoulders so he could barely lift his arms. "I just want to get out of these clothes, Mr. A."

"You'll have your chance soon enough," said Auerbach, and then turned to Jane Larue. "Are you ready, Miss Larue?"

Jane Larue's girlish face had grown round and fleshy in the six months of her absence. She hid the rest of herself beneath an old army greatcoat, which she kept wrapped about like a cloak. "I'm ready, Mr. A."

"Very well, then. Maybe we should take a look."

This was the moment he had been wondering about. He watched her unwrap the greatcoat and let it fall. The pink nightgown took a little longer, as she had trouble working it over her head, but then it too was at her feet. And then there was a general hush, as the three men contemplated the naked figure before them.

Jane Larue—or Miss Melba, as she was called in the catalogue— was the company's best photographic model. The other girls lasted only a year or two before they fell sick or took to drink, or otherwise became unreliable. But for the past five years, Jane Larue had arrived each morning at the stroke of seven and started undoing her buttons. In that time, Auerbach had photographed every inch of her, from every angle, in every conceivable costume and every possible setting, until the Miss Melba archive consisted of over five thousand stereographs.

And yet he barely recognized her body now. The belly changed everything. It was not merely big; it was elephantine, and very possibly crushing. She struggled to support its weight with her hands.

"Ah," he gasped, unable to help himself. It was very clearly a bag, containing something alive; something that was Miss Larue and not Miss Larue; something riding inside her. He could see that whatever it was did not sit quietly. It jutted, brooded, hunched, and strained at the skin.

Despite the nature of his work, there were large gaps in his knowledge of the female body. His experience of women was limited to the studio. While pregnancy was common enough among the models, pregnant models naturally stopped working once they began to show. As a result, he had never seen a naked woman in Miss Larue's condition. "And you're in your ninth month?" he asked her now.

"Yes, Mr. A."

He wheeled a half-turn closer. "So this is as big as you get?"

She giggled, a high-pitched girlish affair that hinted at her age—twenty? Twenty-one? "I hope so," she said.

"May I?" he asked, reaching forward.

"Certainly."

He put his hands to the curve of her belly. The surface was surprisingly stiff. Her stomach felt full to bursting with some kind of heavy liquid, yet there was clearly something solid in there as well, floating within. It retreated from his touch and then surged back again. Impulsively, he leaned forward and pressed his ear to her skin: warmth, her salty body odor, dark interior sounds, vague gurgling.

"Fantastic," he said, feeling his trepidation replaced by enthusiasm. "Just fantastic." He heard that giggle of hers pass through her body.

She was so large that Elijah Grapes had to help her put the nightgown back on. It was like putting a pink drape over a boulder. Henry Twersky pulled at his frock coat, clearly perturbed by what he had seen. "Is she going to be all right?" he asked Auerbach.

Auerbach glanced upward at the great blue of the sky overhead, fortifying himself from his reserve stock of patience. It was not Twersky's place to worry about such things. "Do you have your mask, Mr. Twersky?"

A hint of displeasure in the voice was more than enough. Twersky quickly pulled a black strip of cloth from his pocket and tied it around his head, careful not to dislodge his top hat. His eyes peered out from two eyeholes, looking startled by their own transformation. "Ready, Mr. A."

"Then wait for your cue." Auerbach wheeled back to where Bessie stood on her tripod. From this vantage point he could see the set in its entirety: the three painted flats delineating a very grand bedroom, with wood paneling, French windows leading to a balcony, curtains blowing in the breeze, the moon and stars visible. A few pieces of furniture had been spread around the room: dresser, nightstand, makeup table, a Grecian pediment with a statue of Cupid resting on top. And then there was the bed into which Jane Larue was now laboriously climbing with the help of both Elijah Grapes and Henry Twersky.

Jane Larue settled herself under the covers, a small mountain of blanket in the middle of a large bed. Henry Twersky tiptoed off to the side to await his cue. Elijah Grapes ran back to man Bessie, all but his thin legs disappearing under the black hood. When everyone was in place, Auerbach began speaking in what he thought of as his directorial voice: a voice slower, deeper, richer than his ordinary speaking voice, a mesmerist's voice. "Are you comfortable, Miss Larue?"

"Yes, Mr. A."

"Very good, then. Now listen to me carefully and I will tell you about our little scenario. This great mansion is your home, and this luxurious bedroom is your bedroom. It is late and you are asleep in bed, beneath wonderfully cool satin sheets. Can you feel the coolness?"

"Yes, Mr. A."

"And what about the mink coverlet? Do you like it?"

"Oh yes, I love mink."

"Go ahead, touch it, run your hand over it. Isn't it nice and soft?"

She ran her fingers over the blanket, which was in fact brown velveteen, in general much worn, and completely bald in spots. "Yes, it feels wonderful, Mr. A."

"Good. Now remember, your husband is away on business

tonight, but you are not worried about being alone. After all, there is a high wall around the mansion, and a night watchman at the gate, and many servants asleep downstairs. Tell me, do you feel secure tonight, Miss Larue?"

"Yes, Mr. A."

"Good. And because you feel so secure, you have fallen deeply asleep. You are having very beautiful dreams about the blessed event to come, the birth of your first child. Can you tell me what you are dreaming about, Miss Larue?"

"Last night I dreamed I fell down the stairs."

"Well, yes, but tonight you are having better dreams—you are dreaming of babies. Fat little cherubs, pink and smiling, with blue eyes and wisps of downy hair on their heads. Can you see them, Miss Larue?"

"Oh, yes, Mr. A., now that you describe them."

Jane Larue liked lying on her back, listening to Mr. A.'s voice. With her head propped up on two pillows, feigning the sleep of the rich, she could look out through all-but-closed lids at the dark, fuzzy figure of Auerbach in his wheelchair, crumpled in that pose she knew so well. She had been working for him for the last five years and he had always sat that way—head tilted to one side, as if he were viewing not her but the pictures she would become, and the wrapping they would be sold in.

She had not liked him when she first met him, which was surprising since she had a weakness for handsome men, and even seated in his wheelchair, he was unusually handsome: big brown eyes beneath thick eyebrows, a strong forehead and curly black hair. And it wasn't the legs that put her off, either. If anything, they reminded her of her grandfather, who had lost both of his to a cannonball at Chickamauga. But there was something about the way Mr. A. looked at her, a practical look, like a farmer eyeing a sow at the market. She had known that she would be taking off her clothes, but didn't want him to touch her. She had stiffened when he drew his chair up close. Her eyes kept drifting down to the blanket that covered his lap.

"Well, of course, you're curious," he had said to her, and then, before she could say anything, had removed the cashmere blanket from his lap. She had caught her breath, afraid of seeing something terrible, but the legs were not really deformed, only very small, a pair of legs belonging to a child. They rested straight out in front, dressed in pin-striped pants and patent leather boots, too short to bend over the edge of the chair. "They work," he had said, wiggling one and then the other. "But they're too small to walk on." He stared down at them, and then up at her with a look of sudden intimacy. "You see how it goes. We all have our troubles."

It had drained the fear from her, made him seem harmless, as if he were someone to be pitied, just like herself. It wasn't till months later, when she had seen him do the exact same thing with another new girl, that she realized it was contrived—no, not contrived, but a method he had. Mr. A. was full of methods. But by then she knew him better and did not begrudge him his methods.

Covering up his legs that first day, he had asked her: "Have you ever seen a stereograph, Miss Larue?" She had liked being called Miss Larue.

"No, sir." She had arrived in town less than a week before and hadn't yet been to a theater, or spoken on a telephone, or tasted any of the other wonders of the big city. She didn't know that stereo-scopes were everywhere, that they cost just a dollar, that everyone had one, forgotten in the closet or attic.

Mr. A. had smiled that beautiful smile of his, so pleased with his mysterious toy. "It's like a photograph you can step into," he said, "right inside, like stepping into a room. You can see everything as if you were really there."

He had handed her a small wooden box, no bigger than a sugar tin. She had held the box to her face, and it was like looking through a keyhole into a great, secret room: somehow, the little wooden box contained an enormous space inside of itself. Inside the box was a complex and shady garden enclosed by tall hedges, a waterfall filling a reflecting pool, a table and chair beneath a tree. It was utterly real and completely private, and so beautiful she felt tears come suddenly to her eyes.

"That's how you'll look," he had said. "Men will look and yearn but will never be able to enter. Almost, but not quite."

Later, as she lay naked on the couch, he had given her directions with a gentle, measured flow of words. Without thinking, she had reshaped herself, following the curve of his voice: "Yes, that's good, open your knees, wider, wider, hold it. Okay, now close the knees, that's right. Hold it just like that." The feeling was strangely selfless, as if she had somehow left Jane Larue behind to become this other thing created by the voice: breasts and neck and open lips—an image in Mr. A.'s mind, a step in his chain of production, a miniature woman in his magic box.

A week later, back for more work, she had peered into the stereoscope he handed her. Inside the little box she saw the room she was even then standing in, seemingly more real than the version that surrounded her. The velvet drapes, the couch—all real, utterly real, and nothing more so than the woman lying there, her body in sated repose, a mysterious, carnal smile floating above full breasts and dark nipples. She had never seen a photograph of herself before, let alone this kind of thing, and the sense of loss was immediate, terrible: she could never become the woman on that couch.

"As I said, you are dreaming of little cherubs," continued Auerbach. "Little Renaissance putti. And you hear nothing at all around you, not even the soft padding of footsteps over plush carpeting. Your eyes are closed, and you do not see the shadowy figure at the foot of your bed."

Through half-closed lids, she watched him signal to Henry, who walked on the set, taking up his position at the side of the bed.

"You are a gentleman jewel thief," said Auerbach to Henry, "meaning a man of culture and refinement who robs for sport rather than crude gain."

"Sport," said Twersky, nodding anxiously. "I understand."

"At this point, the gentleman jewel thief turns and sees the rich woman in her bed, and he is immediately struck by her unearthly beauty."

Twersky struck a pose, peering at her with a look of extreme amazement on his face, as if she had grown a second head. Click.

And so began a series of carefully shaped tableaux: The gentleman jewel thief standing by the bed, viewing the sleeping woman. Click. The woman waking, a look of dismay on her face. Click. The woman sitting up and pointing to her belly. Click.

"You are taken aback," said Auerbach. "You are a gentleman first, a jewel thief second, and you are going to leave. But the sight of this beautiful woman has done something to you, and you are suddenly unable to control yourself."

The jewel thief, enflamed, pulling away the mink coverlet, ripping off her nightgown. Click. The jewel thief running his hands over her enormous stomach. Click. Licking her belly. Click. And then a picture of her lying back atop the covers, her feet in the foreground, her long legs filling the middle distance, followed by the great summit of her belly—a composition perfect for stereography, with its extreme rendering of depth. Click. Click.

Jane Larue and Henry Twersky worked together in silence. They responded to Auerbach's commands without speaking, freezing periodically for the click of the camera. For his part, Auerbach gave directions in his slow, syrupy voice, watching as his words made the two bodies on the bed twist and writhe, stop and resume. The stereotyped progression of positions did not bore him, even after twenty years. Rather, he saw it as a form of internal coherence equivalent to the rhyme scheme of a sonnet—a thing to make one quietly rejoice in the world's order.

Indeed, watching them move, he seemed to see the whole universe spread out before him in all its complex interconnections, a great web with himself, Augustus Auerbach, at the very center. Experience allowed him to envision just how the scene being enacted would look in the stereoscope, the two bodies stopped in time, transformed into otherworldly, magical things. He could already read the catalogue copy he would write: "Expectant mother overcome by gentleman jewel thief." He could estimate the price: $3.79 plus second-class postage for an album of thirty stereographic cards delivered in an unmarked brown wrapper. He knew the cost of packaging, as brown wrapper was currently $3.99 for a ream, string $4.15 for a ball of a hundred yards. He could remember the night he had arrived at the method—through long hours of trial and error—of wrapping the six-by-ten-inch boxes he used for slides with a piece of paper exactly fifteen by twenty-three inches, and a length of string no more than forty inches, thus saving himself twelve cents per package. He could see the cards themselves stacked in the warehouse, thousands of them awaiting shipment to customers around the world, in Great Falls and Grand Rapids and London and Calcutta. He could see those same customers with their eyes to the box, all viewing not the actual Jane Larue or Henry Twersky but the imprint of their light, the relic of a moment months or even years in the past. This moment.

Auerbach was pleased. For reasons that were still not entirely clear to him, expectant mothers represented new territory for exotic photography. He had made a quick check of his competitors' offerings and had found not a single visibly pregnant model. What this strange and inexplicable gap meant to Auerbach was commercial opportunity. If successful, his experiment with Jane Larue could create an entirely new category of photograph, which meant in turn a whole new class of things his customers would need to buy from him. In other words, a new desire.

How many men manage to leave their imprint upon humanity in this way—not on the outside, the way we look, but on our very natures, what we *want*? The inventor of ice cream managed it, as did the first horticulturist to domesticate the tobacco plant. Gutenberg did it, and so did Moses—Moses with his tablets, inventor of the desire to be good. It was select company. Auerbach's place in history would be assured.

And then suddenly Twersky leaped off the bed. "Blood!" he yelled. "Oh, God, blood!" He hopped from foot to foot, wringing his hands while Elijah Grapes ran over.

Auerbach's attention returned to the scene only slowly. The models were not supposed to do anything other than what he told them to do. He sat, momentarily speechless, while Elijah Grapes examined the situation on the bed.

Why is it that men who have escaped death become so prosaic? "I think we're done for the day," called Grapes, in his dry, uninflected voice.

"Done?" said Auerbach. "We are not done." Only then did he wheel himself to the foot of the bed, where Jane Larue lay, feeling awkwardly beneath herself with her hand, then examining her fingers.

Her voice was quiet. "I think my water broke."

"Water?" asked Auerbach delicately. He had no idea what she meant, though he could see the dark stain spreading out over the sheet.

"I'm going to have the baby."

"The baby," he echoed, remembering that there was in fact a baby in the equation. He looked up at the sky. Enormous clouds sailed past, casting shadows. The light was losing its intensity. "We need just a few more photographs to finish."

"It's starting to hurt," she said. "A lot." She stared up at the ceiling with a worried look on her face, like somebody listening for approaching thunder.

Auerbach took a deep breath. Dealing with the models was always a trial. They could bring work to an instant halt, and there was really nothing he could do but beg and cajole till they started up again. "Miss Larue, surely you understand that the photographs we have are useless without a proper ending. Tens of thousands of loyal customers will be disappointed."

She grimaced. "I can't, Mr. A. I'm sorry."

"Can't? Can't or *won't*?" He leaned in close, till he could smell the salty odor of her perspiration. He hated this part but it was for her own good—like the commander who shames the cowardly soldier into battle. "Do you remember when your father was sick, Miss Larue?"

"Yes." She nodded wearily.

"Who advanced you the money you needed?"

"You, Mr. A."

"And when your landlord was going to evict you, who gave you the money then?"

"You."

"Then don't you think you owe me at least this much?"

She closed her eyes as if to shut out the question, then released a long, strangled moan.

"That's not an answer, Miss Larue."

Another moan, and then Elijah Grapes drew up beside him, pulling an old rickshaw they occasionally used as a stage property. "Maybe we should move her to one of the bedrooms, Mr. A."

"And what about the catalogue?"

"The light's gone anyway."

That was not quite true, but Jane Larue was groaning now, a deep, guttural sound, more animal than human. There was clearly no going back; a noble experiment had been ruined. "All right," said Auerbach, waving his hand dejectedly at the entire scene. "Take her away."

Elijah Grapes and Henry Twersky lifted Jane Larue into the rickshaw, then pulled her out of the studio and into the hallway. Auerbach followed behind in his wheelchair. They took her to one of the bedrooms, a green and gold affair with a cathedral ceiling and four-poster bed. Auerbach sat with her, while Elijah Grapes went for a doctor. Henry Twersky was suddenly nowhere to be seen. "He probably thinks he killed me," she said, looking up at the bed canopy, grimly amused.

"We don't need him," said Auerbach. "He's completely replaceable because of the mask."

"And me?" she asked.

"*You* are irreplaceable, unfortunately."

Her mouth opened as if to speak but kept on going, into a scream.

This kind of intense suffering was not edifying to watch, and it went on for a long time, receding and then returning with a kind of nerve-wracking circularity that left Auerbach drained and exhausted. The yelling was terrible. At first he tried to reason with her, but when that didn't work, he retreated to a corner, watching with a mixture of annoyance and stoic determination. As soon as Grapes arrived with the doctor, Auerbach returned to the studio. If the pregnancy photographs were a failure, he would have to get something else to replace them in the catalogue right away.

But his mind kept slipping back to Miss Larue. He felt a certain degree of concern—she was his top-selling model, after all. And then there was the question of responsibility. Not that he bore any particular responsibility, of course, but he was president and sole proprietor of the company, and that seemed to imply something, a kind of patriarchal role involving a general air of beneficence. He found himself returning to check up on her now and then during the course of the day, sitting for a few minutes at a time by her bedside. He tried to comfort her, telling her about how Napoleon walked among the wounded at Austerlitz, the great man's extraordinary bravery in the face of such terrible suffering. When that didn't help, he tried to distract her with small talk about the rising cost of bulk-rate shipping to Minneapolis and points west. But a particularly horrible series of screams sent him wheeling back to the studio.

Morning turned to afternoon, and afternoon to evening, and Jane Larue still lay on her back in the darkened room, howling, panting, and cursing. She grabbed Auerbach's hand with such force that he could not get it back, though he tried desperately. She was squeezing his fingers so hard he thought they would break, but the pain did not confound him so much as the sudden intimacy. He had taken pictures of her in what other people would consider the most private moments—squatting to relieve herself in "Chamber Pot Patty," for example—but he had never held her hand.

Auerbach was there when the baby was born: suddenly, between Jane Larue's bloody thighs, appeared a round, puffy face that looked to have been carved from an apple. The ferocity of the little being was overwhelming, intimidating. Jane Larue was not pushing the baby out, despite her screaming—no, it was peeling her off like wet clothes, working one shoulder up, then the other, grimacing blindly with the effort, till the doctor yanked him free in a single long, wet, slithering motion. It was something between pulling a cork—the same obvious release of pressure—and grabbing a fish from a barrel. For one frozen moment, the baby hung in the air, the doctor holding on to him by the arm as if he had apprehended him shoplifting: a little gray man dipped in oil, hairless and irate, with a long pointy head. He glared out at the room through his one open eye.

3. DOES HE DREAM?

Having been awake for two full days, Auerbach crawled into bed after dinner and fell deeply asleep. His first thought when he next opened his eyes was that it was morning—if a little dark—but careful inspection of the clock revealed it was not yet midnight. He had slept three hours.

He tried to get back to sleep, but his thoughts kept intervening. He felt he had seen something important that evening, something terrible and cruel at the heart of things. The baby peeling Miss Larue away with a ruthlessness that was more natural process than human act. The baby's cry, so relentless, so perfectly repetitive, and yet so devoid of individual personality that it sounded closer to machinery or perhaps birdcall than human speech. Miss Larue, her color ashen, her skin glistening with sweat, going into a fit of trembling so intense that Auerbach thought she might die right then and there. There had been so much blood, after all—it stained her thighs and pooled on the white sheets draped over the bed and the floor. Yet she had taken the wet, oily creature and put it to her breast.

Is this what they meant when they said that nature was red in tooth and claw? Is this what they meant by survival of the fittest? Auerbach had stared in horrified fascination, trying to reconcile the smallness of its fingers and the delicacy of its ears with the ferocity of its sucking. That odd combination of rapacity and fragility—he recognized it immediately, intuitively: humanness.

From this one little fact, he felt, the entire world could be teased. Men are just infants with mustaches and pocket watches. Life is a battlefield on which they contend. Whatever one marauder takes, the others cannot have. Over everything hangs what Clausewitz called the fog of war—smoke, confusion, fear. A few extraordinary men, like Vanderbilt and Carnegie, rise above the mass, but for the vast majority the only mercy is death.

He stared up at the ceiling, wide-eyed, the sweat trickling down his back. He recognized these thoughts now. They were the thoughts that came to him on sleepless nights, the thoughts that forced him out of bed and into the office to buzz for Miss Parish. Usually he outran them, but now it was too late and he would have to listen to the very end.

Since his competitors copied his every innovation, he was never more than a single catalogue ahead. Just one month—thirty days— to save himself and his life's work from obliteration, and not once, but twelve times a year, with a double issue for Christmas. Meanwhile, the cost of wrapping paper and postage kept going up, and so did the payoffs: city hall, the Democratic Club, the police, the Clean Living League, a dozen civic and religious organizations. If displeased, any one of them could turn around and destroy him.

Was it any surprise that he could not sleep, that his head ached and his hands trembled? Carnegie was a wolf among men, Vanderbilt a lion, but Auerbach was an invalid in a wheelchair, plagued by uncontrollable thoughts. For how long could he continue to struggle without pity or rest? For how long could he suppress the fear?

Auerbach had read Darwin and Spencer; he understood the inexorable logic of natural selection. To be afraid was weakness, and weakness was doom. He was doomed. Others would triumph; others would take his rightful spot in history. He would get no credit for his genius. Kleinfeldt at Montparnasse Exotic was probably planning a pregnancy series right this minute—the odious Kleinfeldt, with his velvet dinner jackets and silver rings, his conceited laugh, his pockets full of novelty items, photographic key chains and cigarette holders. Kleinfeldt would get credit for pregnancy—the category would belong to him. He would win because he was an animal, a predator without fear or compunction, untroubled by thought or any of the higher feelings that disabled Auerbach, despite his genius. Auerbach would be spat on and then forgotten. The grass would grow over his grave. There would be no monument. Nobody would know that he had lived, struggled, and died.

And yet he could never speak of this to anyone, because if he did, they would know, and then his air of authority would be gone, the models would not twist and arch in response to his commands, and the Guptas would not answer his letters by return post.

But of course, the one antidote to weakness was work, and so he got into his wheelchair, pulled the lap rug over his legs, and wheeled himself down the hall to the office. There he rang Miss Parish's buzzer, rang till his finger ached.

But Miss Parish—the good, dear, servile creature—did not appear. He let go of the buzzer and cast a mournful, frightened look at the teetering stack of correspondence on his desk—the night's requirement. How could he possibly begin? And yet how could he not? Willpower was the only thing that divided him from the John Smiths. He picked up the first letter and started to read. It was from John Smith:

I am writing to enquire about the possibility of buying your fine products on credit. Previous to certain recent reversals,

I was a man of considerable personal wealth. I will not impose on you by outlining the entire tale here. Let me say only that it includes incapacitating back pain of unknown origin, too trusting a disposition, and a loss of connubial intimacy. I expect my fortunes to rebound within the year— certain investments in the China trade. I watch the sea from my window. Until that time, however, I find myself suffering a degree of pecuniary embarrassment.

He let the letter drop. Credit without collateral—the suggestion seemed to carry some terrible contagion of grief. Auerbach felt his eyes begin to sting, and he blinked away the tears. He hated the John Smiths, hated their madness and their stupidity and their doom, but most of all he hated their pigheadedness. They had lost at the struggle of life, yet refused to die. They had forfeited the right to human needs, yet still had them all—needs that grew larger the longer they went unfulfilled, until they could be sated only in fantasy. Auerbach's job was to feed the John Smiths, and he did it grandly, efficiently, nobly, but the effect was contrary to what one might imagine. He fed them till they were hungrier and hungrier, till they wrote him letters begging for mercy, an end to their hungers. But life itself was hunger. He could not shut it off.

He wheeled himself out into the hall and then sat for a moment, not knowing which way to go. It was then that he heard it: a series of strange, repetitious cries, like the cries of a cat. He followed them, drawn onward in spite of himself, down the hall, through the winter parlor, past the bust of Fox Talbot, inventor of photosensitive paper. They stopped short just as he arrived at the room Miss Larue was occupying.

The door was open. She was sitting up in the great four-poster bed, her nightgown lowered to her waist, her breast in the baby's mouth. She looked much better than she had after the birth—

bathed, rested—and so did the baby, swaddled in a clean white towel. The baby's eyes were shut, his puffy face working at the breast. Miss Parish was seated in a chair by the bedside, dozing. He had never considered that she might know Miss Larue.

Auerbach sat in the doorway and watched in silence, at the edge of an act more intimate than any he had ever photographed. He wondered at the source of that passion, the fact that neither of the participants could help themselves. Jane glanced over at him and then returned her attention to the baby, without greeting or comment. Powerful physical processes seemed to be taking place inside her, making her superior to the outside world. She grunted and then arched backward, lifting her face and closing her eyes—in relief or pain, he wasn't sure. One hand squeezed down the length of the breast, increasing the flow. With her big mammaries and fleshy, preoccupied face, with the dark circles under her eyes, she looked heavy, purposeful—not the fluttery, nervous Jane that Auerbach knew from life. No, this was closer to the Jane he saw in his stereoscope, the Jane sculpted around a need.

It was a long time till she acknowledged him again. "What are you doing up, Mr. A.?" She was half asleep, her eyes hooded.

"I was looking for my typewriter," he said, feeling abashed. The scene had done something to him, something he did not understand—like dawn when it came to re–create the garden outside the office window.

"Do you want me to wake her?"

He looked over at Miss Parish, slumped in her chair. "No, let her sleep."

"You can come in if you want."

"There are some things I have to take care of." But he wheeled himself in, till he was at her bedside. The baby seemed to have fallen asleep on the breast. The black hair on its head was surprisingly thick, the cheeks puffed and red. The tiny pugilist's face was set in a grimace of satisfaction. It slept with the seriousness of an idol awaiting offerings.

Suddenly he was overcome with a need to speak what was on his mind. "I have trouble sleeping," he said, staring down at that face in perfect repose. "The weight of responsibilities. I have *thoughts*, Miss Larue." He looked up, struggling to regain his dignity as president and sole proprietor.

She was smiling down at the baby, clearly oblivious to his darker meaning. It was just as well. "Do you think he has them too?" she asked simply.

"Milk, I suppose."

"Does he dream?"

"I hope not." Even the good dreams, the ones where he got up and walked, left Auerbach feeling sad.

"He smells so clean," she said, bending her head down to inhale. "Here, smell." She elevated the sleeping form for him to sniff, as if it were a flower.

Auerbach was not a smeller of roses; his garden was something to be looked at through the office window. But he bent down and put his nose to the hair. The smell was very particular: freshly baked bread, still warm, dipped in milk.

"Does he have a name?" he asked.

"Augustus," she said matter-of-factly.

Alarmed, he drew himself up in his chair. "Augustus?"

"Augustus Jeremiah Larue. Jeremiah is for my father."

"But why?" It felt as if she were making a claim of some kind. Did she want money? Some form of protection? Caution was called for. She was a mere model, after all, and he was—well, himself. There could be no duplicates.

"You were there when he was born, Mr. A."

"So was the doctor."

She looked hurt. "Don't you like it?"

"I didn't say that." There was a part of him that indeed saw the logic involved. Why shouldn't the whole world be full of him? And he would need an assistant someday, when Elijah Grapes got old. "It's an excellent name."

"I think it fits," she said, smiling down at the child. "You're a millionaire, and he's going to be one too."

Auerbach went back to his bedroom and fell deeply asleep. When he woke the next morning, the sun was already streaming from under the curtains like water flowing beneath a door. It was late, but he felt no sense of panic. "Bertha the Bar Girl" could wait—would have to wait while he bathed in the big claw-footed tub, attar of roses swirling in the hot water, its scent rising with the steam. For the first time in weeks, his head was clear, his eyes free of the burning. The thoughts had been silenced, and he did not have to worry where he stood in the great chain of being. Suddenly there was room in his mind for surprising things: water droplets on the bathroom tile, a finger of white light stretching across the ceiling. Tying his tie before the mirror, he pictured Jane Larue's baby, Augustus—the way it had lain, cradled in her arms, lost in something so ferocious it could not be labeled sleep.

Auerbach pulled on his crimson vest with the black stripes and wide lapels. Over that went the serious black morning coat. As a businessman, he prided himself on his command of the logical syllogism, the ipso facto at the heart of the matter. He had seen the baby. He had slept. The baby had put him to sleep. It was as simple as that. He did not have to understand the reason, just as he did not understand the reason silver salts changed color with the caress of light—nobody did. He had corresponded with the leading chemists in the nation, professors at Harvard and Yale, and they did not know. He rang for Elijah Grapes and sent him to Jane Larue's apartment on Cherry Street, to bring back a bag of clothes. He had decided: she and the child would be staying for a while.

That one bag of clothes was all Jane Larue seemed to require of the outside world. No one came to see her; she wrote no letters, sent no telegrams, and did not ask to use the telephone Auerbach kept in his office. She seemed to have no connections and nothing pressing to go back to. She slept or sat in the winter parlor in nightgown and bathrobe, nursing the baby or holding him while he napped. It was as if she possessed a piece of vital information, so ancient it was new. Contemplating it was enough.

As the weeks passed, Auerbach established a routine: he went to the studio in the morning, to the office in the afternoon, and to Jane Larue's bedroom in the evening, to look at the baby. Whatever strange soporific powers the child possessed were still active. Auerbach watched him nurse, watched him wave his hands and feet in the air, and then left. He was asleep within minutes after getting into bed.

That is, until one evening at his desk, when he opened a plain brown envelope and pulled out Kleinfeldt's newest catalogue. As usual, he noted the cheap paper, the ink that came off on the fingers. With great delight, he read the forward aloud to Miss Parish:

> Once again, it is our Sincere Pleasure to offer the Current Catalogue of Fine Photographic Products from Montparnasse Exotic Photography—the Fabergé of Exotic Photography! the Wedgwood of Erotica!—to our audience of Sophisticated Gentlemen—Gentlemen of Discernment—Gentlemen of Taste—Sporting Gentlemen who admire the FEMALE FORM in all its Variety, Plenitude, Mystery, Fecundity, and Power…

"Can you hear the capitals, Miss Parish? Every other word is capitalized. And there isn't a single period." It was a moment to be savored. He lit a cigar, blowing great gusts of smoke. "Bad prose is the outward sign of a boorish mind." But then, flipping idly through the pages, something caught his eye: a photogravure of a naked woman with a belly as big and round as a medicine ball. The caption read: *First Time Ever!!! Pregnant Strumpets PLEASURE Themselves—the Sacred State of Motherhood Degraded by Lust...*

"Oh no." He let his head sag into his hands. When he spoke again, his voice was mournful, dolorous. "I don't understand it, Miss Parish. I try so hard, so very, very hard. But in the end—in the end..."

"Is something the matter, Mr. A.?"

He lifted his face and forced a smile. "What more do they want from me? What more can I give them?"

"Who, Mr. A.?"

"Do I go yachting in the Mediterranean? Do I visit Newport during the season?"

"No, sir."

"That's right. I'm always here, working. I don't even sleep. I have renounced all of life's pleasures—everything—to pursue this one goal: the making of a photographic empire. Is that such a terrible thing?"

"I don't know, Mr. A. I guess not. Not for someone like you."

"Then why *him*?" It was almost a shout.

"What do you mean?"

"*Him!*" He rapped the catalogue with his knuckles. "Kleinfeldt! Why does *he* get the photographs?"

"What photographs, Mr. A.?"

How could a mere typewriter understand? He waived her away and then let his head sink back down to the desk. "You can go. I won't be needing you tonight."

He listened to the rustle of her skirts as she left, then sat up and returned to the catalogue. *A Series of Sixty Stereographs! Never Before Seen!* He threw the cheap rag in the wastebasket and then wheeled himself out of the office and down the hall to Jane Larue's room. He found her sitting up in bed with the baby in her lap. She was looking down at the baby, and the baby was looking up at her—each staring at the other with great, selfless admiration.

"Well, it's happened," he barked at her.

"What has?" She raised her head slowly to look at him. In the last couple of days she had taken on something of a witch-woman look. Her hair was down around her shoulders, uncombed, her nightgown open in front, leaving her breasts exposed. There were big circles around her eyes. Yet in an odd way she was more beautiful than ever.

It slowed him down a little—but only a little. "Kleinfeldt's beaten us. 'Pregnant Strumpets PLEASURE Themselves.'" He re-created the capitals with his voice, making the Kleinfeldtian dashes in the air with his hands. "'The Sacred State of Motherhood Degraded by Lust—'"

She regarded him for a moment with hooded, sleepy eyes and then returned her attention to the baby. Mother and child resumed their mutual admiration. "That's terrible, Mr. A."

It was not much of an apology, considering the fact that she was the one who had ruined his plans. "Don't you see?" said Auerbach. He was nearly bursting with the unfairness of it all. "It belongs to him now. Pregnancy belongs to Kleinfeldt."

She looked up again, eyes drugged with the baby's gaze. "Oh?"

It was like talking to an opium smoker, but he could not stop himself from trying to make her understand. "If I do it now, they'll say I stole the idea from *him*."

She cocked her head to one side. There was a small, quizzical smile on her lips. "Aren't you rich enough yet, Mr. A.?"

"It's not about money. It's about my place in history."

"History?" She actually giggled.

"Does that sound funny to you?" Auerbach drew himself up with great dignity. "A hundred years from now, people will know the world is different because of me."

Her face went blank as she tried to struggle with the idea. "A hundred years just seems so far away."

"That's because you're one of the ordinary people who can't see beyond the moment."

"Maybe so."

"Well, I am the very opposite of that." Auerbach turned and wheeled himself to the door, but the idea of going to the office was so awful that he stopped and turned around again. She was watching him from the bed, and her eyes seemed to stir the self-pity in him. "This is a terrible setback, Miss Larue, a terrible setback. How will I ever get to sleep now?"

"You can stay with us here if you like, Mr. A."

He wheeled back toward the bed. "Too much to do, I'm afraid."

"Maybe you need to take a rest. Things will look better in the morning."

"Do you think Kleinfeldt is resting, Miss Larue?" Nevertheless, he made no move to leave.

Within minutes, mother and child had fallen asleep on the bed. Auerbach sat, watching the rise and fall of Jane Larue's breathing while pondering the law of natural selection. On the surface, he certainly seemed fitter for survival than Kleinfeldt. He used punctuation, his grammar was better, and he insisted that his models wear clean linen. Yet he knew in his bones that he was doomed, that the world would be buying Kleinfeldt's blurry obscenities long after his own elegant concoctions were lost and forgotten. Why? The reason could only be some hidden unfitness, some missing piece inside him, some *lack*.

He stared at the baby, sleeping tucked under Jane Larue's arm. It looked so deeply content that he could not help but think of its inevitable disillusionment. His own mother had been forced to leave him periodically in order to tour, and he had felt her absence keenly. Mr. Newberry, the theater proprietor, took charge of him during those periods, with the help of a housekeeper and whoever else happened to be around the theater—carpenters, actors, musicians—but he was left much on his own. And so he would sit by a window in the apartment above the stage, watching the street, as if his mother might actually come walking up the sidewalk as she did on ordinary days—as if the sheer intensity of his vigilance might make her appear. When not at the window, he would rummage through the costumes in her trunk, sniff at her bottles of perfume, stick a finger in her face powder. He had understood neither clock nor calendar, and so her absence had no beginning and no end; it was a physical thing lodged inside him, like a stone.

And then at some point, without any warning, she would be back: a figure in the doorway, waiting for him to look up and take notice. He could not remember her face, exactly, only the outstretched arms. He would run to her—yes, he remembered *running*, a sensation like music—and she would sweep him up and twirl him about. What else did he remember? Perfume, the warmth of her skin, the softness of her fur collar, her voice, *his* voice, the spinning room. She would put him down and fling open one of her trunks, pulling out presents.

He remembered that she once gave him a wooden steam engine with wheels and a pull string. That night, she sang him to sleep while running her fingers delicately over his forehead. In an excruciating struggle, he held on to wakefulness for as long as he could. The next morning, he camped outside her bedroom, waiting for her to appear. He remembered how he tried to occupy himself with the steam engine, how he pressed his ear to the door, how he looked through the keyhole and saw nothing but carpet. She did not come out until after lunch, wrapped in a silk kimono, black eyeshades pushed up to her forehead. He sat beside her while she ate breakfast, and in his excitement he talked for both of them: to conserve her voice for the evening performance, his mother made a practice of not speaking till dinner. Afterward, they went for a carriage ride in Central Park, and that night she took him with her to the theater. He played in the dressing room and then sat at the back of the house, watching her performance while drifting in and out of dreams.

Three decades later, Auerbach sat beside Jane Larue's bed and wondered if he had not, in fact, found the cause of his unfitness: a too-loving, too-indulgent mother. True, later experiences had hardened him in the way he needed to be hardened: he had been orphaned, and had then lost the use of his legs. But underneath there remained a soft spot, a hidden weakness that disqualified him from true greatness. He felt a rush of something much like despair.

The baby stirred and began a hiccupy cry. Jane Larue sat up almost instantly. Eyes still closed, she gave a matter-of-fact squeeze to her breast, shooting a jet into the air like a doctor clearing the bubbles from a syringe. She put the breast into his mouth, releasing a deep grunt as he began to suck. In a few minutes he fell asleep again, with the nipple still in his mouth. Without warning, she lifted him up and passed him into Auerbach's arms. "Hold him," she said, her voice dark with sleep.

Auerbach tried to give him back, but Jane Larue had already turned away, stretching for an empty glass on the nightstand by the bed. And so Auerbach held the baby stiffly against his chest. The child's physical presence was shocking. There was something raw and feline about him. Naked except for his diaper, he was stringy and lean, rubber bands of muscle strung on a delicate frame of bone. Head, rib cage, fists, and nothing more. His mouth hung open, a clean cat's mouth, pink and empty of teeth. The baby was asleep with one arm raised in the air, like an orator inciting a crowd to riot.

"He looks like an anarchist," said Auerbach.

And then suddenly the baby was awake again, gazing up at him with his blue eyes. The look was indescribable, a kind of clear seeing that seemed to take Auerbach in just as he was, complete and unabridged—and nevertheless to find him good. It was not the way people were supposed to look at each other.

"He's up," whispered Auerbach, unable to remove his eyes from those eyes and whatever it was that they were seeing. "Take him. Quick."

"He won't bite you," said Jane Larue. She was squeezing milk from one of her breasts into the glass—a surprising amount of the stuff coming out. "It hurts if I get too full." When she was done, she held the glass up, admiring.

Auerbach handed over the baby and left. He meant to return to his room but wheeled through the darkened mansion instead. The hallway was of terrazzo, speckled and veined, and filled with artifacts of lost ages collected from every corner of the world: vases from China; carpets from Persia and Turkey; the heads of Roman consuls, pitted and gnawed by time; the torsos of Greek gods. He had bought them to remind himself of the weight of his position, the historical grandeur of his endeavor, but tonight he heard only their silence. They had no idea who owned them.

He took a left and passed through the billiard room. He could not reach the tables, and did not know how to play. He wheeled through the crossed elephant tusks that led to the trophy room, with its lions and tigers mounted in fierce poses—bought in bulk. They made him feel ridiculous—he, who had never been off Manhattan island. He kept going, knowing that he was now hunting his own frustration, through parlors, salons, galleries only half-remembered, like the rooms of a hotel visited for just a single night long ago. The furniture had been sent to him by his agents in Europe, and consisted almost entirely of the heirlooms of distressed aristocrats—people who did not understand the new mercantile economy, in which pictures of naked ladies shipped in brown paper packages were the foundation of empire, stronger than the saber or cannon, more valuable than serfs or ancestral lands.

They deserved to lose what they had, but what was he doing with it? It was all junk. He would get rid of it in the morning.

He ended up by the indoor pool, staring down at his reflection in the water. It was a simple drawing made with a minimum of strokes: an eye, a nose. But this was not what the baby had seen, could not be.

He realized then that it was time for the mother and child to leave. They were ruining his concentration. This was a place of business, not a home for unwed mothers.

The resolution seemed to make him feel better. It is a strange fact that water makes soothing noises even when absolutely still. Listening to the pool's wetness, he fell asleep and dreamed. He seemed to view his dream through a jeweler's glass. He could see every street and alley of a vast city, knew every life lived in each house. Who would kill whom, who marry whom. Each raindrop had a direction and purpose. It was a vision of order that left him amazed and overwhelmed and frightened of his own weakness, because somehow its continued existence depended on him, the fact of his looking, and he did not know if he had enough strength to go on.

The cries entered his dream in the form of a light-footed man, a gentleman jewel thief in top hat and tails. But the thing he was stealing was Auerbach himself—wheeling his chair out of the room with the pool, down the long hallway toward the bedroom where Jane Larue was staying with the baby. And when he awoke, he was in fact there, and the cries were hers, not the baby's. She was standing by the bed with the baby in her arms—cradled in such a way that Auerbach instantly understood something had happened. "Do something," she screamed, holding the baby out to him. "*Please.*"

He knew instinctively that he must not take the baby from her, that to do so would envelope him in something so heartbreakingly sad that he would never find his way out. But his hands seemed to reach up of their own accord. The little creature felt different now, its body slack, as if an essential string had been cut. Its face was blue, the eyes slightly open, showing the whites. A quick glance was all he could take.

"*Oh, please, please, please,*" wailed Jane Larue, hovering over him.

He thought of the pull-cord to call the servants. Somebody might know what to do. He began an awkward, weaving progress across the room, switching the baby from arm to arm so he could direct his chair. It seemed to take forever—there was furniture in the way—and then suddenly he was tipping, sprawling. He gripped the baby to his chest with one hand, broke his fall with the other, and rolled onto his back. From the corner of his eye, he could make out his chair a few feet away, tipped on its side. "Ring for help!" he yelled to Jane Larue, then raised himself to his elbow and watched her run toward the velvet cord. She tugged till it came down in her hands.

He sat upright, his blanket gone, his legs spread out in front of him. A moment later she was on her hands and knees beside him, crying hard. It would take time for anyone to come from the servants' quarters, which were at the far end of the east wing. "*Oh, God, my baby, my baby,*" she repeated, the words no longer language, but a kind of private song. He held the child up, looked at its blue face, and then clapped it on the back, at first gently and then harder. When that did not work, he shook it and watched its head wobble back and forth. These efforts seemed to require all the strength he had; he gasped for air. Finally, he could think of nothing else but to hold the baby to his chest, as if to fill it with the beating of his own heart.

Much later, with the doctor there, and Miss Parish, and three or four maids, and Jane Larue in a deep morphine sleep, he slipped away to the studio. He had never been there at night and was struck by its strangeness. There was no need for a lamp or candle. The enormous open space was streaked silver and blue by the moonlight, crisscrossed with shadow. The old theatrical properties and stage sets looked like they had been carved of obsidian or ice, as if they weighed a thousand pounds or might melt by morning. He tilted his head upward, gazing at the night sky through the glass dome. Stars were everywhere, a latticework of distant fires. Auerbach experienced that strange sense of limitless space—of falling upward—that the mind fights at such moments but cannot completely banish.

A photographer's job is to capture the light emitted by an object, in order to preserve its mark even after the object itself is gone. How many of the women who had modeled for him over the last twenty years were now dead? He counted them out—the ones he knew of—on his fingers: eight, possibly nine. Yet their light remained, traveling into the future in the form of French postcards, a dozen for a dollar. Not the most dignified memorial perhaps, but human—an artifact of their struggle.

He wished he had photographed the baby when he had the chance.

4. MRS. VERENA SWANN, SPIRIT MEDIUM

Verena Swann sat in her carriage, peeking through the curtain at the crowd of mourners filling the avenue. Derbies, bonnets, slick black umbrellas, here and there a pale, wet face like a camellia—pointed straight at her. They were waiting for her to open the door and get out, to become *theirs*—waiting for a woman who loved her husband so much she would not let him go, even in death.

Leopold, her brother-in-law, peered over her shoulder. "Look at this," he whispered. "Thousands standing in the rain, for *you.*"

"For *him*," she corrected. It was uncomfortable hearing the thought aloud. This was Theodore's funeral, after all. They were here to honor him, to recognize the sacrifice he had made for his country.

"There's no *him* without *you*," said Leopold.

In a practical sense it was true: Verena was not only Theodore's wife, but also his voice. Since his death, she had learned how to open herself like a door, so that his disembodied spirit could enter and fill her with his thoughts. She fell into a trance, and the two of them became entwined in a way she could not describe. His hand moved her pen. Her mouth formed his words. She shook with his laughter and cried with his sorrow.

Leopold sat back in his seat, clearly moved by the sight of the crowd. "All our hard work is finally paying off, isn't it?"

The funeral, the crowds—they really were Leopold's achievement. It was Leopold who had enlisted Verena in a campaign to raise funds for a rescue expedition. Under his direction, they had toured the country, lecturing on the history of Arctic exploration and the wonders of Spiritualism.

In the process, they had built Verena's talent into a lucrative business. Verena was now the most sought-after spirit medium in the country. Her public séances were filled to capacity, and her private sittings commanded truly startling fees. She was consulted by industrialists, politicians, and European nobility. She and Leopold moved through the upper reaches of New York society, welcome in the very best salons and most exclusive drawing rooms—places a milliner's daughter would otherwise never have seen.

"You led the way," she told him.

Leopold gave a self-deprecating shrug. "You realize that nothing will be the same after this, Verena. We will be working on an entirely different level."

She parted the curtain and looked out again at the sea of umbrellas filling Fifth Avenue. The newspapers had predicted ten thousand, but it seemed like the entire city was there, waiting for her. "What level is that?" she asked.

"Real influence, real wealth."

There was a knock, and the carriage door opened. A solemn young man in top hat and morning coat stuck his head in. "It's time, Mrs. Swann."

She felt something turn upside down inside of her, but did not falter. She lowered her veil, took the young man's hand, and stepped down to the cobblestones, followed by Leopold.

The crowd was different close-up—powerfully physical. The mourners steamed in the rain like horses. She looked from face to face, stunned by her need for them: to love her, to lift her up like a child and fill her with their electricity.

"Are you all right?" asked Leopold.

"I'm fine."

"You're trembling." He took her arm, moving her down the aisle cleared by the police—with his other hand holding an umbrella over her head. And then he did what he did for her so often: talked her through. "Eyes forward," he whispered. "Head up. Breathe. That's right."

"I said I'm fine."

"Pay attention. The governor's waiting up ahead. Remember to thank him for his support."

The governor met them at the foot of the cathedral stairs. "Mrs. Swann," he said, taking her hand—he was a client. "At last, he's home."

She was surprisingly good at this—polite pleasantries with the rich and influential. "Your help made all the difference, Governor."

She shook hands with the rest of the party: two congressmen, a senator, the mayor, the police chief, various gangsters and millionaires. Seton Bittersley, editor of the *World Dispatch Leader* and president of the Clean Living League, gripped her hand tightly in both of his and wouldn't let go. Police Inspector Wolfscheim saluted, looking martial. Some said the police chief took orders from him, and not the other way around. The Reverend Voorhees murmured something so low and respectful she could not hear it.

Her gaze wandered back to the crowd below. The faces were watching her with a frankly assessing air, as if she were an actor in a play. Of course, they were not mourners, really, but spectators. They had come to submerge themselves in a little piece of history, to be excited and soothed by ritual, to savor the feelings evoked by dead heroes: exaltation, national pride, a sense of the tragic dimensions of life. Some of them may have been in the crowd at the dock when Captain Swann sailed for the Arctic. They may have remembered an indistinct figure at the rail of a ship, waving with great dignity. For most of them, however, he was simply the man in the photograph, a much-reproduced portrait by the expedition photographer, Horatio Portus: Swann dressed in a suit of fur, a noble squint on his handsome, sunburned face. Visible behind him, a landscape of ice, alarming in its white barrenness—a portent of danger and loss.

Did they understand the sacrifice he had made for them? Or the terrible price she had paid to reclaim him?

"Let's go," said Leopold.

Verena began to climb the cathedral stairs, her arm still in Leopold's, her eyes focused on the yellow light of the interior, hazy through the black mesh of her veil. Leopold helped her into the pew, and she was careful to arrange the folds of her dress before sitting. Behind them were the families of the three other expedition members who had not been found, followed by rows of men in black coats, top hats on their laps: the Geographic Society, the Museum of Natural History, the Smithsonian, the Explorers Club. There was a low hum of conversation, echoing in the stone hall.

She lifted her veil to look at the altar. It was crowded with wreaths bearing the names of scientific, fraternal, and patriotic societies: the Elks, the Masons, the Thalassographical Society, the Brotherhood of Arctic Whalers, and the Clean Living League. The casket was off to her left, almost hidden by the wreaths. Poor Theodore, she thought, shoved aside by our love for him.

She reached up, removed the locket from her neck, and opened the lid. The photograph had been taken five years before, just prior to his departure for the Arctic. In it, he was a young man of thirty-three, with thick black hair combed back from his face; high cheekbones like an Indian warrior; and those enormous black eyes.

Verena Swann loved her husband so much that she would not abandon him, even in death: that was the reason the mourners stood out in the rain, watching to see her step out of her carriage. She was their proof that love is not limited to the body; that it can travel ten thousand miles over ice and snow and be secreted in the pocket like a pebble.

Verena envied them their simple proof, because for her, love had become a maddeningly complicated thing. Did she love Theodore? What did that *mean*, exactly? Was it the ache she felt in her chest at night? Or the tingle that moved down her neck when the trance began to take hold? By contrast, she knew she had loved her father—his severe black coats, his fragrance of macassar oil, leather, and wool. She had loved the way he twirled her around and around till her feet stuck straight out in the air.

She had loved her mother too, though it was a different kind of love, voiceless and anxious. After her father died, her mother was always in the shop, cutting velvet, arranging feathers. Her gray eyes would hold Verena for a moment—disappointed, seemingly, that she was not a man, not her husband—and then move on to the next task: sewing, gluing, waiting on customers. Verena worked in the shop after school just to stand beside her, just to hand her things— an ostrich plume, a sewing needle. When she graduated, she began working full days, from seven in the morning to nine at night, six days a week.

The customers came in, resplendent with their complex, interesting lives, radiant with the world outside. She heard little snatches of their life histories, all shaped by the need for a hat—a cousin getting married, a tea party, a trip to Newport or the seashore. Between tasks, Verena would look up and catch little glimpses of their world through the plate glass window: young women walking in groups, wives with their husbands and children, men hurrying on business. Then her mother would call for her—something about silk or feathers—and she would return to the business of making hats.

She met Theodore at a Broadway arcade one Sunday, amidst exhibits of carnivorous plants and two-headed sheep. She was there with two other girls from the shop to see the dancing chicken and the minstrel show, and to ask questions of the fortune-teller. She noticed him in the shooting gallery, a dashing figure in his naval uniform, picking off the mechanical ducks one after the other with a little air rifle. She remembered his icy white teeth, his dark eyes, the sea-black of his hair and beard. He introduced himself in the café, bought her an ice cream, and they walked together through the exhibits—intersecting now and again with her friends, who pretended not to see them. They watched a strange mechanical figure, an automaton, defeat one person after another at chess, and they stopped at a booth where a man displayed a little electromagnetic machine, powered by a hand-crank. He told Theodore to hold the wire in his palm and clasp Verena's hand in his. The man cranked, and she felt some strange force shoot through Theodore's hand and into hers, a kind of prickly excitement.

"Now let go," said the man, but neither of them could, their fingers would not move. Their hands were melded together, and they laughed—a little wildly, as if riding a runaway horse.

She had expected marriage to be the start of her real life. She thought it would give her what the customers in the shop possessed—a life worth buying hats for. In a sense, it did. She became Mrs. Theodore Swann, wife of the noted explorer. There were balls, galas, and public appearances, all to raise money for one expedition or another. But Theodore was prey to terrible black moods, periods of lethargy and despair, and her life was soon ruled by the signs of their arrival: her husband at the window, staring out for hours at a time; at the dinner table, chewing his food in silence. He looked at her as if she were a stranger. He slept fitfully, woke crying from nightmares, then began consuming patent syrups in order to rest— more each night, to less and less effect. She lay in bed alone, listening to the creak of floorboards as he paced out in the hall. His face grew haggard, the eyes sunken, bleary—the face of a stranger. Eventually, he locked himself in a room with a Bible and a bottle of whiskey—for two days, three. She put her ear to the door and heard him talking to himself, the sound of virulent argument.

Most of the time, he was away at sea, his absence a constant presence in the house, punctuated every three or four months by thick letters smelling of the ocean. She stayed up nights, frightened of receiving bad news—of shipwreck, drowning, or avalanche. If she had ever lay awake in the early-morning light and daydreamed of his death, it was just because she could not stand fearing it any longer.

Soon after learning of his disappearance, Verena attended her first séance. She did not go with the intention of locating him; she still wanted to believe him alive. But there was a feeling inside her, a kind of grief that seemed to partake of everything that had ever happened in her life. It sat in her throat and nothing seemed able to dislodge it, and so she wanted to be among people who cried.

She was not disappointed; there was much weeping at the séance, and though she sat in granite silence, she found that it helped to watch others release their tears. She began frequenting a number of regular sittings about town; it was at one of Miss Fabricant's that she first made contact with some kind of unseen force that used loud rapping noises—sharp as the sound of knuckles against hard wood—to answer yes or no to simple questions. Do you miss me? Do you love me? Later, at a Ouija board, the cup had spelled C-O-L-L-D. That was how she felt, cold, numb with cold. A few days after that, the Warren sisters had brought out what they called a planchette, a little heart-shaped board supported by two caster wheels with a nub of pencil at the narrow end. They had placed the device upon a sheet of brown butcher's paper and then rested the tips of their bitten fingers upon the device, and it had skittered from right to left and back again. Afterward, on the paper beneath, they had found the letters S-N-O hidden among the scribbling.

Theodore, she assumed. So began an immersion as passionate and confused as their earthly romance—more so, in fact, because it lacked the man himself, with his mysterious blankness, his love of ice, whiteness, and cold. She traveled the country to attend the most celebrated séances: to Chicago to meet Mrs. Lovejoy, to St. Louis to speak to Miss Aphra Raines. She read Machtinger on the theory of transmigration and Canaday on electromagnetic evidence for the soul. In Utica, Professor Braithwaite said he detected an unusually strong magnetic force around her, and that night suggested a laying on of hands. In the morning she found her gift. To say that Verena came to believe would be misleading, as it would imply that some form of doubt or disbelief had been overcome, some state of conviction reached. The two things existed side by side: she believed, and she disbelieved. She *felt*.

Soon after that, she had left with Leopold on their tour of the country. It was a strange, dreamlike time, of dresses going into the trunk, coming out again, and then going back in, of midnight trains and woozy dawns met on railroad platforms, of winter skies seemingly hammered from iron, enclosing little towns where trees and buildings were sheathed entirely in ice. Settled in the middle of vast prairies or endless fields, the towns looked like little glass sculptures arranged on a child's dresser top. The windows of the trains were iced over, her view of the countryside as it passed distorted as through a kaleidoscope.

She and Leopold lectured in opera houses and town halls almost daily. Their performance was part lesson on the natural history of the Arctic, part dramatic narrative of the Swann expedition, part patriotic exhortation, and part sentimental hymn to marriage. Afterward, they would hold a séance, either in a private home or in the grange hall or Masonic lodge. The trances came right away—she never failed. The gift wholly consumed her. Hardly sleeping or eating, unsure just where on the map she was or where they were going next, knowing no one, utterly dependent on Leopold, she seemed to be floating through the world, halfway toward becoming a ghost. The feeling was both frightening and strangely thrilling. She had dreams in which she was still riding on that train, neither knowing nor caring about her destination.

They succeeded in raising enough money to mount an expedition to search for Theodore's remains, and when it was forced back by storms, a second one the following year. By then they were back in New York, renting a town house on Washington Square. At Leopold's suggestion, she had begun offering sittings for a fee, turning their philanthropic enterprise into a business venture. But what else could she do? Her mother had died shortly after Verena's marriage, the hat shop was gone, and Theodore had left nothing but a small naval pension.

There were people who accused her of profiting from her husband's disappearance. She understood their distaste all too well: Captain Theodore Swann, a national hero, entered her body and utilized her voice to tell paying customers where to find the lost pocket watch and the missing ring. To the philosophical, he gave long disquisitions on Swedenborg and the nature of the afterlife. For the bereaved, he located lost relatives among the great masses of the dead. While Theodore did these things, Leopold moved about the scene with a camera, taking pictures of the participants in which the forms of discarnate spirits appeared in the background, floating in the air. The pictures were both proof and souvenir.

There was no denying that Theodore's death had conferred certain benefits, and that to enjoy those benefits put her in a certain position. His voice, calling to her from the other side, had revealed a talent dormant within her, a talent that would have otherwise remained hidden. It had given her what she always lacked: work, purpose, independence.

It was exciting to be the center of attention in the room, to be so desperately needed. And yet it did not feel good. The sittings were exhausting; they left her nauseous, sick and drained. When she closed her eyes at night, she saw the sitters staring at her, felt their hungry touch. There were side effects, strange episodes when she came awake from the trance and could not move her legs. Leopold would have to carry her up to bed. This might last hours or days, the feeling completely gone from the limbs. There were also bouts of intense weeping, of incoherence and waking dreams, fits of anger during which she would lose control of her hands, pummeling and scratching herself wildly—her face, her breasts—till she raised welts and drew blood. It was the price of being caught between the living and the dead; they were both very difficult customers, full of demands, and they would not let her rest. She told herself that she was nothing more than a kind of telephone or telegraph, but nevertheless, the work left her feeling hollowed-out.

And then there were the times when *it*, the trance, did not come—increasingly frequent now. Leopold had taught her how to work around this, but fabricating was even harder to do, and left her trembling with fear, too anxious to sleep. What if *it* did not return? What would become of her? All she had was *it*, the ability to open like a door.

She was taking things for her nerves now, just like Theodore had done, little glasses of sherry, teaspoons of syrup that left her woozy, adrift between dreams.

She spent the night after the funeral walking from room to room, too overwrought to sleep. Dawn found her in the parlor, looking over Theodore's Arctic curios: the stuffed polar bear, snowshoes and whaling harpoons, scrimshaw and Eskimo carvings. He had, in general, no interest in possessions, but these pieces of rock and bone were important to him. He would not let anyone else touch them, and insisted on dusting and polishing them himself.

When had they degenerated to the level of décor? Their sole purpose was to impress the customers now, to make certain they knew they were in the house of Captain Theodore Swann, and that Verena Swann was really the great explorer's widow. She picked up one of the penguins he had particularly liked. He had nicknamed it Winters. It was the size of an infant, but unexpectedly light, fragile-seeming. She guessed it was stuffed with straw. She sat down on a couch and hugged it to her, careful not to squeeze too hard, and was soon so busy weeping that she did not notice Leopold, standing in his dressing gown in the parlor entrance, framed by the whale's jaw. "Can I get you something?" he asked.

"It's Winters," she said, through her tears. "You remember? He called this one Winters."

Leopold came forward to look. The dressing gown was paisley, the pajamas striped. "That's one of the new ones," he said. He had bought a load of objects from a dealer in St. Louis about a year before, to replace the things that had gotten broken as they moved about the country, raising funds for the rescue mission.

"Are you sure it's not Winters?" she asked. She put the penguin down on the coffee table and looked it over. It did look a little less shabby than she remembered it.

"Winters started to molt in Chicago," he said, kneeling down on the floor beside her. "Do you want something, Verena? A glass of sherry?" His handsome face had turned oddly complicated. He looked embarrassed but also determined, and his eyes seemed to watch helplessly as the rest of him plunged onward. "You know how close we've become. I feel like I know your every thought, your every feeling."

Verena had a pang of alarm. She had feared a moment like this, but she had not thought it would come so soon. "I'm all right. Go back to sleep."

"How can I sleep if you're down here weeping over a penguin?" He smiled a pained smile.

It was not his closeness. She was used to that. His robe was loose and the top of his pajamas unbuttoned, showing the base of his thickly muscled neck. She could smell his cologne, his hair pomade. Under normal circumstances these things were soothing to her, tokens of his physical solidity. Leopold was real, not a voice or a prose style, not a tingle in the back of her neck.

"I'm not weeping for a penguin," she said.

He looked chastened but determined. "He's home now. It took three years, but we brought him home. The funeral ended that phase for us. We have a chance to start something new."

"What about Theodore?"

"He wants us to live, Verena."

"Does he?" She had never gotten that feeling. Theodore's communications were full of information about the other side, thoughts about his past life, fragments of philosophy, but they rarely touched on her. He mostly worried about whether she was writing fast enough. *Get that down?* and *Are you listening?* were frequent interjections.

"He wants us to be happy," said Leopold with great conviction.

Verena felt the emotional balance shifting dangerously between them. She had been aware for some time that Leopold's feelings toward her had become hazardous. The ordinary word was *attachment*, but in truth they were already doubly attached: not only brother- and sister-in-law, but partners in the act of calling up voices.

Nothing would be more natural than to marry him. But if she did, she would disappear into her strange function as a speaking tube between the here and the gone. Leopold would hold her to his ear like a seashell in order to hear what Theodore had to say. She would be lost between the brothers.

She could not allow Leopold to upset the balance. She could not say yes to him, could not marry him, but was afraid to say no and anger him. The more she wished to be free of her current mode of life, the more she feared that freedom. What if Leopold left her? What if she lost her ability to speak for the dead? What other life could she have? On her own she would be nothing. It would be like the years before she met Theodore: perpetual waiting for something to happen.

No, it was better to make *Leopold* wait, and so she tried to change the subject. "They think we're using him," she said.

"We're helping him." His face was earnest, utterly sincere; she knew he believed this absolutely. "He's a lot more famous because of us."

"But they think we're helping ourselves," she said.

"And what's wrong with that?" He took her hand in his, very gently. It was a large, supple hand, a hand that could make playing cards disappear and silver dollars travel from finger to finger like a caterpillar. "I want to help you too, Verena. I want to help you get everything you deserve. Money, fame, happiness."

She could not find the strength to draw her hand away but let it go limp—a compromise. Her chin sagged to her chest. "It's too soon."

"It's been three years." He spoke very quickly, as if trying to get it all out before she stopped him. "I know this is poor timing, Verena, but you know me. You know that I loved Theodore too. The two things are not in conflict. Quite the opposite."

She managed to pull her hand out. "Everything will be ruined."

"Our work will go on as before. Better than ever."

"We're brother and sister, Leopold."

He winced, and then a hardness crept into his face. "I'm tired of being the brother." She knew this applied to Theodore more than to herself. Leopold had struggled in Theodore's shadow for so long, struggled still, even now that Theodore was dead.

There was nothing she could say. Leopold gave her a resentful glance, and then heaved to his feet and left.

She kept to her room the rest of the day, avoiding him. In the evening she asked the maid, Maisie, to bring her dinner up on a tray, but Leopold sent word that she must come down; they had a sitting at ten and he wanted to make sure she ate. She found him practicing card tricks with his usual methodical patience. He could be cold sometimes when he was unhappy with her—she dreaded his silences—but he seemed to have chosen to simply forget about their earlier talk, and she was grateful. She lay down on one of the couches, beneath the glassy gaze of the stuffed polar bear. "I'm not well," she told him.

"We can't cancel, if that's what you mean. Mayhew is coming."

They had been discussing the inevitability of this visit for months now. Dr. Morris Mayhew was a member of the Society for the Study of Psychic Phenomenon, but he had recently diverged from that organization's usual scholarly mumbling to declare public war on Spiritualism and Spiritualists in an editorial in the *World Dispatch Leader*. His movements were now closely tracked by the half-dozen or so newsletters that circulated among professional mediums.

"I'm not well enough," said Verena.

"Rest a little."

She got up at eight-thirty and had dinner in her bathrobe. Leopold pushed her to eat a little boiled chicken, some mashed potatoes, a couple of spoonfuls of rice pudding. Eventually he grew impatient, took the fork, and fed her himself. She liked being fed by him; his hands were large and hairy but surprisingly delicate as they wielded the fork. "This Dr. Mayhew," she said to him between bites.

"You met him once," he said. "A very small man. Open."

She swallowed a bit of chicken. "You said he wants to send us to jail?"

"Nobody's talking about jail, Verena. Open."

She ignored the clump of mashed potatoes at the end of the fork. "What are we talking about, then?"

"He thinks we're frauds."

"Isn't it obvious?"

"Not to him, apparently. Open now."

She took the mashed potatoes and chewed. "He's going to see right through me."

"There's nothing to see."

"Well, that's the problem, isn't it?"

"That's the beauty," said Leopold, stretching out the word in his rich chocolate baritone.

She took her bath and dressed in the clothes Leopold had laid out for her on her bed, a white velvet gown and red silk shawl, pearls, gloves, and tiara. She was ready on time—a very rare occurrence—but ten fifteen found her hiding in the kitchen, pouring sherry into a water glass. Leopold came and took her by the arm. "I can't go in there," she said, glancing in the direction of the front parlor, where the weepers were milling—*weepers*, their private word for the clients.

"Of course you can," said Leopold. He was in a cutaway, his hair brushed back with pomade.

"I can't and I won't," she said, and then gulped from the glass till he pulled it away—both of them careful not to spill on her dress.

"These people are depending on you, Verena."

"For what?" she gasped. The sherry was heavy and sweet in her mouth, sharp at the base of her throat. She felt dizzy and panicked, as if the ground were slipping from under her feet.

"For whatever it is they get from you." He put an arm around her shoulder and led her out of the kitchen and through the hallway. The noise filtered in from the room beyond, making her shiver: the hungry murmur of voices, the impatient clinking of teacups and saucers, the muffled pawing of shoes on the carpet.

"I can't," she whispered. "Please." They were standing at the double doors that led into the parlor.

"Breathe," said Leopold, breathing in deeply himself. "From the diaphragm. In….Out….In…." And then, before she could say anything else, he pulled open the doors.

She stood for a single beat, blinking at the light from the electric chandelier. The room was full of people, holding teacups and butter cookies in postures of exaggerated civility, like children playing at a tea party. They looked toward her now, their faces forgotten in expressions of such desperate need that they would not normally have worn them, even when alone.

Silence fell over the room. Leopold took her arm and together they started forward, practiced as actors. She kept his slow, stately pace, careful to stand straight, to nod and smile, to breathe from the diaphragm. The strange, inexplicable thing was that she was good at this game, this playacting. The weepers turned to watch her as she moved, human sunflowers following the sun, eager to be noticed, to be singled out for a greeting, to be given a chance to speak and unburden. "Over there," whispered Leopold, barely moving his lips. He signaled the direction with his glance. She saw, standing in front of the polar bear, an older man, very small, with a white imperial and a bemused, kindly face. Dr. Mayhew.

"I see him," she whispered back.

"Stay away from him," said Leopold. "Leave him to me. Understand?"

"You always treat me like a child."

"Why is that?" And then, "Time to mingle."

They split with practiced ease, Leopold moving off to the left, shaking hands, bowing, making his way toward the photographic equipment set up in the corner. While she mixed with the weepers, soaking up their sadness and confusion, he would take their portraits.

And then Mrs. Wheeler was upon her, and Verena made her voice as grave and steady as she could manage. "How are you?" she asked.

Mrs. Wheeler gave a sad smile. "Better, Mrs. Swann."

"And the nights?"

"The nights are not good."

"You miss her," said Verena. Mrs. Wheeler's daughter had taken arsenic some months before.

"Yes." It was a sound like a rusty hinge.

"You feel as if half of you is gone."

"If only I could bring her back," said Mrs. Wheeler, reaching beneath her veil to cover her eyes with her hands.

"What would you do then?"

"Tell her I'm sorry."

"Why?"

"Because I am." It was a howl, but no louder than a whisper.

Verena took Mrs. Wheeler's arm in a curious gesture, as if testing her doneness. "You will get your chance. One of these nights, I promise." And then, as if caught in a fib, she glanced over at the corner where Dr. Mayhew had stood. He was still there, still looking amiably content to observe the scene.

What an earful she would give him if she ever decided to confess! She would tell him that it was all a lie, that the search for the dead had nothing to do with love. She would tell him that the weepers cried not for the departed but for themselves, because they had to stay and live on with all the needs that living people have. She would tell him that she too was wracked by those needs, to the point where she sometimes thought she would go mad.

But of course, she would not confess; it would be an absurd act of self-destruction. And so she moved on, touching people lightly as she traveled through the room, saying hello as if offering news of immortality. From the corner of her eye she saw Leopold taking Mrs. Wheeler's portrait—Mrs. Wheeler sitting stiffly in the chair, obviously a little frightened. Images of discarnate spirits appeared floating in the background of Leopold's prints, and Mrs. Wheeler probably expected a double portrait with her daughter. No doubt Leopold meant to oblige her. He was a magnificent photographer.

And then she was speaking to Mr. French, cupping his hand in both of hers. "How are you, Mr. French?" asked Verena.

Mr. French had entered into a suicide pact with a young woman. "I need to speak with her," he said.

"We will find her for you—in time."

"It's been months." His face went through a series of contortions as he tried to master his feelings, finally collapsing into an expression of abject befuddlement. "I'm not a coward, Mrs. Swann."

"On the contrary," said Verena, pressing his hand. And then she could not help but glance over to Dr. Mayhew's corner—that is how she thought of it now, his corner. He was still there, watching her, a genial smile on his lips.

She disengaged from Mr. French and moved toward Jane Larue, who was pushing a man in a wheelchair. Verena knew that the seated figure must be Augustus Auerbach, the millionaire; Leopold had already done a great deal of research on him. "Jane, dear, I'm so glad you could come," said Verena, taking both her hands. She fought the urge to look back and check on Dr. Mayhew.

"Thank you," said Jane, her voice frothy with emotion. "Thank you so much for everything." She began to cry despite her broad smile. "You've given me back my Augie."

"You never lost him." Verena reached out and wiped away the tears with a finger. "Nobody is ever lost, Jane, only misplaced." She put her finger to the tip of her tongue, as if tasting a dish she were cooking, and then turned to address the man in the wheelchair. "I'm so glad you could join us tonight, Mr. Auerbach."

He did not look like she imagined somebody in that line of work might look like—neither sinister nor seedy, but rather shy. He was handsome too, with wavy black hair and sensitive dark eyes, and elegantly dressed in a black silk coat and white vest. A cashmere throw rug covered his legs. He sat very straight, with an elegant sort of formality. When he spoke, his voice was soft. "Miss Larue has told me you perform wonders, Mrs. Swann."

"Is there somebody in particular you would like to contact?"

He seemed startled by this, as if he had not considered the possibility. "No, no, I'm simply here to listen and learn."

"Oh, it is never that simple," she said. "The spirits pull you in."

"Look this way!" cried Leopold, and then there was the explosion of the flash powder.

5. THE SWANNS POSE A DANGER

Auerbach did not normally allow his picture to be taken. He most especially did not want a crudely doctored photograph of himself with ghosts in white togas superimposed on the background. He had spent much of his apprenticeship in the darkroom, retouching plates, and he knew just how easy a trick it was. But he did not protest, because he had struck a very advantageous deal with Jane Larue: he would accompany her to see the Swanns, and in exchange she would return to work. He was determined that she should have no excuse to back out.

That wish was not entirely self-serving. After the funeral, Jane Larue had moved out of the mansion, back to her apartment on Cherry Street, where she apparently did nothing but brood on her loss. Auerbach was convinced that work would provide the distraction she needed, before her grief hardened into morbid obsession. And so he had felt hopeful that morning, when Mr. Grapes opened the office door and ushered her in. She was dressed in mourning, layer upon layer of black, with a great black saucer of a hat atop her head. It made her look paler than she already was. "I'm so glad to see you looking better, Miss Larue," he said.

"I came to thank you for your help with the funeral."

"Yes, of course." He tried to wave the subject away—the whole matter was too odd and confusing for words. "All I want to know is that you are feeling better."

"Yes, much better."

She looked terrible, in fact, haggard and wasted, but there was no telling when he would have another chance. "I think you should consider coming back to work, Miss Larue. Work can do wonders in a situation like yours."

She blinked in a dazed sort of way, her head cocked to one side as if listening to a conversation next door. "I should tell you, I've spoken with him."

He assumed she meant Henry Twersky, who had been missing since the day of the birth. "I'd like to speak to him myself."

"He says I don't need to worry, he's very happy now. There was no—" Her face contorted, fighting off tears. "No pain at all. He says he's never lonely, he's with me all the time. Even here, even now." And then she really did begin to cry, a terrible gushing of tears.

Only then did Auerbach realize that she meant the baby. "Would you like some tea, Miss Larue?" He reached for the buzzer to call the butler. "And a piece of cake, perhaps? Let me get you some cake."

"He says the only thing he worried about was me, because I didn't know he was here. But now I know." She laughed, wiping at her tears with the back of her hand. "Oh, Mr. A., I've met the most wonderful woman. She's the one who put me in contact, and I thought of you, thought of you first thing." She looked at him earnestly, with a kind of naïve benevolence, wanting to make him a repository for her good news.

"Me?" he asked, genuinely puzzled.

"She can do wonders, Mr. A."

"But I don't need any wonders, Miss Larue."

"But you do. We all do." She actually fell to her knees in front of his desk—an actress, after all. "Please let her help you."

He did not know why this mattered to her, but he could see the opportunity it presented. "Perhaps I can, but I'll need something from you in exchange."

They understood each other in an instant. She sighed, stood up, and dusted off the skirt of her dress. "If that's what it takes."

Auerbach should have been greatly satisfied by this conclusion, but he had, in fact, fretted the rest of the day, until the appointed time for their journey to Washington Square. To begin with, he hated leaving the mansion, and did so only when absolutely necessary. A trip outside meant being lifted into and out of the carriage, and then up and down stairs at his destination, all the while being gawked at by fools. Even more important, it wasted time better spent on work.

But that was not all; he had a particular antipathy to the idea of a séance. An interest in ghosts, angels, and the life hereafter were symptoms of weakness to him. He had never wasted a minute imagining his mother in heaven, and had never sought her ghostly comfort. He did not even miss her—he did not have the time.

Yet here he was, on the whim of a photographic model, in this strange parlor with its polar bear and penguins, and its air of a betting shop right before the big race, trying his best to fit in. He let the crowd in the parlor stare as much as it wished, and kept a smile fixed on his face, as if he did not mind being gawked at like a carnival exhibition. Occasionally he would even nod in a stiff sort of greeting.

And then he met the spirit medium, Mrs. Swann. He had read of her in the newspapers, of course, but there she was, completely different from what he had expected: younger, prettier, dressed in white velvet instead of gray wool, her delicate face full of a watchful intelligence. It had been so long since he had talked to anyone other

...ian an employee; he felt clumsy and slow, annoyed with himself. And then the flash powder had exploded.

"It's time," said Mrs. Swann, and directed the company to the far end of the parlor, where a large table stood ready. Large as it was, the table was inadequate for the number present, and seating arrangements were complicated, with both Swanns fielding entreaties and complaints. Auerbach inserted his wheelchair between Mr. French and Jane Larue and waited for the others to get settled.

The lamps were extinguished and candles lit. Incense made the air foreign, peppery. Mrs. Swann asked them all to hold hands. Auerbach greatly regretted not wearing gloves, but did as he was told, taking a stranger's hand in his left and Jane's in his right. Jane's was warm and small and clasped his own with the naturalness of a child. This was only the second time he had ever held her hand.

Mrs. Swann recited a "Prayer to Light," each line beginning with the invocation "O Light! O Blessed Ray!" Mr. Swann then led the group in an ecumenical "Hymn to the Sky," his mellow dark baritone dominating the singing. Auerbach alone remained silent, but watched with interest. He sensed a professional overlap with the Swanns. Like him, they charged money in exchange for emotion.

The hymn ended and there was a moment of silence. "Now," said Mrs. Swann, "I ask you all to close your eyes and picture the spirit you wish to contact while I prepare to enter my trance."

Auerbach kept his open, staring at the other sitters as they went through these mental exertions. Their faces were all radiant with the same kind of dark excitement—a greed for feeling. He imagined the John Smiths looked that way while thumbing through the Rive Gauche catalogue. Beside him, Jane Larue squeezed her eyes shut and leaned forward in her chair, as if rushing to meet baby Augie.

He turned to look at Mrs. Swann, directly across the table. She sat back in her chair, chin thrust out, face angled upward toward the ceiling. The pose accentuated the line of her neck, which was long and shapely and vulnerable.

And then a voice spoke out. "Who is she anyway, and what do you really know about her?"

It took him a moment to realize that it was in fact her, Mrs. Swann. The voice was darker, rougher, ever so slightly slurred at the edges—the voice of a drinker who has finally found his subject, deep in a long night of drinking—a male voice. And yet Auerbach could not specifically say what was drunk about it, or male about it; it remained Mrs. Swann's. She seemed to be talking to someone in particular, to have picked up in the middle of a conversation. It was loud enough, yet hard to follow, like eavesdropping through a door.

A dirty smoker's laugh. "Why do you make her do this? Just give it to her. Empty your pockets and go." Pause. "Go ahead, stop gawking. Walk out on her, leave, leave her alone. She doesn't need you."

She sat still in her seat, her chest pushed out, her shoulders back, her head tilted up and to the side—as if someone were pulling her up by the scruff of her neck. Her face was stretched in a bitterly amused grimace. Her eyes were all but closed. "For God's sake, don't you see she's laughing at you?" she cried. The movement of her lips and the sound of her voice seemed oddly unsynchronized, like a kinetophone in which music and pictures have fallen out of step.

A murmur went around the room. Auerbach distinctly heard the phrase "disruptive spirit" and forgot about looking for signs of fraud. Though he considered himself wise to all tricks, his real talent was for credulity—for believing in the picture before him. Somebody was wearing Mrs. Swann like a suit of old clothes, and he was afraid. He looked over at Jane Larue. Her eyes were open and she was staring at the medium. Things were going wrong; she would not be speaking to her baby. Her hand tightened around Auerbach's.

"An errant spirit," said Mr. Swann, at the other end of the table. "There's no danger. It happens all the time." And then he said directly to Mrs. Swann, "There are people here waiting to speak to their loved ones."

"The loved ones have the night off."

"Then we might as well send everyone home."

There was a long pause, Mrs. Swann with her eyes closed, but much going on in her face—a thinking face. Around the table, the congregants stared at her, the upset still in their eyes. They looked like children watching their parents fight at the dinner table. They were still holding hands, hunched forward but ready to spring up and run if need be.

When Mrs. Swann spoke again, her voice was changed: clipped, clean, a bit officious. "I would have clapped him in irons. I put the cook in irons once, when he complained about the provisions. Can't have complaining. It undermines morale." She sat straight in her chair now, her chin up.

"It's the captain," whispered Jane, her hand relaxing in his.

"Who?"

"Captain Swann." She seemed greatly relieved. "Her husband."

Mrs. Swann continued. "Discipline is everything. There is nothing more beautiful than a group of men united to achieve a worthy goal. Self-sacrifice is the requirement. Even the bonds of sentiment—wives and children, for example—must be severed." And then switching abruptly: "There is a child here waiting to speak."

Jane tensed in her seat. "Augie," she keened, without further preliminaries. "My baby."

"Mama," said the medium. Her voice had changed once more, grown lighter, softer, breathier—and something else too, something he could hear but not describe. Somebody new was speaking through Mrs. Swann.

The medium sat forward, her hands grasped in front of her chest. "Do you miss me?" she asked Jane. Her lips were drawn up in a smile, though her eyes were still closed.

"Yes, oh yes." Jane looked at her as if she were looking at her baby.

"I'm with you all the time, Mama. I go wherever you go. I ride on your shoulder or in your hair. I touch your face with my hand."

"I wish I could see you."

"There's a lady here for him." There was an air of departure, a fading.

"Stay for a while," Jane pleaded.

A new voice, majestic. "Augustus, dear."

Auerbach did not respond—not because it was counterfeit but because it was so obviously genuine. His mother's air of authority permeated the room, her perfume rose out of the soapy smell of incense.

"Has it been so long that you do not remember me?"

He looked to Jane Larue for help, but she had her head in her hands. His eyes traveled around the table from watcher to watcher, looking for a cue that this was a fabrication, a magic show.

"Or are you too proud to own me? I was just a singer, after all, and now you are quite the gentleman." This was meant satirically; the medium's face had an expression that could only be called saucy. It was his mother, looking into her makeup mirror, admiring her handiwork, and then shifting her eyes ever so slightly to take in the little boy reflected beside her—admiring him admiring her handiwork.

"Mama?" asked Auerbach, very softly. He was embarrassed to use the word but had nothing else to call her—the last time he had spoken to her, he was ten years old. "Is that you?"

Laughter. "Oh, it's me all right. Still touring the hinterlands, waiting for a decent engagement." She gave a long, dramatic sigh. "I'm glad to have finally found you."

Auerbach answered tentatively, feeling his way forward, as if he were reading a play script he had just been handed. "You were looking for me?" he asked.

"Does a mother ever let go of her son?"

"I saw you fall." The memory was there, in the back of his mind, a shard of something larger. He was in the audience, as usual, watching her perform. The play was called *God's Newest Angel,* and her final scene required that she rise up to the rafters on a pulley to sing her last song of the evening. She was floating high above the stage, suspended by a rope and harness, when something snapped and she dropped.

"Do you blame me for that?" she asked, sounding amused.

He felt angry—she had, after all, left him an orphan—and then regretted the thought. "No, of course not," he told her.

"You didn't need me anyway, Augustus."

"I was a little boy, you know."

"But look at all you've achieved since then, entirely on your own."

"I'm a millionaire!" he howled, a cry of unquenchable sadness.

"But your legs," she whispered.

"Useless," he hissed. A fever had set in just days after her funeral, and he had been bedridden for months. Later he was beset by terrible soreness in the legs. He lost his sense of balance and began to stumble and fall. Soon he was unable to walk without crutches, and then even crutches were not enough. But by then the unnatural shortness of his legs was evident to anyone who looked—even himself. They had stopped growing while the rest of him had continued on toward adulthood. "The best medical minds in the country—" He was out of breath suddenly and could only manage fragments. "Some say glandular—others traumatic—"

"What does that mean?"

"I'm not sure." But of course he knew: they had meant the shock of watching her fall, at such an impressionable age. It was a notion he had rejected out of hand.

"This is nonsense," she said, imperious. "I want you to stand for me."

"What?"

"I said, stand for me. Stand up, this instant."

He struggled to do as she asked, and his last thought was that something terrible was happening. He was dizzy, lightheaded; little flashes seemed to sparkle around the room; and then his consciousness dissolved into blackness.

Auerbach woke to a blunt, aching pain in his nose. He was slumped low in his wheelchair, one arm hanging over the side. Looming over him was a half ring of faces: Leopold and Verena Swann, and an elderly gentleman with a neat, white imperial and a kindly smile. It was he who spoke. "Are you awake now, Mr. Auerbach? Do you need another sniff?" He waved a little blue vial of smelling salts. "No? Good. You had a little shock, but there's no reason to worry. You're fine now."

Auerbach found it hard to speak. He had been dreaming something very important and did not want to lose it, though he could not say what it was because it was already gone. "Who are you?" he whispered.

"My name is Mayhew, and I am a physician. Shall we sit you up now?" He gestured to Leopold Swann, and together they helped Auerbach right himself in the chair. "How do you feel?" he asked, smoothing the front of Auerbach's coat.

"Better," said Auerbach, though in fact he felt strange, as if still half dreaming. A small crowd was standing about, some people staring at him, others preoccupied with their own thoughts, brooding. It looked like a highly emotional gathering had just split up, and he feared that he might be the cause. But he could not remember what had happened.

"Do you know where you are?" asked Dr. Mayhew, as if reading his thoughts.

It was swiftly coming back to him. He recalled a complicated series of events: the coachman had carried him up the front stairs, then Jane Larue had grasped his hand at the table, and Mrs. Swann had pretended to be Jane's lost baby, Augustus. Jane's face had glowed in the candlelight, wet with tears and a kind of ecstasy of grief.

"A séance," said Auerbach. Yes, he remembered now. Before it began, Jane had wheeled him around the room and he had eavesdropped on the conversations. There had been much talk about rappings, levitations, automatic writing, and materializations—all of it in hushed tones of greed, like prospectors discussing the rumor of gold.

"And do you remember what happened?" asked Dr. Mayhew.

"Yes, yes, I do." But in fact his memory was confused. He had a nagging sense, for example, that he had just spoken to his mother. He must have dreamed about her while unconscious, and yet dreaming did not seem to fit the feeling of exhaustion that sat in his chest, a sense of great distances traveled. He felt as if he had wheeled himself thousands of miles away and then quickly returned, faster than the electrical pulse through a telegraph wire. Her voice still lingered in his ears, much as her perfume once lingered in his nose, many years before, when he was a boy. The words themselves had evaporated, but the sound remained behind as a shape in his memory, a gap, a hole to be filled: *Walk*, she had said, or something much like that. *Get up and walk.*

"How did I faint?" he asked.

Dr. Mayhew's smile carried a hint of smugness. "These events can create a great deal of nervous excitement, even for the most stable of individuals."

"I would put it differently," said Leopold Swann. "Speaking to the dead takes some getting used to."

"And then there was the physical strain," added Dr. Mayhew

matter-of-factly. "You tried to stand."

"Stand?" murmured Auerbach, feeling his face heat up.

Dr. Mayhew's eyes were almost merry: little blue half-moons above his white imperial. "Yes, it looked quite painful."

They had seen his legs—had seen him try to stand on those stunted, feeble limbs. Auerbach could think of nothing but escape now, as if the house were on fire. He would have raced to the door if Mrs. Swann had not blocked the way.

"I'm so very sorry," she said, looking guilt-stricken. "Can you ever forgive me? It's not me. It's the forces moving *through* me. They have to get out and I have no say, and sometimes the effects are terrible."

"Must go," he muttered, hardly knowing what he was saying. "Late for another appointment." He maneuvered around her, but his strength was gone, and the chair moved as if plowing through sand. It seemed to take forever to get to Jane Larue, who stood with a handkerchief pressed to her nose, an expression of grim exaltation on her face. Her eyes were red and her cheeks streaked with tears. "Let's go," he said to her.

"Not now," she said.

"Yes, now."

In the carriage they rode in silence. Auerbach brooded while Jane Larue sniffled into her black handkerchief. It angered him that she did not notice the distress she had caused him. That was how it was with the models: they took his ministrations for granted, as if he were their mother. He could die and they would not notice, till they needed a new dress, or help with the rent, or funeral expenses.

He dropped her off at her rooming house. "I kept my side of the bargain," he said to her as she climbed down to the sidewalk. "Now you keep yours."

She looked at him with sympathy. "It's like taking off your clothes, Mr. A. The first time is always hard."

"Just be in costume by eight."

She went without a word, her long black dress dragging along the sidewalk.

Back at home, Auerbach sat up by the fireplace, unable to coax himself into undressing for bed. He knew he would not be able to sleep. There was too much swirling inside him. He watched the flames and saw Mrs. Swann standing before him in white velvet and a tiara, radiating a strange sort of glamour. He felt again the need to say something clever, to best her. He wanted her to know that he did not need her help or her wonders, that he, for one, was in no need of spiritual comfort.

He thought of his mother. The voice he had heard could not really have been hers, but why then did it bring her back with such unusual clarity? He remembered how she had dressed him in velvet suits, fed him bonbons, and taken him for carriage rides around the Battery to wave to her admirers. She had let him help with her costumes, applying the brush to her lips and arranging the great towering wigs on her head. She was gone much of the time—on tour—or silent as a marble goddess, but there had also been nights when she sang him to sleep while stroking his head....

He tried to think of something, anything else, and ended up imagining his fainting spell: a lurching attempt to stand, followed by the fall back into his seat, like a puppet with a broken string. He pictured his lap rug on the floor and his legs exposed, the pants hiked up to display his bare shins. It was true that he showed his legs to the models whenever some empathy was needed; at such moments he delighted in the power they gave him. But this was different. The image of those people staring at his stunted limbs put him in an agony of shame, and the thought of Mrs. Swann seeing—he could follow the idea no further.

And that was when everything suddenly became clear: what had happened was no accident. The Swanns had tricked him, perhaps even drugged or mesmerized him, knowing that if he tried to stand he would inevitably fall down and pass out. Their plan was to humiliate and discredit him, and thus to wrest Jane Larue from his influence and take her for their own. They knew how important she was to Rive Gauche. They knew they could demand money or even a share of the business and he would be powerless to resist. Once having insinuated their way into the company, they would reduce him to a figurehead, a prisoner, a secret slave.

But there was actually a worse possibility, wasn't there? What if they decided to not even bother with mere blackmail? What if they simply put Jane Larue under contract to Kleinfeldt?

He felt himself growing hot. His head felt light. His heart was pounding like a fist on a door. And yet in truth he was relieved. After a strange and most stressful night, he was once again on familiar ground: he had enemies, and he would have to take action to protect himself against them. He wheeled himself to the office and buzzed for Miss Parish. When she got there, he barely gave her time to compose herself at the typewriting machine. "Letter," he said, not lifting his gaze.

"Yes, Mr. A."

He began dictating. "Dear Mr. and Mrs. Swann, I am writing to express my disgust at the display I saw tonight. I don't profess to know how you perform your little tricks, but I do recognize them for what they are: tricks. Parlor tricks. I want you to know that I was not fooled."

He stopped for a moment, listening to the clack of the keys—the sound of his words incising the paper. "In any case, my outrage is not for myself but for those actually vulnerable to your predations. I think of Miss Larue, frankly, a woman of great talent but small means and little common sense, blinded by grief at the loss of her only child. I give you notice that I will do everything in my power to stop this from continuing. Usual close."

He lit a cigar, considering what he had just dictated. The more he thought about the events of that evening, the more inadequate it seemed. It did not even touch on the outrageous manner in which he himself had been treated. The Swanns seemed to have assumed that he was some sort of crippled idiot, sentimental about his mother, ashamed of his deformity, imprisoned by his wheelchair, secretly yearning to walk. "Rewrite," he said.

The snap of paper going into the machine. "Ready, Mr. A."

The voice was darker this time. "Dear Mrs. Swann," he said. "If you really knew me, you would know that the past is of no importance to me whatsoever. Nor is my mother, the unfortunate Mrs. Auerbach. I never think of her. The woman to whom one is born is an accident over which one has no control, and therefore no more relevant than the color of one's hair. I have been the master of my own destiny since the age of ten."

Of course that was not to say that it had been easy. The loss of his ability to walk had made him useless around the theater, and his apprenticeship as a photographer had also been difficult. It was thought that his wheelchair was unsuitable for the studio—a place of much bowing and scraping, of potted palms and gold picture frames, of ladies and gentlemen dressed in their finest, expecting to be admired. He was relegated to the darkroom.

"As for my so-called infirmity, it is likewise irrelevant. The topic is so utterly without interest that I will not say another word about it, other than to note that every one of your preconceptions is wrong, wrong, wrong."

He stopped short and then sat very still, breathing slowly. Miss Parish seemed uncertain as to whether he was finished. "Usual close?" she asked.

"Read back," he growled, and then listened as she repeated the words in her high, piping voice. It was all wrong. Anger was an amateur's mistake. The Swanns would believe that he had been wounded—that he was bleeding—when he had only been a little shaken. What he needed to do was regain his composure. He pulled the lever on his wheelchair so that the back reclined. He was now looking up at the ceiling, in a posture of relaxed mastery. In this posture he would talk through his plans. "Strategy session, Miss Parish."

"Yes, Mr. A."

She turned from the typewriting machine to give him her full attention. He sometimes used Miss Parish as a sounding board. The poor creature did not really understand, but it was helpful to hear his thoughts aloud.

"I have always thought of Rive Gauche as a family, Miss Parish."

"That is how we all think of it, Mr. A."

"And that is why I am so deeply affected. The Swanns pose a danger to an important member of our family."

"I know how that must upset you."

"Furthermore, they have insulted me personally in the grossest and most indecent manner possible. They have laid down a challenge, and that challenge must be answered."

"I have never known you to fail at a challenge, Mr. A."

"The problem is Miss Larue. They have entangled her so artfully that anything we do to them might turn her against us."

"I know you won't let that happen, Mr. A."

"Indeed, I won't." Auerbach puffed his cigar. He had already decided that the best way to hold on to Jane Larue was to avoid open conflict with the Swanns. Instead of trying to fight them off, he would hug them close, so close that they would not be able to make the smallest move without his knowledge. If they tried to turn Jane Larue against him, he would know right away. "If there's one thing that I've learned over the years, Miss Parish, it's that you must keep your friends close, and your enemies even closer." He closed his eyes to savor the beauty of the sentiment. It meant that he would never be alone. "Rewrite," he said.

Miss Parish turned and put a fresh sheet into the typewriting machine. "Ready, Mr. A."

"Dear Mr. and Mrs. Swann, I am writing to thank you for an extraordinary experience. I am of course well aware of your fame, both here and abroad, but after witnessing your powers, I cannot help but feel that you are not yet as famous or as rich as you deserve to be or could be, with my assistance. I will call on you this afternoon. Deluxe close." The deluxe close—"Trust Me to be Your Most Obedient and Devoted Servant"—was used only for the most important correspondents.

He checked his pocket watch. It was only half past three, which meant that he had the rest of the night to consider what exactly to offer the Swanns. Whatever it was, it would be something much like the stereoscope he had promised so many years ago to Jane Larue.

6. ONLY SPACE FOR ONE

It was nearly two in the morning when Verena Swann saw the last group of weepers to the door. The need to leave seemed to trigger something in them, and they became suddenly, desperately loquacious. They stood in their overcoats by the coat rack in the hallway, running their hats through their hands as they relieved themselves of one last burst of words. Exhausted, Verena did not try to respond—they did not seem to expect it. They looked as if they had been locked behind a glass door and were trying to impart some vital information as to their rescue, but without real hope that it would be heard.

Verena Swann hated the weepers. She hated their naked and hungry faces. She hated their quivering voices as they asked their selfish questions: *Does he remember us? Can she see us? Will they tell us what to do?* She hated the way they stood too close to her, clasping her hands in theirs so she could not get away, demanding answers: *I need to know if he still loves me. You need to tell me if he misses the children...* Yet she hated them even more when, temporarily sated, they finally went home, leaving her to her loneliness.

Verena walked back to the front parlor and sat down on the couch beside Leopold. He was in his shirtsleeves, vest unbuttoned, a pack of playing cards spread on the coffee table before him. He shuffled, drew a card from the center, put it back, shuffled, drew the same card, put it back, did it all again and again, in exactly the same, quiet, workmanlike way, as if taking a machine apart and then reassembling it, just to see how it worked. Leopold was always serious about illusion; it was not only his profession, but also his way of moving through the world. He had left home as a young man to work in a carnival, had sold patent medicines after that, and he understood the human need to be convinced. This did not make him cynical, however, but reverent.

"I don't think I can keep this up much longer," she said to him.

Leopold's answer was to shuffle the deck in silence, and she passed the time contemplating his broad shoulders and back. Leopold had once self-published a book on salesmanship centered on a principle he called "massivity of presence," and to that end built himself up with Indian clubs and a medicine ball. He would have survived the Pole. Theodore, forced to pull a sledge over the ice on half rations of pemmican and hardtack, had been delicately built.

"You might as well say it," she said finally.

Leopold looked up but did not turn to face her. It was as if he were addressing the snowshoes above the mantel. "Will those errant spirits be making many more appearances, Verena? It's probably best that I know." At times such as these, he specialized in a tone of pained rationality.

"I had to say something, Leopold. It had been ten minutes and nothing was coming out. You don't know what that's like."

"I know exactly what that's like." After his career in patent medicines, Leopold traveled the country, giving public lectures on temperance, mesmerism, vegetarianism, and free love. He was immune to silence and unafraid of speech.

"But you don't know what it's like for *me*," she said. She saw again the circle of faces, their eyes closed, mimicking the off-center and naked expression of the blind. They had looked like they were giving themselves to be kissed. Their faces had fizzled with emotion like glasses of champagne. They had brought long lists of questions, recriminations, promises, and self-justifications aimed at the dead. Two of them had old treasure maps that needed explaining. They would have torn her to pieces if they had thought a bit of her flesh might have restored Aunt Mabel or solved the mystery of their parentage. She had opened her mouth to speak to them but nothing had come out, and the silence had roared in her ears. She had become afraid of what she might say: *Stop making me fleece you! I don't like it! I'm not even good at it! I have my own private dead to worry about!* And then she had told herself: *Quickly now, say something before they get up and leave.*

"I feel like I'm going to shrink away," she said to Leopold.

"How long do you think these people are going to let you do that?"

"Do what?"

"Tweak their noses like that."

"Not long, I hope."

"Well, your wish may be granted. You did a wonderful job of making us look like fools in front of Dr. Mayhew. I can guarantee you he'll be back to poke around. And then humiliating that poor crippled millionaire—I don't know how we'll smooth that over."

"I thought I'd do him some good while I was busy fleecing him." This was a pose, of course, meant to enrage Leopold while keeping her own remorse at bay.

Leopold closed his eyes. "He's a millionaire, Verena."

"Theodore never talked about money. It was of no interest to him." Comparisons to Theodore were calculated to wound both herself and Leopold.

"At least I don't leave you to starve while I go off to the North Pole," he said.

"True," she said. "You have the virtue of being alive."

He gave a snort. "Which means you have to be dead to be appreciated around here."

"Well, that's how we make our living, isn't it?"

"No, that's where you're wrong. Ghosts don't pay the bills, Verena. Weepers do."

Verena Swann went to her bedroom and sat down on the bed, suddenly too exhausted to stand. She looked down at her hands and was surprised by their appearance, as if they belonged to someone else. Their bonyness, their veins—these were the hands of a middle-aged woman, not her hands. This was not her body, her legs; these were not her breasts.

Perhaps something about Mr. Auerbach's good looks had bothered her. She felt so ugly herself. Or maybe it was the way he sat in his chair, coolly taking in the farce that she orchestrated for the others. He had seemed so free of the frustration that drove them, their hunger to speak, to be heard by their silent, invisible dead. By what right did he feel himself superior to her little circus of yearning? Perhaps she really *had*, in a certain sense, wanted to make him fall— to show him that he too was susceptible. Yes, yes, she had wanted to punish his arrogance. But once she saw him sprawled in his chair like that, with the blanket gone and his legs exposed, she realized with horror that it was not what she wanted at all.

On the wall opposite hung a photograph taken by Horatio Portus, the photographer on Theodore's polar expedition. It depicted a vast snow plain, at the center of which stood a group of men pulling a sledge. For all she knew, any one of those men could have been Theodore—it was impossible to tell. The men were harnessed like horses and leaned forward into their task with great determination, their legs disappearing into the deep snow. Their tracks could be seen stretching off to the left, a fragile trace obliterated by the picture frame. To the right, nothing but unbroken whiteness.

She had never understood why Theodore wanted that. She had never understood how he could trade her for it. And so maybe she had never understood Theodore. There was a part of him that was blank to her.

She had seen him laid out in the coffin the evening before the funeral, dressed in white tie, morning coat, and striped pants, the Explorers Club's Order of von Humboldt—a large gold star—pinned to a red sash strung over his shoulder.

This was not what he had intended, of course. The point of the danger was that he would survive it. He loved risk, because surviving confirmed his specialness.

Standing beside the coffin, she had looked down at his face. The man in the box was most definitely Theodore, but of course was not Theodore, not *her* Theodore. It was like the string that held all the beads together had been removed, though the beads were still there. The eyes were closed, the forehead waxy, the strong nose powdered, lips and cheeks painted with rouge. Beard and hair glistened with pomade. There was a heavy scent of perfume, clearly meant to mask other smells, of sea wrack and bodily decay.

Leopold had stood beside her, his large hands gripping the edge of the casket. "My God, Theodore, Theodore," he said, addressing the body. "I never thought I'd see you again." His eyes were bleary with tears. Over the last three years, since the expedition had failed to return, Leopold had become an expert at extravagant mourning. He was much better at it than she—and they both knew it. Over time, he had become the chief mourner, and she had been relegated to supporting roles—fanning him when he grew overheated, handing him handkerchiefs when his were soaked, patting him sympathetically on the arm.

He had brought a handkerchief to his nose. "He looks wonderful, doesn't he?"

She wasn't sure if "wonderful" was the word. Underneath the makeup on Theodore's face were rough patches, something like scabs or burns—frostbite, she guessed—and he was clearly much thinner than when he left. She could see the pins the mortician had used to take up the slack in his cutaway and striped pants. The white carnation in his lapel seemed impossibly large, a weight to keep him from flying away. The enormous gold star on his chest looked like it might crush him.

Oddly, Theodore, the professional explorer, had always been on the delicate side. It was Leopold, the stay-at-home, the mourner, who followed a regimen of physical cultivation: rare beefsteak, calisthenics and Indian clubs, monthly baths in olive oil. She had seen him in the hallway of the house they now shared on Washington Square, wearing nothing but a bathrobe, face shining like polished brass after one of those baths. The strange foreign scent of olive oil everywhere.

She got up and went over to her desk, opened the drawer and removed another, smaller photograph. This one was definitely of Theodore. It had been taken by a crewmember of the *Independence* and was dark and blurry, with some kind of stain or discoloration at the bottom where the plate had been spoiled. It showed Theodore standing on the deck of the ship, a day before the expedition went ashore. He was different from the man she had married five years earlier—bearded, sunburned, thin, the bones showing in his face. A strange look in his eyes, which were focused not on the camera but on the shoreline beyond the ship's railing. Looking away from her at something she could not see.

This was the photograph Verena used as an aid to trance—not the trances she entered on behalf of the weepers, but the private ones she entered in secret, in her bedroom, at those times of utmost despair when she could not bear to be alone.

Her method was to place herself inside the photograph, as if she too had been present on the deck of the ship, as if she were present at this very moment in the little square of time preserved inside the picture. She imagined what Theodore would look like if she were standing to his left—the sight of his ear, the shape of his profile, the bump at the midpoint of his nose—and then to his right, the view subtly different. She imagined standing behind him, and suddenly she could see what he saw: a land of blue ice lit by the sun.

She took out paper and a lead pencil, and then returned to the photograph. She tried to follow Theodore's gaze, directed at a shoreline she could not see. She felt the return of her exhaustion, anger at the way she expended her energy for other people, to feed their grief while hers starved. And then, at some point, she realized that she was writing—or rather, that the pencil was moving over the paper and her hand was following. The letters were his: small, spiky, crude. Nobody knew how to work the balloon.

The pencil continued to move, and her eyes followed it across the page. I mean the reconnaissance balloon. The writing was so perfectly transparent that she did not need to read it; it was like listening to Theodore's voice with her eyes, even as her hand brought that voice into being.

A long red tongue, unfurling in the snow, and a wicker gondola the size of a picnic basket. Boyle read the instructions through his goggles. I get it now, he said. Strap A to buckle B. Icicles in his beard. An hour later it was standing—an exclamation mark in all that whiteness. Boyle gave me the instruction booklet. There was a valve you had to turn. Left or right. Yankee ingenuity.

"Why are you telling me this?" she asked, whispering the words out loud.

Didn't you ask me why? Why go to such a terrible, empty place? I had never felt anything like that before, the rising. The floor knocked me off my feet. I was falling upward into the open mouth of the balloon but never getting there. Pieces of sky came and went between the straps. When I grabbed the lip of the basket, I was facing south, back to where the ship had dropped us off. I could see where the black water began. Farther out were the icebergs, as big as whole cities. Then I turned north to the Pole and the ice was like fire frozen into rock. Blue, green, red, orange, gold. Radiating light.

"Did I mean anything to you?"

One question at a time. If you listen, I will tell you how the ponies hated the ice, and how we had to put burlap sacks over their heads or else they wouldn't move at all. In a week all sixteen were dead. Two tons of forage brought all the way from New York, wasted. The dogs were just as useless. They pulled in different directions, tangled up and began to fight. Nobody knew how to make them go. Boyle wanted to shoot them, but I would not allow it. No, you know how I feel about dogs. Their loving natures, their loyalty, their simple faith. They rode on the sleds and we pulled.

The equivalent of laughter, a tremor or wave in the pencil, a long squiggly line. "Do you think that's funny?" she asked.

Do I have a choice, Verena? It's a little too late to cry. The trip north was relatively easy till we passed the last supply depot. From that point on, something changed inside of us. We were in uncharted territory now, past help, past our own understanding. The going was slow— snow up to our knees—the sledges heavy. We kept our eyes down on our feet, so as not to become confused. The landscape was lit from within like a magic lantern, throwing off fantastic shapes and colors. Sometimes these shapes turned out to be the peaks of distant mountains, and sometimes ice boulders just a few yards away. We thought we saw human figures any number of times, only to have them dissolve into the atmosphere, phantoms—until suddenly, without warning, they were right in front of us. We half expected them to disappear, but they did not. A man and woman, two children on a sledge—a family of some sort, here where nobody should be. They were surrounded by dogs, dozens of them, their long coats crystalline with ice, baying at the wind.

"Did they mean you harm?"

The male came forward to meet us. He was shapeless in furs, silvered by ice. Eyes hidden behind Eskimo snow goggles—slits cuts in a flat piece of bone. A rude figure torn from prehistory, a rough clay model of ourselves. And then he held out a gloved hand, a shapeless sealskin mitten, and displayed a strange object.

"What was it?"

A boot heel, torn from the boot. Nails still in it. And they had other things—a metal spoon, a brass button with the imprint of an anchor. A leather belt. Relics from some past expedition. Franklin, perhaps, or some other doomed group, now wholly forgotten. We could only afford the boot heel. It cost us two sewing needles. And then we watched the family travel swiftly away, carried by their dogs. Who thought dogs could pull like that? said Kitely. And then we got back into our harnesses and began hauling again.

"Isn't that us now, selling relics? We could have spent our lives together."

Aren't we doing that now?

"Did you ever want a baby?"

I'm your baby, Verena. There is only space for me.

7. DR. MAYHEW AND MR. SPUFFORD

The observation tower had been designed by Dr. Mayhew himself and was unique to the Mayhew Asylum, an integral part of its unusual treatment regimen. In itself it was not overly impressive: just a narrow circular shaft at the center of the building, rising six stories to a skylight. But the tower had a certain beauty to it. On a fair morning, like this one, the light streamed down like water into a bottle, splashing against the curved walls, with their rows of small circular peepholes, and down onto a heavy wooden chair stationed in the middle of the floor. The chair could be raised all six stories to the very top of the shaft by way of a pulley suspended from a circular steel frame immediately below the skylight. A ball joint allowed the chair to rotate 360 degrees to face in any direction.

The new night attendant was waiting beside the chair, looking rumpled and deflated—Spufford was his name, Josiah Spufford. Over the last couple of weeks, Dr. Mayhew had become increasingly disappointed with Spufford. He was large enough, with a face like a brick wall, but soft and crumbly inside, like rotten plaster. Working with lunatics required that one be impenetrable as stone.

Dr. Mayhew climbed onto the chair and strapped himself in. "Anything unusual overnight, Mr. Spufford?"

Spufford shrugged deferentially. "Miss Fitzwilliams grew very agitated at about two this morning, Doctor. She began yelling and wouldn't stop."

"Oh?" Fitzwilliams was a Spiritualist from Utica who claimed to communicate with a dead Indian named Chief Rainwater about the price of pork belly futures.

"She said she was being held against her will and wanted the police."

"Did you tell her why she is here?"

"I told her that she is insane, as you instructed."

"It's crucial that she accept that fact, or the cure cannot take hold." Dr. Mayhew reached over to detach the brass telescope that stood at the side of the chair. When fully extended, it stretched five feet to the row of peepholes that ran the circumference of the wall at each floor. He gave the signal to ascend. "Ready to rise," he said, and watched Spufford begin turning the hand crank that ran the pulley. Almost immediately the floor fell away.

For Dr. Mayhew, the trip up was the very best part of the morning. There was the sensation of rising like a pearl in water, of being lighter than air, of being able to turn complete circles with just the tug of a cord. There was the blue above his head and the light silvering the space around him. But most of all there was the exalted sense of mission it gave him. The observation tower was a key element in his therapeutic approach. As it allowed him to look into any patient's room at any time, patients could never be sure that he was not observing them—because he *could* be. Indeed, he encouraged them to think that he was, day and night. After a while, they could feel his gaze on their skin, and the fact that this was an *imagined* gaze did not make it less potent.

Dr. Mayhew had himself grown up in a house of shut doors and keyholes. His father, the Reverend Mayhew, was given to harsh, terrible glooms, during which times he locked himself in his study, meditating upon the Bible, or talking to the air with great vehemence. His mother had suffered from headaches that required darkness and silence. Both were strict disciplinarians. In general, it was never strange or unexpected to be shut in a room, or shut out, or to find oneself looking through a keyhole.

The chair stopped its rise at the first row of peepholes, swaying ever so slightly, and with a single practiced motion, Dr. Mayhew extended his telescope to its full length, resting its front end on the contoured lip of peephole number one. Inside he saw Fitzwilliams laid out on the bed, swaddled in a cotton sheet like a newborn. She writhed, thrashed, and bucked against the thick leather straps that held her to the bed. Dr. Mayhew could see the outline of her arms and legs, struggling against the sheet. Her mouth was wide open, the muscles in her neck visibly taut. No doubt it was very loud in there, but one of the joys of the observation tower was its silence.

Dr. Mayhew made a mental note to speak with Fitzwilliams later that day. He would of course impress upon her that anger was out of place in a hospital devoted to healing, that such feelings were therefore not allowed, that they must not be indulged, and that they would be punished. He then signaled to Spufford to take him up to the next level.

Spufford turned the hand crank and watched the chair ascend. He had not quite recovered from his interview with Miss Fitzwilliams earlier that morning, but he told himself that it did not matter, because he had only an hour left on duty, and then he would be going to the post office. It was the first of the month and there would almost certainly be a new package waiting in his box.

Nevertheless, he was having trouble getting Miss Fitzwilliams out of his mind. It had not been pleasant telling her that she was insane—even if she really was insane. She had begun talking very rapidly, trying to convince him otherwise—starting in the middle of a story so long and convoluted, so full of digressions, that he could not follow its twists and turns, its additions and subtractions— something about a sick mother and a gift for finding lost relatives, and a kind old gentleman willing to invest. He could not slow her down long enough to make sense of it, and in any case had not wanted to. He stood at the little sliding plate in her door, looking from one side to the other—anywhere but at her glistening wet, desperate face—feeling the upset and the anger rise within him. What are you doing? he wanted to ask. Don't you realize that this is my work, and that as such it is not in fact real? I am here to do the absurd and meaningless tasks to which I'm assigned, until it is time for me to go to the post office and collect my package. But if you continue to insist that you are in fact real, like anyone else, a real person, and that the person standing here in my white orderly's uniform is likewise also real, is in fact me, and that this moment is actually happening between us, then I will—not quit, because I owe too much money to quit, and because I would not otherwise be able to afford my packages—not quit, but become *upset*.

And so he had, begging her through the wire mesh to be quiet, his voice louder and more threatening each time—which had only made her talk faster, and in an even more circular fashion, something about paying the kind old gentleman back and buying a house for her mother, which she would nevertheless gladly sign over to Dr. Mayhew, or even to him, Mr. Spufford, what a good idea, why hadn't she thought of that before—till in sheer horror he snapped shut the slide on her door and walked away, trembling.

But his mood was lightening now that the end of his shift was approaching. Even working the crank had become less of a chore— had become in fact oddly satisfying, as if it were one of the tasks in a fairy tale that the hero must complete in order to win the princess. Dr. Mayhew's chair took forever to descend, and then Spufford had to change from his uniform to his street clothes and walk down the long gravel drive to the gate. He got through all these delays in a kind of pleasurable agony of anticipation. But once on the street he was too jittery to wait for a streetcar. He started walking.

At the post office, he made a conscious effort to prolong the wait, walking slowly among the post boxes. The path to his box was so familiar that he did not even have to look at the number stamped in brass on the little door. His hands shook as he turned the key in the lock. Yes, a package had arrived. It was no larger than a book and considerably lighter, wrapped in plain brown paper. He put it in his satchel, pulled his derby down low, and walked out onto the street, suddenly afraid that the truth of what he was carrying might be written on his face. He bolted recklessly across one thoroughfare after another. It occurred to him that if he were trampled by a cart and killed, his wife would find the package in his satchel and open it. This would almost certainly inspire her to search his desk, in which case she would find the hidden drawer too. The possibility filled him with a mixture of panic and relief.

By the time he reached home, he was in a sweat, breathing out clouds of steam in the cold air. His wife met him just inside the door, the baby in her arms. "The heat was off half the day," she said with an air of pent-up grievance. "I had to take him to my mother's."

It doesn't matter, he thought. Because in a minute or two I will be unwrapping the package. "I'll speak to Janusch," he said, meaning the porter.

"While you're at it, he needs to fix the sink."

"I'll tell him that too."

"The butcher sent his boy over with the bill."

"I'll pay it tomorrow." The package cost almost four dollars, plus twenty-two cents postage—enough for the butcher and green grocer combined. And then a sudden inspiration: "I've got a report to finish for Dr. Mayhew."

He went to the windowless closet of a room that he called his study, lit the lamp on the desk, and then closed the door. Locking it was impossible; the lock made too much noise, and in any case it would be an unusual thing to do and he did not want to do anything suspicious. So he propped the wastepaper basket against it instead—not so much as a barrier but as a warning device. He removed his hat and coat, sat at his desk, then opened his satchel and placed the package before him. His hands shook as he opened the wrapper, careful not to make any noise. Inside was a second wrapper, inside that a cardboard box, and inside that a set of twenty-six stereographs wrapped in tissue paper. He opened the bottom left-hand drawer, pulled out his stereoscope, and placed the first card in the bracket. He then lifted the device to his eyes.

What he saw inside was a man standing beside a bed and watching a woman sleep. The man was masked, signifying that he was an intruder, like Spufford himself. Spufford went to the next card, in which the woman woke and saw the man. She had a look of ridiculous dismay on her face. He liked that, the bad acting that made plain that this was all just make-believe, and that he need not worry about the man and the woman because they were really actors—nothing would actually harm them. He went to the third card. The woman sat up and pointed dramatically to her belly. The unexpected thing was that her belly was huge beneath her nightgown. She was eight or nine months pregnant, Spufford realized, and his heart started to smash against his chest. He had no idea that pregnant women—that they let pregnant women—but then, who would *they* be? He moved quickly to the next card, in which the intruder ripped off the woman's nightgown, exposing her naked belly to view. It was certainly real. It looked much like his wife's did, toward the end of *her* pregnancy: a sack of something heavy and wet, about to burst.

He remembered the night his wife and he conceived their son—he was certain he knew the night it happened. His wife wanted a child and seemed to have some great natural force on her side. He argued against it, saying they should wait a little while longer, citing money, debt, the small apartment they had rented, but he knew he was merely making a gesture, that the objections sounded weak even to him. She left the little rubber cap they had been using—the *womb veil*, it was called—on the nightstand by the bed, then got on top of him and rode him with a kind of utilitarianism that was strange, both intimate and impersonal. This wasn't about him; it was about the baby that did not yet exist.

In the heat of the summer, she lay naked in bed on her back, the mosquito netting down around her, in communion with the thing inside her, a self-sufficiency of nesting dolls.

There was no way to know that the baby inside her womb would soon be an infant, crawling around the house with something strange in his fist, a ladle or spatula taken from the kitchen—just as there was no way to know that he would have Spufford's mother's eyes, and that he would make Spufford ache with a feeling he could not name. Sometimes Spufford could not stop watching him; sometimes he could not bear to look him in the face. The great human tragedy of the thing was that Spufford stared at the baby and thought, *If only I could be more like you*, while the baby gazed back at him with those midnight eyes, the decision imprinted on his face: *I will be just like you.* Spufford wanted to warn him that the greatest danger comes from the forces acting inside us, forces inside us that control our behavior, that make us do things that are not right or good, that tend toward pain. And because they are inside us, there is nothing we can do to resist them. They are *us*.

Suddenly he was startled by a voice—his wife's voice. At first it seemed to be right in the room with him, but in the next moment he realized it was just outside the door. "We need some milk," she said, so loud it sounded as if her mouth were to the keyhole.

"Yes, right," he said, putting down the stereoscope. "Milk." The situation was problematic. His wife was not, in general, a respecter of closed doors. He thought she might try to push it open, in which case the wastebasket would rattle and give.

"And a loaf of bread," she said. To his great relief she seemed willing to remain just a voice.

"Can I finish this first?" he asked.

"What are you doing?"

"A report. They want it tomorrow morning." He had already placed the stereoscope to his eyes once again.

"How long will you be?" she asked.

"Two minutes," he said, changing cards.

8. WHATEVER IT COSTS, I'LL PAY

A uerbach's carriage made slow progress downtown. He kept the window curtains shut, as he could not bear to see the chaos that reigned outside: the carriages competing for right of way; the pedestrians sprinting across the avenue; the delivery wagons spilling their cargo as they lumbered along. The city was awful—dirty, cramped, disorganized, full of ignorant, incompetent people going about their business in the most wasteful ways possible.

And yet he did not feel as superior as he normally did—not nearly so superior. Even in the darkness of the carriage, the noise from the streets rankled. Perhaps it was because this was his second time out in less than two days, when normally he might leave the mansion only twice in a year. Or perhaps it was because he felt sick with exhaustion. He had been too agitated to sleep the night before, trying again and again to unravel the tangled intentions of the Swanns. Not that he had gotten too far with that task. There had been moments when he thought he had them—finally—but then some new consideration would present itself and they would slip away into the murk once again.

Nevertheless, he did not consider turning back. He had a serviceable plan, and he intended to put it into effect. It was the kind he liked best: a bear hug that worked like a punch. He would tie the Swanns into golden knots that would make them utterly harmless, and before they realized it, he would *own* them. In short, he would propose a partnership. He had a number of ideas in mind, but the one he liked most was a mail-order business in spirit photography. Customers would indicate the spirit they wished to see, and Leopold Swann would then create a photograph for them.

The wonderful thing about this idea was that it would keep Leopold Swann shut up in the darkroom all day. For over the course of the night, Auerbach had become convinced that it was Leopold who had engineered his fainting spell. No other interpretation made sense. Tall, strapping Leopold Swann had seen the wheelchair and the lap rug and assumed he could humiliate Auerbach into relinquishing Jane Larue. He had then forced Mrs. Swann to do whatever it was that she had done. Her look of mortification, her pained apology, made it clear that she had been coerced.

Auerbach did not know what power Swann had over his sister-in-law, but he had decided to make an ally of her. He would woo her away, and when Swann was taken care of, he would set her free. It would be part of his revenge.

The Swanns were engaged with a client when he arrived, but the housekeeper led him into the parlor to wait. It was the same large space in which the séance had been held the night before, but to his surprise, everything that had seemed so strange and menacing then—the harpoons, the animal trophies—now seemed perfectly harmless. Perhaps this was because the curtains had been pulled back from the windows and the room was full of sunlight, sunlight splashing on the carpets, striping the walls, and bouncing off the glass display cases.

Looking around, he felt himself relax; this would not be as difficult as he had feared.

"Mr. and Mrs. Swann will be down in a moment," said the housekeeper.

She was a sensible-looking young woman in black serge and a white apron. Auerbach remembered her from the night before, collecting coats and hats, and asked her name.

"Maisie, sir." She gave a quick curtsy. She had a broad, freckled face and small gray eyes.

He groped for something that would put her on the subject of the Swanns and their little game. "Do you believe in spirits, Maisie?" he asked, unsure how exactly to direct his probing.

She nodded vigorously. "Oh yes, sir."

"And you are convinced that they are real?"

"I have seen them, sir. Standing before me like a living person."

"But of course they *are* living," added a voice from across the room. He turned to look. It was Verena Swann, coming toward them from the big double doors. She wore a white dress that seemed to glow in the afternoon light, and walked with a slow, stately gait, an enormous white tulip in her hands. The effect was so dramatic, he felt like he was standing inside a play—perhaps one of his mother's. "Just not as *we* think of living," she said, and then walked up to his chair. "It is good to see you again, Mr. Auerbach."

He shook her hand lightly and let go, suddenly as nervous as the night before. Telling himself to treat her like a model did no good, because she was clearly not of that species. He straightened his lapels and then smoothed the blanket over his legs, conscious of his inadequacy outside of work.

"Leopold will be down in a moment," she said. "The Thursday sittings are always so crowded, I wonder if you had a chance to look around. Let me show you our Arctic photographs. They may interest you, as a photographer."

She led him over to a long row of pictures in simple black frames. The pictures consisted of gigantic ice formations carved by the elements to make strange white cities that glittered and smoked in the sun. The human figures at the bottom were tiny and absurd, and always in some futile form of transit, manhauling sledges or leading strings of hooded ponies through deep snow.

"These were taken by Mr. Horatio Portus, the expedition photographer," she told him.

"Ah, yes, very impressive," said Auerbach, pretending to scrutinize the photograph on the wall. "Very impressive indeed." The problem was that Mrs. Swann was standing beside his chair, one hand resting lightly on his armrest. He could feel the heat of her body—it felt like sunlight.

"Mr. Portus stored hundreds of plates at base camp before leaving with Theodore for the Pole," said Mrs. Swann.

"I see." Arctic exploration seemed an absurd waste of time to Auerbach, a stunt one step above bicycling or ballooning, but he could see that the picture was meaningful to Mrs. Swann, who stood before it with evident respect. "They must have been very brave men," he said.

"Oh, they were."

"You are every bit as brave, Mrs. Swann—braver, I would say." She gave a dismissive laugh, but he insisted. "Believe me, it is always much harder to be left behind."

She bent her head, affected. "I'm glad you decided to give us a second chance, Mr. Auerbach. I thought we had lost you."

"I am not easily discouraged," he said.

"I am glad. I would have blamed myself."

They looked at each other and then looked away. He felt the sweat break out on his brow.

"Have you seen the whales' teeth?" she asked hurriedly. "They are on the other side." She indicated the far end of the room. "Here, let me." The next thing he knew, she was pushing his wheelchair toward the display cases.

This did not take Auerbach by complete surprise. The models often pushed his chair; they found it comforting, and because it did them good, he had reconciled himself to the strange physical intimacy of the act: the sound of their breathing, the scent of their perfumes, the sense that he could almost feel their muscles working beneath their clothes. But Mrs. Swann was most definitely *not* a model, and the ride felt very strange indeed. He was on the verge of asking her to stop, when the door opened and Leopold Swann walked in. Mrs. Swann stopped pushing, and they stood motionless, as if caught in the midst of a theft.

"Sorry to keep you waiting," said Swann, taking it all in. "I had something to get from the studio." He held up a large envelope as if it were a kind of apology.

"I was just showing him Theodore's things," said Mrs. Swann, sounding guilty.

"Yes, very good," said Swann. He was a big man, groomed to a high sheen, with a yellow vest and brown checked pants. Great black mustachios swept upward from his muscular face.

Auerbach looked him over and felt both anger and a touch of fear. "It was an extraordinarily impressive performance last night. I have never experienced anything so stunning."

Swann gave a slight bow. "It can be overwhelming the first time." He handed Auerbach the envelope he had been holding. "This will be of interest to you, I think."

Auerbach opened the flap. The envelope held a photograph, which he took out and held up to the light.

It had been so long since he had seen a picture of himself that it took a moment to recognize the figure in the wheelchair. "I didn't authorize this," he said, then remembered the séance, the burst of flash powder. The picture showed the Swanns' parlor, the very same room in which he was now sitting, but it was crowded, with people pressed in among the cabinets. And there he was, a man in a chair with a blanket on his lap, no legs visible. He looked tense, even frightened—despite the grimace on his face, which tried to pass for a smile. To his right was Jane Larue, and to his left a woman in a type of dress he had not seen since childhood: his mother.

He gave a barking laugh. "A crude double exposure," he said. "Nothing more." But he felt little pinpricks up and down his back.

"The truth is true, Mr. Auerbach, whether we choose to believe it or not," said Swann.

"The whole thing couldn't have been more obviously contrived," he said, only belatedly realizing that he was arguing against his very reason for coming, the mail-order business in spirit photographs.

Leopold Swann was not listening, however. His attention was on Mrs. Swann, who seemed to be having some kind of trouble. Her face was dull, her mouth open, her eyes glassy. It occurred to Auerbach that she might be having an attack of some kind. This seemed perfectly credible, some extension of the sickening feeling now swirling inside of him too.

Swann helped her over to a couch and then sat down beside her, staring into her face with great concentration, as if reading the level on a bottle. "I believe she's slipping into a trance."

And then Mrs. Swann spoke. "I know you think I wasn't a very good mother to you, Augustus, but I tried to learn the role. I had acted the daughter, the beautiful, doomed daughter, thousands of times, in a thousand different plays, by gaslight, by candlelight—by torch. It's all I knew how to do." Her eyes were closed, her voice and face changed. She seemed to be struggling in a dream—no, it was as if someone else were dreaming herself Mrs. Swann. "I held you in my arms. Like holding a piece of the sky. Clouds passing through me." There were gurglings from deep in her throat. Laughter? Tears?

Auerbach could not tell. Her head rolled from side to side. She gave a prolonged moan.

"There were nights I thought of smothering you in your crib. Not to hurt you, you understand, but to save you—to save you from my failure. It was winter, ice on the windowpanes, and I carried you back and forth from one end of the room to the other, till the sky grew blue. It's not that I hated you—I was frightened. I lived by the strength of my voice, my ability to make them weep in the balcony. If I lost that power, if I made myself sick taking care of you, who would take care of *me*? And if I collapsed, who would take care of *you*?"

The medium's face was not at all like his mother's. Aspasia's had been long, fleshy, regal, with a tall forehead, strong cheekbones, and a powerful, commanding nose. A face made for the stage. Mrs. Swann's was smaller, more delicate, an inverted triangle leading down to a sharp chin. Yet the two seemed to coexist now, one on top of the other, as if Aspasia's features had been impressed upon Mrs. Swann's, like a mold pressed into soft clay: the big eyes, closed as with an excess of feeling, as if the hugeness of her interior life claimed her complete attention. The wounded, indignant expression. The chin thrust outward in challenge. The dramatic, flaring eyebrows. The strong line of the lips. The muscular hair piled atop her head.

It was her in one of her moods, when the reviews had been bad or the audiences small. She would then reassess her life. He would be woken up to serve as audience, given hot chocolate at the kitchen table, warmed by the stove. He would sit, excited by the strangeness of the house at that hour, by the unusual privilege of having her all to himself, without friends or suitors or theatrical protégées interjected, buzzing about her like bees. She would stand at the stove, stirring a pot of milk, dressed in a padded silk kimono. She had been the victim of betrayals, she told him, poor guidance, bad advice, ungrateful management, her own good impulses, and her naïve generosity.

He had felt overwhelmingly fortunate to be included in the circle of her suffering, had yearned to help, to vanquish her enemies, even while understanding the implicit criticism that he could not, would not, acknowledge: that he was in fact part of the problem, an extra burden, yet more ingratitude to be borne.

Mrs. Swann's face was damp, flushed. She lay back on the couch with her eyes closed, tossing her head, arching her back, parting her lips to speak, then closing them again, elongating her neck as if to dislodge the words stuck within her. It looked much like the scene he had photographed that morning, while giving directions in his gentle voice: *Now open your legs, yes, a little more. In the eyes, show it in the eyes, that's right. Hold that.*

"Your willpower," said the medium. "Never forget it comes from me. I kept an old trunk full of scripts, fifteen years of scripts. Tattered and curling pages, pencil marks in the margins. I read them all, memorizing the mothers' parts this time. And so it was done. I was a mother." Her laughter managed to be both self-mocking and self-congratulatory. And then her voice was sad. "But what I've found is that the mother's part never ends, you see, unlike the beautiful doomed daughter who gets to die and be done with it."

Auerbach had begun to tremble. He would have wheeled himself out if he could have gotten a grip of the wheels. "Call my coachman," he said to Swann. "I think I'm taking ill."

But it was Aspasia who answered, not with words but with a song. It was little more than some nonsense syllables and a simple melody, circling and returning, as if moving back and forth between past and present, but his eyes began to fill with tears. She reached out and touched his cheek as she sang, gently stroking his face.

"Oh, no," he said, feeling himself in danger of being swept away.

"I'm tired," she said, her voice faltering. "I have to go." A gentle sigh, and then Mrs. Swann sank back against the couch, once again what she had always been: herself.

"For God's sake, get her back!" cried Auerbach. "Whatever it costs, I'll pay."

Swann looked peevish. "This is not a carnival trick, Mr. Auerbach."

Just then Mrs. Swann began to stir. Her face was her own again, but older: pained, confused, and creased with exhaustion. "Leopold," she called, seemingly unaware that he was sitting next to her, holding her hands in both of his. "I can't move my legs." The sweetness with which she said it sent a chill through Auerbach.

Leopold Swann turned to explain. "A temporary effect of the trance." He put a proprietary hand on Mrs. Swann's forehead, as if feeling her temperature. "The poor thing suffers terribly for her gift. If you will excuse us, Mr. Auerbach, Maisie will see you out."

"I will be better tomorrow," said Verena Swann. "We can continue then."

"Tomorrow, then," whispered Auerbach. He was barely able to find the strength to wheel himself out of the room.

9. YOU ARE THE NOVEL I AM WRITING

Leopold swept her up in his arms and carried her upstairs to her room, as if she weighed nothing at all. She smelled the pomade in his hair, redolent of cloves. A good, safe smell. It had been a long time since he had carried her in this way, and she realized now how much she had missed it. She felt hot and muzzy, a word her mother had used to describe the blurry after-state of fever.

The feeling that came after a trance had always been in a certain sense familiar, even nostalgic, a reminder of lying in bed as a little girl, sick with fever. And it was doubly nostalgic now, since trances like the ones she had experienced early on hardly ever happened anymore. In the early days, going into a trance had been like falling down into a well. She would wake confused, as if she had been plucked out of time and then placed back in it, farther downstream. Days may have gone by, or only moments, it was impossible to tell. She was just a leaf, a twig, carried by the rushing water. She liked giving herself over to a higher purpose she could not see or know. It did not matter what it was or where it took her, as long as it took her and she was gone.

Leopold put her on her bed. She lay on her pillow, feeling wonderfully empty, her mind soaked through with something clean and warm and obliterating. It was as if the sun had burst inside her head. She watched Leopold straighten out her legs, smooth out her dress, then begin to unlace her boots, though she could not actually feel the working of his hands.

She was not frightened, because she had been through this a hundred times before and knew her legs would be back in the next day or so. For whatever reason, the spirits sometimes took a piece of her with them after a visit. The maddening thing was its unpredictability. They didn't always take something, and it wasn't always the same thing. She had woken from trances with her hearing gone, or her voice gone, or once even her eyesight gone. But they always returned it later if she was patient and did not panic.

This was less of a problem now that her powers seemed to be waning. It had been almost a year since the spirits had taken anything from her, and so the loss was strangely welcome. She liked watching Leopold care for her in this way. She could tell he was satisfied with her performance by the great gentleness with which he began unlacing her boots. Of course, she could never have allowed him to do these things if the boots had been on her own legs.

"You were wonderful, Verena," said Leopold. "It just poured out of you, like the old days."

"What did I say?" After a trance she could typically remember only the melody of someone speaking, as if heard through a door, speech resolved to pure music. When she woke, all that was left was Leopold's recounting of what had been said. She had no idea how accurate it was; for all she knew, he was making it up. But she needed it. It was a small cup to hold the vast feeling inside her. Without it she could not drink.

He began telling her the strange, intimate details of another woman's message to her son: the nights spent carrying him back and forth, the reading of the play scripts. She listened, recognizing nothing of herself in the story, feeling only discomfort at the words that had been furled up inside her. How could a mother not know what a mother is? Then she remembered her own mother's swift, silent hands working on one of her hats while the shop window blazed golden in the sunlight. Her mother did not speak unless she needed something—a needle and thread, a pot of glue—and never looked up from her task.

"Was Mr. Auerbach pleased?" she asked.

"Delighted, absolutely delighted."

She smiled. This was the solution to everything. She would make Mr. Auerbach a part of their little circle, an intimate, a regular. He would come two or three times a week, to the big séances on Thursdays, and to her public appearances, and maybe to some of the special meetings she did for the governor. He would write little notes in between, and send little gifts. He would take her out for rides in his carriage. And he would pay lots of money, which would make Leopold happy. Leopold was so much easier to live with when he was happy. He would forget his ridiculous fantasies of being in love with her. "And are *you* happy?" she asked.

"Of course I am. You hooked him. We just need to pull him in carefully now."

"He seems like a sad man."

He pulled off her boots and placed them neatly beside the bed. "Well, he's a cripple."

"You and Theodore, with your barbells and Indian clubs. But there are more important things."

"That is true. He is extremely rich."

"He seems lonely."

"They all are."

Yes, that was true, but she thought of Mr. Auerbach and his

beautiful dark eyes, of the way he had looked at her in the parlor, in front of the photograph. It gave her the feeling she sometimes had on the street when she caught a glimpse of herself in a shop window: that sense of thereness, among other people, at a particular point in the course of her individual day, at a discrete moment in the history of the world. *I am here, in my new bonnet. I am I, nobody else.*

"But he's a little different," she said.

"You swing back and forth like a pendulum, Verena. Just the other day, you practically pushed him out of his wheelchair."

She did not want to be reminded of what she had done before. Her moods were so extreme—she was a victim as much as anyone else. "I thought you would be pleased," she said.

"I am, but what I would like most of all is a little professional detachment. We are professionals."

"I don't want to be a professional." She looked down and noticed Leopold massaging her toes through her stockings. She could not feel it, but she could see the long fingers working back and forth. "Let go of my foot, please."

"It increases circulation."

"Let go, please."

He withdrew his hands. "Verena, at some point we are going to have to talk. You can't avoid the subject forever."

Normally she would have closed her eyes, done anything to avoid this moment. But the sunlight in her head made her feel almost drunk, and the words slipped out. "You don't want me, Leopold, only my gift."

"That's absurd." He looked genuinely startled, then angry. "That's cruel."

"You can't see it, but I can."

He was about to respond, then obviously thought better of it. "You're exhausted," he said. "I'll send Maisie in."

She watched him leave, his powerful back disappearing through the door. She felt hot, her muscles rubbery, her eyelids heavy and swollen. She worried that she had hurt him, and that he would brood.

Maisie helped her out of her dress and into her nightclothes, and then covered her with a quilt. But Verena knew she would not be able to sleep. There was still something in her; she hadn't been completely emptied. She asked for paper and pencil, and Maisie brought her little cherrywood invalid's desk, the one she used in bed during periods of convalescence. She had an unavoidably large correspondence with her clients. They were dependent on her guidance.

The desk formed a solid wooden bridge over her missing knees. Maisie helped her sit up. "Leave me," said Verena. She held the sharpened pencil in her hand. She already felt the tingling in the back of her neck, the pressure in her throat that meant the pencil would soon begin to move. She closed her eyes.

Theodore would have felt nothing but disdain for a man like Auerbach. She was painfully aware of that. Her husband's definition of manhood was based on a few simple requirements, all of them physical. For Theodore, the test of manhood was cutting ice blocks in temperatures so cold that his beard froze. So cold that exposed skin burnt as if seared with a hot iron, raising big red welts. It was manhauling a three-hundred-pound supply sledge through chest-high drifts of snow.

It was all a test of how much and how little: how much work, how many miles, how little food, and how little sleep. How much fear, how little hope.

The pencil began to move, but not in the usual way. Normally, the feeling was empty or hollow: she was a reed, a pipe through which something rushed on its way to somewhere else. But this was different; it moved against, not through her; it was hard, it hurt. She was being dragged like a sledge. She tried to resist, to pull back, but it was impossible. The pencil scratched and ripped, its sharp tip cutting open the white skin of the page to show the black ore beneath.

His legs, it said.

I didn't mean to do that to him, she responded, though of course she *had* meant to, had done it quite deliberately to get back at Leopold, before she truly knew Mr. Auerbach.

Dead branches, wrote the pencil. It was often this way; the paper became a collage of the irregular scraps of language available to him in the spirit world. *Rotten stumps.*

She was surprised by the intensity of Theodore's feeling. Infirm, she said, choosing the most neutral word she could think of.

She had seen Mr. Auerbach's legs clearly after he fainted. Leopold had turned on the gas lamps and Dr. Mayhew had gone to retrieve some smelling salts from his medical bag. Mr. Auerbach sat slumped in his wheelchair, the blanket he wore on his lap draped over one of the wheels, his legs exposed. Is that all? she had thought, used to clients with much uglier secrets.

It was then that something changed in her feelings toward him. She had filled with sorrow for the strange man with his poor sad blanket, and she had understood the cruelty of toying with him. She tried to apologize when he woke, but he was frantic to get away. So when Leopold had shown her the note that morning she had felt strangely giddy. It was rare that she got a chance to make amends.

A poor crippled man, she said to Theodore. No harm to anyone.

Pictures of men and women, scrawled the pencil, indignant.

Well, yes, there was that, of course. One night after all the other patrons had left, Jane Larue had confessed her true occupation— had done so kneeling on the carpet, hands together in supplication, long hair thrown down over her face like a veil. Verena could hardly hear her for the wailing. The story had come out in fragments: how she had met a man who had introduced her to a man in a wheelchair who had shown her how.

To what? When they had finally put the pieces together, it was almost dawn, and Jane was curled on the couch like a child, Verena stroking her hair. Leopold sat by the fire, sunk deep in an armchair, lazily squeezing his grip-o-meter. She could see he was thinking of the possibilities, and sure enough, the next day he began doing what he always did with potential clients: compiling a dossier. But he would not show it to her, and she had to wait till he was out to peek in the file. As she suspected, there were examples of the photographs Mr. Auerbach's company produced. She flipped through them quickly, her face half-averted: photographs of things she had done with Theodore when he was still alive, things so intimate they had felt invented, so private they did not have a name. When she recognized Jane Larue's face, she closed the file and put it away. She was breathing heavily.

Obscenities, scratched the pencil.

It doesn't matter, she replied, and then repeated what Leopold always said about problematic clients: It's none of our business what they do in the day. She did not, in fact, believe this, however. The postcards had shaken her. It was as if she were standing outside at a window, looking back into the past, at her most intimate conjugal moments—parodied by strangers.

She realized now that the photographs were one of the reasons why she had lashed out at him: he had made those things. He had shaken her.

The pencil continued across the page: *Men and women spliced together in that way we once.*

We: the word created an empty space in her chest. She remembered lying beside Theodore in bed, arms and legs tangled; she remembered his weight on top of her, making her solid, a part of the world. I miss your touch, she said.

I reach.

And I keep waiting to feel.

I can't.

My body aches to be held. I'm not an old woman yet.

The pencil clawed its way across the page. Anger was always his substitute for sorrow—they were alike in that way. When alive, he would tip vases to the floor and then kick through the shards. But it was worse now that he could break nothing but her. *Pornographer,* he wrote.

He's rich, she said, parroting Leopold.

Flesh, wrote the pencil. *Enemy of spirit.*

But I can't just get rid of him, she said. Leopold would be angry.

Leopold has waited half a lifetime just to strip my corpse and dress himself in my clothes.

She had never told Theodore about her troubles with Leopold, and yet he knew about them, as if he were in the house, listening. He's not interested in me, except for my ability to talk to you, she said. You're the one he loves. Look how he's kept your memory alive.

Maggotmaggotmaggot, he wrote.

You will never lose me, she said.

And then came one of his sudden bursts of eloquence, the words forming quickly, fluidly, without resistance: *Imagine having a mouth that can't speak unless pressed to another mouth a hand that can't write unless entwined in another hand nothing but borrowed words to catch the things that swirl inside me.*

The flow of words stopped but she was overcome with an image so vivid that it seemed to be right before her. Her entire head was a window. She looked out on a searing blue sky, so blue it made her dizzy; so blue she could taste it on her tongue, the color of a cold so intense it could not be named. The view was cropped in a peculiar way—in a flash she realized she was looking out of an open tent flap. *Have you ever seen something so blue? I should write a novel about it.*

She thought she felt his hand on her arm, his breath on her neck. Her head was swirling. Dictate it to me, she said.

When I was a little boy. Fingers on her neck pointed her head upward to a new shade of blue. As her vision reeled, she caught a glimpse of windows, gables, rooftops, and finally the sky, flowing like fast-moving water. She was running—or he was, the little boy—with that little-boy abandon, lampposts careening past. A musical vibration moved through him, an ascending chord: laughter. *It was blue like that,* he said.

The laughter spiraled through her, but she felt the opposite, a sadness like wood smoke and fallen leaves. Dictate and I will write it down, she said.

You are it, Verena, the novel I am writing.

With that, her hand was her own once again. She sat, weeping silently so Leopold or Maisie would not come in. She was empty now, exhausted, her eyes almost closed, but she looked over the piece of paper on which she had been writing.

Obscenities.

Men and women spliced together in that way we once.

I reach.

I can't.

The conversation over, her answers missing, her intuitive sense of Theodore's meaning gone—all that was left was a series of jagged fragments running down the page. She began to doubt how much was real and how much was in her mind. Was she mad? Was she wasting her life on an illusion? And yet how otherwise to explain the words, the handwriting, the lingering feeling of his breath in her ear? There was no answer. She folded the paper and hid it under the blanket, then lay down and closed her eyes.

She woke after a long sleep. It was dark in the room; the window was a rectangle of city night. The house was quiet. She pushed herself up to a sitting position and then ran her hands down her thighs to remind herself of her legs, which still had no sensation. And then she remembered a dream: Theodore was kissing her. Her eyes were closed and her mouth open, but when she opened her eyes again, it was not Theodore but Mr. Auerbach, and standing to one side, glaring at them with great fury, was Jane Larue.

She looked about the room, as if someone might have heard. She told herself that her dream was just that, a dream, and meant nothing at all. Certain dreams were important; they could act as portals to the spirit world. But most dreams were absurd, merely jumbled thoughts left over from the waking hours. This was one of those.

Nevertheless, she could not help dwelling on the image of Jane Larue's angry face, twisted with jealousy. What exactly was her relationship to Mr. Auerbach? Given the nature of her work, it was hard to believe it was simply one of employer and employee; unless, of course, his ailment made it impossible for him to—but that did not seem very likely. Mr. Auerbach had an air about him, one that she recognized because Theodore had it too: a definite masculinity. And then the kiss seemed like a kind of proof, even if it happened in a dream. She stopped herself, embarrassed.

What would a man like Mr. Auerbach want with someone like Jane Larue, she asked herself: a poor, sweet, pathetic creature, to be sure, but so ignorant and so silly? Perhaps he felt unworthy of a more substantial woman because of his infirmity. And yet that was exactly what he needed—a woman who could show him the way out of the shadows he now inhabited, into the light. Jane Larue was not that woman. Intentionally or not, she was keeping him tangled in depravity.

10. YOU DON'T HAVE TO BE AFRAID OF ME

Riding home, Auerbach could not control the shivering. It was as if an icy river ran through him. He drew down the window shades and then unfolded the blanket he kept over his lap, pulling it up to his chin. He suspected a fever.

Of all the spirits that could have claimed him, his mother made the least sense. Napoleon, Caesar—they would have had something to offer. But she had died when he was only ten, and had no understanding of business or the world of affairs. All she knew was the theater, a place of tinsel and greasepaint and shoddy make-believe. When she died, she left behind a trunk of old tattered scripts—just as the voice had said—and a pile of gowns; nothing of value.

If she had not reappeared, he could have continued thinking of her as the beautiful voice that sang him to sleep when he was a boy, rather than as a casual and neglectful parent. No, *neglectful* was not the word, he told himself—he had always been well-fed and well-dressed, and she liked to have him with her, backstage or in her dressing room, or in the audience watching her sing. *Inattentive* might be a better word, though he recoiled from that too, as it smacked of bitterness or blame, wholly inappropriate when discussing a young woman killed onstage in the prime of life. She had, in fact, given him a considerable amount of attention at times, showing him the new costumes she would be wearing in the next play, or the ball gown she would be wearing out to some special event. And she listened to him, she really did. After the show, she would ask his opinion of her performance and then listen to his critique with solemn attention, as if she were talking to the critic from the *World Dispatch Leader* and not a ten-year-old boy. Of course, his reviews were always glowing—that may have helped.

No, *mercurial* might be the right word, a basically affectionate word. She meant well, but her attention was sometimes drawn away—which, he hastened to add, was wholly understandable, given the demands of her career and the sensitivity of her temperament. She herself had had much to say on just those topics—her career and her temperament. The young Auerbach had listened to her thoughts with great attention, feeling inexpressibly lucky to be in her confidence.

And then she had died.

Auerbach stuck an arm out of the blanket, picked up the envelope the Swanns had given him, and removed the photograph. He still had trouble recognizing himself as the man at the center of the composition: a man whose lower half seemed to disappear into a blanket; a man seated on some sort of wheeled contrivance halfway between a throne and the electric chair that Mr. Thomas Edison promoted as an alternative to the noose; a man surrounded on three sides by women: Jane Larue, Mrs. Swann, and his mother, Aspasia.

Aspasia was standing to his left, facing the camera. Her dress was of the kind he remembered her wearing, far different from the current fashions: a heavy silk tea cozy of a gown, puffed out with stiff petticoats. Her expression was relaxed and utterly natural—completely without the pinned quality evident in her other pictures. Everyone looked pinned in the old pictures; the exposure times were so long that the sitter had to be kept immobile with a metal brace.

No, this was not an old picture, and he saw no other evidence of collage or double exposure. The image of Aspasia sat exactly where it should on the picture plane, in perfect proportion to the others. It was the same intensity, the same shade. There was no border or outline, no spotting.

Though he told himself he did not remember the night of his mother's death, he did; he had in fact simply stored the memory away. There was a certain door he had to open in the back of his mind, and the memory was there, happening. The Majestic Theater was behind that door. It was an old theater, impossibly old, but it gave off a sort of tragicomic dignity, like an ancient widower in tight pants and a corset. The walls were a sooty pink, the ceiling blue, with a galaxy of stars painted on. The stars glittered dimly when the house darkened. The plaster walls were so soft you could burrow into them with a penknife. There were no straight lines left. The walls bellied outward, the floor sloped, the balcony sagged in the middle like a strip of taffy. The structure seemed to be held together by the little plaster putti in the corners.

Backstage, the dressing room was no bigger than a closet, lit by a single gas lamp and stuffed with costumes, towering wigs, boxes full of jewels as big as pecans—glass and paste—pots of face powder and eye paint. Mother and son sat side by side, staring into the mirror before them—a large mirror in a heavy gilt frame, propped on the table and leaning against the brick wall behind. She brought her face right up to the bubbled glass, working with her brushes. "Well, what is your verdict, sir?" she asked, batting her eyelashes.

"Full house."

"That would be nice." She began pinning up her hair in preparation for donning a great pineapple of a wig. "Because I'm not going back to backbends." She had started her theatrical career as an acrobat.

His job was selling sheet music at the end of the show, for which he was paid five percent of his take. This required that he stand at the back of the theater for the last scene of the last act. When his mother finished the final lingering note of her deathbed finale, "O Mourn Not, Papa! Mourn Not!" he was to begin marching down the aisle, hawking the sheet music that he held against his chest. On his way back up toward the exits, he would be followed by members of the cast and orchestra, all singing the chorus as they trooped in the funeral procession while his mother presided from above, arms outstretched in benediction, an ethereal spirit in white satin robes, suspended twenty feet above the stage by an invisible cord.

He loved standing at the back of the theater, waiting for his cue. The stage glowed, a box of yellow light. His mother seemed both very close and very far. He felt the power she had over the audience, and conversely, the power they had over her, a volatile form of love. *God's Newest Angel* was utterly shameless in its hunger for tears, and it produced an extraordinary silence in the audience by the final scene—all the more surprising because theaters were not quiet places. The two-penny seats in the balcony were full of mechanics and laborers, drinking beer from pots and buckets. The stairs and aisles were crowded with newspaper boys, chimney sweeps, and the Street Arabs, who slept on the hay barges on the river, feral creatures who poured in the side doors and hung over the balcony railings, dropping peanut shells on the paying customers below.

On the night the rope broke, she was especially beautiful. As always, there was the collective gasp as she rose from her sickbed up into the air with the slow effortlessness of a balloon. The long white gown unfurled beneath her, a waterfall of satin glowing in the footlights. She raised her face to the rafters—to heaven, that is—and then pressed her palms together in prayer. The sobbing spread throughout the house then, and a wail rose from the seats in the balcony. At twenty feet she leveled off, turning in midair like a swimmer in water to look down at the deathbed scene below, the relatives circling the bed in postures of grief, her own lifeless body—a mannequin covered in a sheet. The gaslight caught the smoke that hung in the air, creating a luminescent haze. A single violin began a wintry melody. She spread her long arms and began "Mourn Not."

He had his eyes on her when she fell. She dropped about a foot or so and then jerked to a halt, like a puppet on a string. Her voice warbled in surprise. She held there for a moment, her arms still outstretched, and then dropped all the way to the stage in a flutter of white satin. The sound of the impact was masked by the orchestra, which played on, unaware of what had happened—till the crowd erupted. Sweeps and Arabs jumped from the balcony and ran toward the stage. The other cast members huddled over her with a new and different sort of earnestness taken directly from life. Mr. Newberry, the proprietor, ran down the outer aisle, turning up the gas lamps, filling the candy-box theater with panicked light.

By the morning, Auerbach had come down with a rampant fever that kept him bedridden for several weeks. Mr. Newberry's apartment was above the theater, and Auerbach slept on the couch in the study. The orchestra roared beneath him. In his dreams he could hear the final notes of "Mourn Not," his cue to march down the aisle with the bundles of sheet music. This was not a hallucination. Attention from the accident had saved a production that had otherwise run its course, and the crowds had swelled again, much more than the theater could accommodate. The understudy filled his mother's role, and God's Newest Angel did not miss a night.

Later that month, when he was better, he went back to selling sheet music at the close of the performance. The understudy would rise from bed into the air, spreading her arms just as his mother had, and he would feel a wild, dreamlike joy, as if it might actually be her.

Back at the mansion, he went straight to his bedroom and got into bed. The chills, the lassitude, the pressure in his head—it had all the earmarks of illness, and yet he knew it was something else. He stared up at the mural on the ceiling—a swirl of clouds and cherubs. Images of his mother moved through his mind: his mother falling; his mother lying on the stage; his mother sitting beside his bed, singing him to sleep. These were followed by an image of Mrs. Swann, laid out on the couch in the parlor, barely conscious, her eyes glittering out of half-shut lids, her skin pale. It looked as if *she* were the one who had fallen and was hovering near death.

He could not rid himself of the picture. She had made herself sick in order to allow him to speak with his mother—had lost the use of her legs, in fact, a sacrifice he understood so well it made him shudder. Worse, he did not even know why she did it. She hardly knew him. He had paid her nothing, had not even had a chance to explain his business proposition. Thinking back, he could not remember the last time somebody had done something for him without being paid. The only people he ever saw were employees—models and servants—and they required payment for each little service they performed. The trouble was getting them to do even half of what they were supposed to do.

Once, as a young apprentice, he had fancied himself in love. Eliza Chiswick was his master's daughter: fourteen years of age, two years older than he. Whenever he was released from his labors in the darkroom, he would wheel himself to the studio's back entrance and watch her move about the drapes and columns and canvas backdrops with what seemed to him a magical freedom, as if the world belonged to her. She greeted the customers with a curtsy, and chatted with them like a society belle, cocking her head to one side and languidly fanning herself. It seemed impossible that she would ever notice him; the very thought was so excruciatingly wonderful that it terrified him. But one day she simply walked across the studio to where he sat pretending not to be watching her—reached him so quickly, in fact, that he did not have time to turn his chair around and escape. "You're one of the apprentices," she said.

"Yes," was all he could manage.

"What do you think of this dress?"

It was green velvet, with a collar and cuffs made of white lace. He wanted to tell her that it was the most beautiful thing he had ever seen, but that seemed impossibly, unimaginably forward. "It would photograph well," he told her. "The folds would fall just right."

She seemed satisfied by this and began examining his wheelchair. "Can you go fast?" she asked.

"Very fast."

"What about downhill?"

"Even faster."

They circled each other for weeks like this—little snippets of charged conversation, each wave of the fan, every flutter of the eyelashes a cataclysmic event, each word an echo that lasted for days. He started to neglect his work, rushing out of the darkroom at the soonest possible moment; and when she was not there, or when she was there but ignored him for the customers, he felt as if a heavy stone were slowly crushing his chest. He would have continued like this forever, without any thought of change, but one day she gestured him toward the storeroom. "I don't think you're allowed back there," he said.

"I'm allowed everywhere."

He took her, of course, though with trepidation. There were the noxious chemicals to think about, and Chiswick's anger—for he would certainly be angry if he found out—but most of all the fact of her, standing in a dark blue dress in that shaded, quiet place. He sat in his wheelchair, not knowing what to say, while she looked at him with that intense expression she practiced—*practiced* being exactly the right word, for she was an actress at heart. "Can I see them?" she asked.

"See what?" he asked, though he understood immediately.

"I want to see them."

His hands moved ahead of his disappointment, removing the wool blanket draped over his lap. He watched her face, which was dreamy, hungry. His legs had only stopped growing two years before, and were not nearly as out of proportion as they would later become, but they were nevertheless strange—*wrong*. He could see that it was the wrongness that interested her.

"I want to touch them," she said, and then reached out her hand and very lightly pressed an index finger, first to the tip of his shoe, and then to the wool of his pant leg.

It was over in a moment. There was a noise out front; he replaced the blanket, she ran back to the studio, and he wheeled himself to the darkroom and closed the door. In a sense, he never reemerged. He avoided her after that, coming early, staying late, and using the back exit to leave at night. Of course, he had glimpses of her carrying on with the customers; he could hear her laughter. But she never tried to seek him out; she had clearly satisfied her curiosity and moved on to other entertainments.

It was years before he understood the power his legs gave him, and years more before he learned to use that power on the models that filled his photographs. Nevertheless, Eliza Chiswick planted the seed. She was the one who showed him that life had singled him out for greater things.

That thought did not invigorate him as it should have, and after a while, lying in bed became unbearable. He got up, wheeled himself to the office, and shuffled through his stack of correspondence. But his mind still drifted back to Mrs. Swann stretched out on the couch after her trance, a deathly pallor on her face. Finally he did what he knew he would do all along: picked up the telephone receiver on his desk and placed a call to the Swanns' residence in Washington Square.

"Good evening," he intoned, after the operator connected him to Leopold Swann. "I am calling to inquire about Mrs. Swann." Talking on the telephone always felt strange, as if he were throwing words down a well and listening for the echo—except the echo came back entirely different.

"Thank you," said Leopold Swann. "She is resting comfortably now."

Auerbach was surprised at the relief he felt. "Would it be all right if I paid my respects tomorrow afternoon?"

"If you want to contact the spirits, evening is better."

That was exactly what he did *not* want to do, but with the words materializing out of nowhere, seemingly unspoken, it was easy to confuse them with the thoughts in his head. "What time?" he asked.

"Ten."

"Very well, then."

He spent the night tossing in bed, regretting that he had given in to the suggestion. His plan to tie up the Swanns seemed more urgent than ever, but he wanted those ties to be businesslike. He did not want anything more to do with trances and spirits, at least not directly. And yet he could not bring himself to commit to the idea of canceling his appointment. Each time he remembered the voice of his mother issuing from Mrs. Swann's mouth, something powerful moved through him, turning his thoughts upside down.

It was not till dawn that he found his solution: he would *not* go to the séance; *Miss Larue* would go. He would simply accompany her, out of a sense of duty.

Auerbach waited most of the next morning for a chance to get Jane Larue alone, but it did not come till the lunch break, when Mr. Grapes and the others retreated to a bench a dozen or so yards away and opened their lunch pails. Jane Larue remained by the bed, tying the belt on her dressing gown, a sad and dreamy look on her face. She was as striking as ever: tall, with broad shoulders, a great torrent of hair down her back, and those sharply defined features that translated so well to film—the high cheekbones and large eyes and long straight nose, the impossibly large mouth.

"Do you have a moment?" He spoke very softly, so as not to be overheard. He wanted to ask her if it could be true: that people contain something in them that can live on after the body dies. That people do not just disappear. That he will not have to leave all this behind—the great glass dome of the studio, and the light pouring down.

"I have been giving some thought to your friends," he said to her.

"My friends?"

"The Swanns."

Her face took on a tearful, frightened expression that he recognized immediately; it had grown common with her since the baby died. "I'm so sorry for what happened, Mr. A. Please forgive me."

"Not your fault," he said quickly, hoping to change the subject before the others came back.

"I've seen it before. People swoon and their limbs start shaking. I fainted once myself."

He frowned, and his tone grew more formal. "My concern is only for you and your speedy recovery, Miss Larue."

"Yes, Mr. A." She nodded with great vigor.

"I have heard that they offer private appointments. I was wondering if something like that might help you through this difficult time."

"Just me and Augie?" Her expression quivered and reformed itself into a look of radiant gratitude. "Oh, Mr. A."

"I've made the date for tonight. I hope that fits your schedule."

"Yes, yes. And you'll come with me, won't you?" she asked.

"If it makes it any easier for you," he told her, and then smiled in a way that signaled his willingness to push more important matters aside.

"You're so good to me," she said to him now, beginning to cry.

"Nonsense." He held out one of the handkerchiefs he always carried in his jacket pocket for the models.

That night, they rode together down to the Swanns' town house. Jane Larue was in her black dress, so elaborate that, except for the color, it could have been a wedding dress. The frills and ruffs seemed to take up half the carriage. She was excited, flushed, fidgety. She shifted back and forth in her seat, crossing and recrossing her legs, making the black froth of her dress undulate. She talked so much he wondered if she might be feverish. "I've heard about these private sessions," she said, fingering the locket around her neck, which held a bit of baby Augie's hair. "They say that amazing things happen. Materializations and levitations and musical instruments appearing from nowhere and playing music."

"Did you say materializations?" he asked, as offhandedly as possible.

"Spirits can make themselves visible, Mr. A. It's been scientifically proven."

"Is that so?" he muttered. The thought made his stomach tighten.

Leopold and Verena Swann greeted them in the foyer, he in white tie and tails, she in black chiffon and a long string of pearls. Auerbach was taken aback by the look on her face: blanched, exhausted. Her eyes were beads of black glass. "I'm glad to see you back on your feet," he told her, worried that she might collapse right there.

"I'm sorry to have caused any concern," she said.

"But you look like you could use a little more rest. Perhaps we should do this another night."

"But you've come all this way," she said, looking from him to Jane Larue. "And I feel inspired tonight."

Indeed, the atmosphere in the parlor felt strangely charged, like the air before a thunderstorm. He assumed it was due to all the weeping that had taken place there over the course of the business day, all the finding and parting. Leopold Swann led them to a small round table at the far end of the room, lit a candle, and then turned off the gas lamps. Even with the candle, the dark was oppressive. It reminded Auerbach of insomnia and the punishing thoughts that came to him in the midst of sleeplessness.

"Mrs. Swann informs me that conditions are exceptionally good," said Leopold Swann. "We may even have a rare chance at the most profound experience available to spirit seekers." He paused for dramatic effect. "A materialization."

"Is that really necessary?" asked Auerbach. His voice sounded different in the dark, smaller, lighter. When he spoke, he liked to see bodies intertwine, faces contort, photographs taken, money made. None of that was possible in the dark.

"There's nothing to be afraid of," said Mrs. Swann.

"It just seems excessive," said Auerbach. It would be more than enough for him if she did what she usually did, that strange form of reverse ventriloquism.

"I don't think we get to choose," said Mrs. Swann.

There was some wrangling between the Swanns after that. Leopold Swann seemed to be saying that a materialization was, in fact, optional, Mrs. Swann that it was up to the spirits. Jane Larue started to quietly weep.

"Look what you've done," hissed Mrs. Swann.

"Me? *You*," said Leopold Swann.

"I just want my baby," whispered Jane Larue.

"Fine," said Mrs. Swann. "Let's get on with it." She sank back in her chair, and her face, removed from the circle of light, blued like the moon in shadow. There was a long interval of silence, filled with breathing, the flickering of the candle. Auerbach felt himself suspended precariously over a tiny island of light. He looked out into the darkness and thought he could make out shapes, areas of volume, but they sank back into the mass almost immediately, as if trying and failing to be born.

What Auerbach wanted was very simple: to be unhurt; to be unmoved; to go home the exact same person he walked in as. But what happened was this: a figure stepped out of the nothingness. It was wrapped in white drapery of an archaic feel, but the shape of the body underneath was clearly feminine, and though the clothing formed a cowl over its head, much of the face could still be seen.

His eyes struggled to pierce through the gloom, even as his memory fought to travel back through the years. He found himself unable to remember anything definite about his mother's features, other than the face in the photograph by Swann. Yes, the long forehead, the high cheekbones, and sharp chin: the makings of his mother, the raw material of her. It was all there, but as strange and inhuman as a tongue of moonlight. And then it was gone. He had merely blinked, and there was a flutter of cloth, replaced by darkness. He could not find the breath to call it back.

"My God," exclaimed Jane Larue. She was frothy with excitement, a volatile mixture of grief and joy. "It's true, all true."

"But you knew that," said Leopold Swann. He sounded exceedingly pleased, as if he were accepting a personal compliment.

"I could have touched her," said Jane Larue. "I could have stretched out my arm."

"You would have felt a material substance very like flesh."

"Flesh." There was awe in her voice. "Flesh."

"When you get to know them, they will let you touch them," said Swann.

"She came here to see Mr. A." There was a hitch in Jane's voice now. "A mother's love doesn't end. It doesn't go away."

"Love is immortal," murmured Leopold Swann. "It's what makes us immortal."

"But it doesn't stop," said Jane Larue through her tears. She sounded strangely indignant, angry. "It doesn't break, it doesn't even bend." The last word became a sob. "I'm sorry, it's just that it keeps on—"

"Hush, child, the trance isn't finished yet. There's more coming."

"I want to see him too. I want to touch him."

"He will show himself when he's ready."

And then without warning, there was a third voice in the conversation: Mrs. Swann. "Hello, dear." It was that voice, the one Auerbach had learned to call his mother's.

He turned to look at the medium. She was still leaning back in her chair, and though her face was in the shadows, he had the sense that her eyes were closed, and that she was asleep. "There's no need to be afraid," she said.

His heart squeezed closed. He held his breath. Leopold Swann leaned toward him. "You can speak to her. She will answer you." His throat went dry. He shook his head no.

"How I wish I could have been with you all those years to guide and protect you," said the voice. "But you did not need me. You have become a handsome, impressive man, Augustus, all by yourself. You make me very proud."

He felt a sudden intense pressure in the front of his face: tears. He struggled mightily to keep himself together.

"You don't have to be afraid of me, or of the woman who speaks for me," said the voice. "We will always tell you the truth."

He inhaled deeply and looked up at the ceiling, or rather, the blackness where the ceiling would have been. How often did he hear the truth from anyone?

The silence stretched on. The medium rocked from side to side, as if in a troubled sleep, and then spoke. "Hello, Mama," she said. "Your little Augie loves you." Her voice had completely changed. His mother had left. It was now the baby voice Auerbach remembered from the first séance.

"Mama, I'm walking now!" said the baby. "I hold Mrs. Auerbach's hand, and we go for walks. And then sometimes I hold on to your skirts and walk right next to you when you go to the store. Can you feel me holding on?"

Jane Larue leaned forward with a look of exquisite pain, approaching exaltation. "Yes!" she said, her face awash with tears. "I can feel you!"

"I love you, Mama!"

Jane's head reared back, as if slapped. "I love you too."

"That's why I have a message for you. Will you listen to it?"

"Yes, yes, tell me."

"You have to do as I say."

"I will, you know I will."

"You can't take your clothes off anymore, Mama," said the medium. "You have to stop."

"Stop?" Jane sat back, obviously stricken.

"You can't let him take pictures of you anymore. It's embarrassing. People here know."

Jane was crying now, very quietly, the sound of a stream at night. "Is that why?"

"Or I'll have to go away."

She shook her head violently. "I won't ever again. I promise."

"Then I'll be back." There was an air of departure in this phrase.

"Please don't go," she moaned. "It's very lonely without you."

And then something was dropping from the ceiling—pieces of cardboard, it seemed, hitting his head, piling up on the table, slipping to the floor. No, they were stereographic cards: cardboard rectangles with two near-identical photographic images printed side by side.

One fell onto the candle; its edge caught fire, and began to curl, and by the extra light Auerbach got a better look: identical pairs of naked women—lying on sofas, standing by fireplaces, eating spaghetti with their hands. They were his cards. They were Jane.

Auerbach rubbed his temples, trying to make sense of what was happening, though the thoughts were confused and slow in coming. Could it really have been the baby who did this? A two-week-old baby who never got beyond mewing like a cat? But who else could it be? After all they had just witnessed, he was disinclined to see it as a simple magician's trick, though a part of him could not completely discount that possibility, either—in which case it would have to be Leopold Swann, arrogant, swaggering Swann. Yet the spirit photographer seemed more panicked than triumphant. He was already up, busily trying to sweep the cards into a pile on the floor.

"We'll leave the light off," said Swann, taking off his jacket and placing it over the heap of cards, as if covering a corpse. Only then did he turn on the gas lamps. "This is not all that unusual," he said, surveying the area for stray cards. "Discarnate spirits can be—" he glanced over at the medium, slumped in her chair, "inappropriate at times, by earthly standards." He seemed flustered, and not a little chagrined. "That is, they are free of certain restraints."

Auerbach looked at Jane. She was sitting completely still, her hands clasped. A card had gotten wedged into the back of her dress collar. Auerbach pulled it out and stole a quick look—the pregnant Jane, astride Henry's thin legs, a collector's item, now selling for as much as three dollars each—before stuffing it in his coat pocket. The only hope, he realized, was to convince her that Leopold Swann had done this to her, that Swann took advantage of his sister-in-law's powers for his own profit. But how?

His attention was pulled to Mrs. Swann, who looked to be waking from a bad dream. She had her hands over her eyes. "Forgive me," she said to no one in particular, tossing back and forth in her chair. "Forgive me. I'm so sorry, so very sorry." Yet it wasn't clear that she knew what had happened or why she was sorry. A card lay face down, unnoticed in her lap. Then she started to laugh, a high hysterical keening. Aspasia's laughter.

Leopold Swann stood over her. "How do you feel, Verena?" The tone of concern failed to mask his fury, which came through in the grim set of his face. It looked like he might start to pummel her with his fists.

"Not well." She giggled and then abruptly stopped.

Swann slowly shook his head, clearly trying to regain self-control. "It's the strain of mediumship, Mr. Auerbach. As a rule, they don't last very long."

Mrs. Swann took her hands from her eyes and then looked around as if she had a painful hangover. "It's just that I have no idea what happened." She let out another burst of giggling, devoid of merriment. "What is that?" She was looking at the stereograph that had fallen into the candle's flame—the charred curlicue that remained of it.

"Enough," said Swann.

Auerbach felt an obscure need to come to her defense. "She can't be responsible for what she does in a trance," he said. "Isn't that right?"

"Well, yes, of course," said Swann, looking up. "I'm glad you understand that."

At that, Jane Larue sprang up, almost upsetting the table. "Ah, now, Miss Larue," said Swann. He stood with his arms open, as if asking her to be reasonable and forgive the spirit world its moment of spleen. "I know this has been a very difficult experience." But she did not seem to hear or see; her eyes were focused on the door. She walked with concentrated fury past the exhibits and was gone.

11. LET HIM GO

Verena sat at the table while Leopold paced back and forth. He was so furious he could hardly speak. "What," he stammered, "what do you think you are doing?" He came circling back. "What gives you the right? What gives you the right to do this?" And then back the other way. "The photographs—where did you even get them? Did Maisie help you?"

Verena hunkered, hands in her lap. She believed that, cruel as it may have seemed, she had in fact done a noble thing by driving Jane Larue away. Both Jane and Mr. Auerbach would now be free to improve their manner of life. Jane could find honest, dignified work as a seamstress or maid, and Mr. Auerbach could look for a more suitable field for his business talents—railroads or steamships, perhaps. Or maybe he would simply retire from business and use his wealth for philanthropic purposes. Verena would show him how. They could start an orphanage. Verena would give up mediumship to run it; she would be a mother to all the motherless children. This would be a much better thing than letting Leopold fleece Mr.

Auerbach. But she could not tell any of that to Leopold. "I'm just sick of all the grieving mothers," she said to him. "They make me ill."

She hated the bereaved mothers in their black dresses and black veils, with lockets and rings containing sacred remnants: curly locks of hair, nail parings, even baby teeth. In their handbags they carried booties and mittens and lacy baby caps, to pull out and sniff like posies, to put in their mouths and press against their eyes. The sheer physicality of their worship was awful, oppressive. And Jane Larue was the worst of them. The silly thing wept at every proof of immortality, no matter how contrived, wailed every time that little child spoke—a physical outpouring that shook the table. She was a little too ennobled by her loss, a little too happy to be miserable. And then there was the comically proud, possessive way she pushed Mr. Auerbach's chair into the room...

"She's not just a weeper, Verena. She's the thing that brought him here."

"We don't need her anymore."

He stopped and glared at her. "Why are you trying to sabotage everything? I am breaking my back to pull in the most important client of our career, and you are doing everything you can to prevent me from succeeding. Is it because of *him*?"

"Who?" Her heart sped up, thinking he meant Mr. Auerbach.

"He was always destroying whatever I built. He wanted to be the big man, the famous explorer. I threatened him."

"That's ridiculous."

"Is it?" He caught himself and began doing his breathing exercises. He had learned them from an Indian Yogi who had traveled with him in a carnival. When he spoke again, his voice was soft, but his eyes were still full of his injuries. "Listen to me, Verena. I go out and find the weepers, I listen to their pathetic stories, and figure out how to please them. I stand in saloons with newspaper reporters, buying them drinks all night, and then holding their heads for them as they vomit into the gutter. And what is the result? I make you famous, and I make Theodore immortal. Are those things so unforgivable?" He stared at her with those gigantic, wounded eyes.

"I don't know," she said, looking away. She had meant to help Mr. Auerbach, not to hurt Leopold. Or perhaps she *had* meant to hurt Leopold, just a little bit—not realizing how badly it would pain her to do so.

"What's more, I take the blame for it all, for all the dirty, disgusting favors I've done for you both, so that you can remain pure and unsullied and enjoy your wealth and fame without the slightest taint—the sainted explorer and his wife, the sainted spirit medium." He mimicked her flicking her hands in the air, a look of dandified disgust on his face. "Yes, I do it all. I take it all upon my shoulders so that you can say to yourself, I do not lower myself for money. No, I just humor Leopold a little bit, the poor, money-grubbing vulgarian!"

"That's not true," she said, hunching her shoulders with shame.

"Let me tell you a little story, Verena. When Theodore left, he took me aside. This was on the dock, right before he went up the gangway. He said, if anything happens to me, I want you to take care of her, Leopold. Swear that you will. And I swore." He looked at her, his eyes brimming with emotion. "And I will keep that oath, Verena, even if you hate me for it."

She looked at him, chagrined. The tears, the swelling of the lips, and the brave set of the jaw: it all looked absolutely real. But of course it *was* real. *That* was how he did it. "I don't hate you, Leopold."

"But you don't love me, either."

"Of course I love you. We're family."

"Then you won't keep me from helping you."

At moments like this she pictured herself caught in a hunter's net: struggle would only tangle her more. "No," she replied.

"Very well then," said Leopold. "I am going to think about what we can do to fix things with our friend Auerbach. Why don't you go to bed?"

She did as she was told, but sleep would not come. She heard footsteps in the hall and on the stairs, the creak of floorboards. She told herself that life had become unbearable. Whatever path she tried to take, the way was always blocked. Theodore had told her many stories of men lost without compasses, how they wandered in giant circles till they came to their own starting place and crumpled in despair. Better to sit and wait for rescue, he had told her, as if she might someday actually be in that situation, a woman who had never set foot in a wild place. Build a fire. Signal. Wait.

She began to remember how reassuring Theodore's physical presence had been, especially at night when she couldn't sleep. She would lie on her side, staring at the square of blue night framed by the window at the far end of the room, and he would fit himself to the curve of her body. His arms would reach around her, one hand cupping her breast. She would feel his chest against her back, the tops of his thighs against her legs.

She wanted him, suddenly, wanted to hear his words in her throat, wanted to be filled with his voice. The desire was overpowering, like the lost explorer's yearning for home. She had some sense that he was very close, just the other side of the coffin lid that had closed on her—just the other side of invisibility.

And then it came: the tingling in her neck and shoulders, a fullness in her chest. It deepened, and then took a new and different direction: a feeling of words; a feeling that he was writing on her body with the tip of his finger. She could feel the words forming, not on her exactly, but *in* her. She could not describe it to herself any better than that, because there was no precedent in ordinary life. It wasn't writing; it wasn't touch; it wasn't speech. It arose from the space between those things.

But of course that's only if there's somebody looking for you, he said.

What is? she asked.

The bit about building a fire. If there's nobody looking, then it doesn't do much good. And of course you never really know whether there's somebody looking or not. But you have to assume there is, otherwise you would head out on that walk.

Leopold thinks I lost him Mr. Auerbach. And maybe I did.

Leopold can't break free of your pull, Verena. But he doesn't understand why he's orbiting. So he goes round and round.

This caught her off guard. He wants to be rid of me? she asked.

He wants to stop walking in circles.

I have nothing to do with that. I've never asked him for anything.

Let him go.

The accusation sounded outrageous, absurd. She was accustomed to thinking of her situation in exactly opposite terms: she as a kind of captive, and Leopold as her jailer. I'm not holding him here, she said. That's insane.

She waited for a response but none was forthcoming. The touch of his finger was gone, and with it the words he had drawn on her skin, insubstantial as breath. If Leopold was not her jailer, perhaps it was Theodore, who came and went at his whim, leaving her always lonely, always yearning for more. Perhaps this was her fate, and she would never escape it; she would live the rest of her life alone. If so, it was all the more reason to help Mr. Auerbach. An act of disinterested kindness might redeem some of what was to come in the years ahead. She had been cruel for a purpose this evening; she would pay him a visit in the morning and see how he was fairing.

12. THE DOOR IN THE GARDEN WALL

A uerbach sat with Mr. Grapes by the stage set in the studio, waiting for Jane Larue, who was now ninety minutes late. Mr. Grapes kept himself busy tinkering with a broken camera, but Auerbach had long ago abandoned the stack of invoices on his lap to gaze out at the garden beyond the glass wall of the studio. He had gotten no sleep and felt headachy, dreamy, listless.

"This isn't like her," said Mr. Grapes. "I don't think she's ever been this late."

"She stalked out of the house and disappeared. I had the coachman drive up and down the street but we couldn't find her. We went to her boardinghouse but she wasn't there."

"What happened?"

"The spirit of her dead child told her to quit posing."

There was no response. The only sound was the dry clicking of the broken camera shutter as Mr. Grapes toyed with the mechanism. Auerbach took this as a reproach. "I thought it would help cheer her up." He could not explain to Mr. Grapes how complicated things had become.

"She's not coming," said Grapes, checking his pocket watch.

"She'll be here," said Auerbach, with a certainty based on need. If she came back, they could start over. The Swanns, his mother, the baby—all would be forgotten, and they would once again become what they had been: happy.

"I can get somebody else here in an hour," said Grapes. "There's still time."

"You don't understand, I don't *want* anybody else."

Grapes put down the pieces of the camera and got up to leave. "I'll be in the darkroom," he said, and walked out.

Alone, Auerbach gave himself over to his study of the garden, with a care he usually expended only on stereographs. He could see a stone path twisting through grass, then a stretch of the high limestone wall that surrounded the mansion. The path disappeared through a decorative arch threaded with vines and into a grove of trees.

He could not allow himself to consider whether she might not come. Instead, he wheeled over to the glass wall of the studio. It contained a glass door, distinguished only by an iron frame and a long iron handle, cool to the touch. He had never once used it or seen it used, but the handle turned easily, and the door swung open without effort. Unlocked, all these years.

He paused on the threshold, looking out: the stone path started from this point. He wheeled himself forward, feeling the sun on his bare head, hotter than in the studio. From somewhere came the scent of flowers, impossibly sweet. He passed along the limestone wall, wheeled through the arch, and entered a kind of natural amphitheater, shaded by trees. The light was soft and brown, the air almost chill. A small waterfall tumbled from an artificial grotto into a pool, filling the space with the sound of falling water. By the pool stood a wrought iron table with chairs, looking as if they had never been sat in.

He felt suddenly melancholy. Yes, it was beautiful, but that did not explain the bittersweet longing he felt, an overwhelming sense of nostalgia so intense it made his chest ache. He had never been here before, and yet he felt that he knew the place, that something very important had once happened to him here. And then he understood: this was the garden in the stereograph, the one he had shown to Jane Larue. Mr. Grapes had taken the photographs; Auerbach had never asked where. But it was *here*.

When he looked up, she was standing in front of him. Her eyes were red, her face blanched. Her hair was pulled back in a severe bun. She was wearing an ugly black sack of a dress with a high collar and long sleeves. Her hands gripped an old carpetbag. "I've come to say goodbye," she said.

He was a little confused by the sight of this new Jane Larue—so grave and dignified. If he were to stop her, it would have to be done carefully, in the gentlest way possible. And so he gave a long sigh, and a bittersweet, wistful smile, and pretended not to have heard. "Do you recognize this place?" he asked, intending to surprise her.

She lifted her chin, a slight gesture, but defiant. "I come here often."

It took him aback. He had never considered the possibility she might know something he did not, and now felt foolish—all the more so because he was not used to being wrong when it came to the models. He tried to make a joke of it. "Not quite as nice as the stereograph, is it?"

"The difference is that it's real."

"Photographs are real, Miss Larue."

"Not like people, Mr. A."

He looked at her, suddenly frightened. This was not just about the baby, he realized; it was about him too. She blamed him for not saving the baby. "There was nothing anybody could have done for him," he whispered. "You heard the doctor."

"You did what you could," she said, eyeing him coldly. It was as if she could see right through him to the hidden truth of his weakness.

"Then why not stay?"

"Because my baby has told me to go."

"But Miss Larue, please be reasonable. We don't even know how much to believe." It sounded inexcusably weak, even as he spoke.

"Of course we know." Her face softened slightly. "I used to think flesh was all I had—till I lost Augie. Now I know it's just a little bit of what there is."

"And what is there?"

"Our feelings are too big for our bodies. They don't all fit inside."

He could tell this was not a useful direction to pursue. "How will you support yourself?" he asked her.

"I'm sorry, Mr. A., but I've already made my decision." She turned and began walking up the path, away from the studio.

He followed behind, through the trees and out into the sunlight. The path wound through flower beds and bushes toward a wooden door in the limestone wall. He spoke to her back. "You're leaving me in a difficult position, Miss Larue. Exotic photography is a *collaborative* art."

"You'll find somebody else."

"No, you don't understand. It requires a very particular sympathy between model and photographer." He did not have the heart to tell her the rest.

She reached the door. He watched her open it, as if the act were nothing. He wheeled up behind her, frightened by the swath of city that came into view. He saw carriages drawn by enormous, muscled horses—carriages he would never ride to the ocean or the mountains or any of the other mysterious places beyond the mansion walls. He saw women in elegant dresses and great swooping hats—women he would never speak with, kiss, or hold. No matter how rich or famous he became, they would all look at him with disgust: the crippled pornographer.

"Goodbye, Mr. A.," said Jane Larue. She stepped through the gate and disappeared into the fast-moving crowd, like a leaf taken by a stream.

13. MRS. SWANN SITS FOR HER PORTRAIT

Auerbach retreated to his office, but found he was unable to concentrate. He picked up a letter, then put it down; picked up a pen and did the same. He reached for Miss Parish's buzzer but withdrew his hand. He pushed away from the desk, returned to it, and then pushed away again.

He thought it absurd that he was upset at losing Jane Larue, and yet if this was not sadness, it was very close, a sharp-edged, broken feeling at the base of his throat. He was aware of a strange kind of elation too, as if Jane Larue had suddenly levitated away in his presence, floating upward on a beam of light. She had said wild, heedless, foolish things, but the strangest thing of all was that he was almost—almost—ready to believe her. Perhaps, he thought, the flesh is not everything. Perhaps there is something else, something that does not stop at the border of our skins, that flows out and around, that joins and stays.

Ever since his mother's death, he had known himself to be alone in the world. That understanding had been confirmed by the years spent working in Chiswick's back room, and it had hardened after he created Rive Gauche. But what if he were wrong? What if he were not truly alone? What if his mother were with him all that time—with him even now, though he could not see or hear her?

He thought he felt something brush his cheek. Startled, he looked around as if he might actually see whose hand—

What he saw was the room itself. The dark green wallpaper had a dense forest pattern—leaves overlapping leaves. The leather sofa had a low, hunched shape. The wastepaper basket was made from an elephant's foot. But he had never noticed any of this before. He was too busy staring into his stereoscope, contemplating, judging, manipulating the little human figures it contained—as if arranging the dolls in a dollhouse.

There was a knock at the door. He picked up a sheaf of papers from his desk and pretended to be reading, but it was only one of the little maids. She curtsied and spoke down toward her shoes. "I can't hear you," he said, which only made the mumbling worse. "Why don't you come over here?"

She shuffled toward him, staring with great intensity at the floor. Up close, she was nothing more than a child: unhealthy rings around the eyes, sunless complexion—one of the horde of little creatures in black dresses and white aprons that was always scouring, buffing, polishing. Could it be that she too had something inside of her, something that could slide through time and space, something that could not be contained by that thin little body? The thought confused him. What would you call such a creature, a creature that is not fully material?

An angel.

"Look up," he said.

She raised her chin. Her eyes were large, dark, her skin lightly freckled. There was a scar of some sort, barely visible, at her hairline. She could be ten but was more likely thirteen. She reminded him of

himself when he was working for Chiswick in the studio on Laight
Street, and that discomfited him even more. He did not like the
memory of that little boy, paid a dollar a day to mix combustibles in
a metal vat. "What is your name?" he asked.

"Jane, sir."

Another Jane. "Do you like it here, Jane?"

"Very much, sir."

But then why was she trembling? "Are you sick?" he asked.

"No, sir."

He watched the slight tremor in her chin, the wilt of her shoulders. She looked frightened, but why? What could she possibly be
frightened of? Him? The thought took him by complete surprise.
When had he become the sort of man that frightens a child?

He reached into his pocket and offered her a silver dollar. Only
then did he notice the little tray she held in her hands, and the visiting card that lay on it—her mission. He picked up the card and
read the delicately embossed letters standing in an expanse of white:

MRS. VERENA SWANN
SPIRIT MEDIUM

It was perfect timing. He had so much to tell her, so much to *ask*
her. He left the little maid and wheeled himself down the long hall,
picking up speed as he went. By the time he found Mrs. Swann in
the parlor off the foyer, he was out of breath, his heart bouncing in
his chest. He wheeled forward then stopped, overcome by the swirl
inside him. "Thank you" was the best he could manage. He meant
something in the area of "thank you for coming."

"I hope I'm not interrupting anything," she said.

"No, of course not."

She looked worried—it was in the eyebrows and those remarkable
eyes. "I am here to apologize for what happened last night," she said.

"But why? That wasn't you."

"But it *was* me."

"You can't be responsible for what the spirits say."

She looked uncomfortable, on the verge of protest. "Nevertheless, I felt I should tell you. And if it's any help, I can talk to Miss Larue."

"She quit this morning," he said, feeling the truth of this with new force.

"I am sorry."

"She was an unusual resource," he said, knowing it did not sound right. "A valued employee."

"You were a good and generous friend to her," said Mrs. Swann.

He gave a rueful laugh. "That is because you do not know photography, Mrs. Swann. I have read that the savages in the jungle will not allow themselves to be photographed. They think it will steal their souls."

"I am the one she should be angry at, not you."

He shook his head. "No, the fault is with photography itself. Photographs are perfect things, and people are not. It is maddening to have to live with that discrepancy, day in and day out. She was not strong enough. They never are."

"Maybe she is better off then."

The idea was a novelty; he had never considered what might be best for Jane Larue, only for Rive Gauche. He nodded his head and then sat, unsure what to say.

She too seemed to be struggling for words. "If you will forgive me, Mr. Auerbach." She hesitated, looking away. "In my profession, I cannot avoid involvement with the most private aspects of my clients' lives. But you must believe that it is because I care about them, and wish to help them."

"Yes, of course." He nodded, a little worried about what might be coming.

She took a breath. "I had the sense that Miss Larue was a particularly close friend."

"She worked here five years." It was the best he could do; there were no words for the connection between photographer and model.

"What I mean is a close *personal* friend."

Her eyes latched onto his, impressing her meaning, but it was still two beats before he realized what she was hinting at. "Oh no, of course not." He sputtered in confusion, his face heating up. "That would be—would be—" Unthinkable, he wanted to say.

She cut in. "You mean?"

"Absolutely not." His destiny as a titan of industry precluded it.

"I see." She nodded with great force, clearly embarrassed. "Well then, I'm sorry for having—"

He cut her off. "Not at all." In any case, Miss Larue would have been shocked at the idea.

They fell back into a long and awkward silence. Auerbach fussed with the blanket on his lap, smoothing it over and over. Women did not think of him that way. That entire area of life was closed to him. Mrs. Swann of all people, with her powers of clairvoyance, should understand that.

Mrs. Swann walked very deliberately toward a tall red vase that sat atop a table. "Oh, is that Chinese? It's lovely." She examined it for a moment, and then began looking about the parlor. "You have an extraordinary house," she said. "I was hoping for a tour."

"A tour." He hesitated; there were whole sections he had never visited. "Yes, of course, a tour. Allow me to show you around."

They traveled side by side down the long marble hall, Auerbach careful not to exceed the speed of her walk. "Um, that is the clock room," he said, pointing to a chamber filled with clocks of every size and shape. "That is the bird room," he noted, waving his hand toward a room filled with caged songbirds, trilling loudly. "This is the sculpture gallery," he said, as they moved through an atrium filled with nude marble flesh.

His voice seemed to come from far away, as if someone else were talking in another room. Mrs. Swann's question continued to preoccupy him. How could she think it possible that he would become entangled with Jane Larue? Kleinfeldt had a wife, of course, but unlike Auerbach, he was not a figure of historical importance. Auerbach had been set aside by nature for a special destiny. This line of thought was complicated, however, by the late-morning sunlight, glowing in Mrs. Swann's hair.

Verena Swann had stopped for a moment to gaze at a statue of a Hindu deity with many arms. Whatever residual embarrassment she may have felt was gone, dissipated by the easy conversation about the house. The mansion was extraordinary, something between a palace and an amusement arcade, filled with exotic furnishings and odd contraptions. She smiled and laughed and asked many questions, enjoying the fact that Mr. Auerbach seemed uncertain about the answers. Had he really never looked at all the precious things he owned? Had he never been in all these rooms? He was an absentminded, unworldly man, but she liked that about him; it made him less intimidating. He seemed content to follow her wherever she led, making up the answers she needed. "You do not seem to care much about the luxuries, Mr. Auerbach."

"I am entirely devoted to my work. There isn't any leisure left over for frivolous pursuits."

"I hope it isn't lonely."

"At times. But then I remind myself of the things I want to accomplish."

They walked on to the end of the hallway, and stopped before a door. "We can turn left here and see the ballroom," said Mr. Auerbach. "And then circle back through the loggia."

"Oh? But what's through the door?"

"Nothing, really—the corridor that leads to my photographic

studio."

She actually caught her breath. "You don't want me to see it, I assume."

"It isn't suitable."

She had in fact worried that she might stumble across something from that other world—naked women, or worse, naked men. But with each successive room filled with artifacts and curios her anxiety had lessened, replaced with a sort of giddiness at the success of her adventure. She felt strong enough to conquer anything; indeed, wanted more to conquer. "I am not a conventional person, Mr. Auerbach. You must know that by now." Nevertheless, her heart was beating hard.

"You are a most extraordinary person, Mrs. Swann. There is no doubt of that."

"Then treat me as such."

He began fussing with his blanket yet again. "Very well then," he said, and pulled open the door.

They proceeded in silence down a long hall. Almost immediately, she feared that she had overreached. She was, after all, just an ordinary woman, a sheltered housewife, a widow, not an adventurer. It was almost time for luncheon, and Leopold would be wondering where she had gone. But then they passed through a second door, into what appeared to be an enormous winter garden made of glass. The effect was extraordinary: space, light, great clouds rolling overhead. "This is it?" she asked, laughing with relief. It was the very opposite of those dark and cramped photographs with their furtively coiled bodies.

"This is it, the furnace that drives the engine."

A vast expanse of empty floor led to a simple stage set: three painted canvas flats with a bed in the middle. A camera stood in front, perched on its three wooden legs. She approached the bed as if it were the sacrificial altar in some pagan rite. "And this is where?"

"Yes."

The bed was ordinary in every respect, as were the linens, which were fresh. "And Miss Larue?"

"Of course."

She tried to imagine Miss Larue naked on the bed. "Why would anyone?"

"For money."

"And yet certainly there must be other ways?"

"To earn money? Sometimes there are, but not always." He sounded weary and sad. "The very best of them have a second motive. They come here feeling invisible, you see, and they want me to make them visible. Miss Larue was of that type."

"Like the weepers," she said, feeling that she might as well have said, *Like me.*

"I'm sorry?"

"Just a little joke." She sat very carefully on the edge of the bed and composed herself as she might have for one of the Spiritualist publications: back straight, head up, hands in her lap. "Take my picture."

"Are you sure?"

"Are we going to argue again, Mr. Auerbach?"

He wheeled himself to the photographic camera and ducked under the black hood, then came out again. "Softer," he said. "More natural."

"This *is* natural."

"No, it has your intensity but not your kindness," he explained.

She laughed. "You don't know me at all, Mr. Auerbach. If you did, you would know that the kindness you speak of wasn't ever there."

"You've been very kind to me," said Auerbach. And when she frowned: "You have shown me things I could never have dreamed of."

She let the frown go. She would try to be what Mr. Auerbach

thought she was, at least for this one moment. She relaxed her pose a bit and watched his hands adjust the tripod, then the lens. He was neat and sure in his movements. When everything was in order he stopped to look at her. She noticed a very particular sort of expression on his face, one that she recognized only dimly from the past: a man looking at a woman.

14. MRS. SWANN RECEIVES HER PHOTOGRAPH

V erena Swann walked out of Mr. Auerbach's gate, into the
soft spring air. She felt too excited to get right into a cab
and decided to walk a little, even though she knew Leopold
would be wondering where she was. Ever since Theodore's disappearance, she had been living from moment to moment, without
considering the future or pondering the fact that she might have
choices. Each step had felt determined by forces outside of herself:
Theodore's disappearance had made her seek out the spirits, and the
spirits had made her become a trance medium; the need to raise
money for a rescue expedition had forced her to perform in public;
and then Leopold had pushed her to continue against her wishes.
Lacking an independent idea of what her life might become, she had
followed along.

It had never occurred to her that she might walk through an
eccentric palace beside a millionaire with soft brown eyes. Or that
she might help him free himself from a degrading connection, help
him remake himself into something better, perhaps even noble. She

had grown so used to fleecing people it had come to seem inevitable—but it was not. She could still be useful to somebody who truly needed her.

When she saw the big department store, she suddenly decided to go in. She wanted to be in the middle of that bustle, in the thick of life, choosing. It also occurred to her that buying something would provide an excellent explanation of where she had been, if Leopold were to ask her. She walked among the glass display cases, looking at all the things she could have, and felt suddenly very excited. She quickly bought two pairs of gloves, a handbag, and a scarf. She then wandered over to the millinery department and browsed among the hats, thinking about her mother and their hat shop. She had felt trapped in that store—trapped as much by the example of her mother's silent, angry, blinkered love as by the long hours. She had yearned to be like the customers who came in for only a moment, to buy a new hat for a special occasion. And so she stood at the counter, trying on one after another: a straw boater with red and yellow silk roses, and then a swooping thing shaped like a giant bird's wing, and then something that looked like a wedding cake with a veil. With each she went to the mirror and saw a different Verena, a different set of possibilities: flushed, cheerful, dramatic, silly, but all very much *alive*. She bought the most absurd of the bunch—a basket of flowers, essentially, with a chin strap—because it made her look innocent.

It was late afternoon when she returned home. Leopold was in his study and did not come out till dinner. She thought she would tell him about her shopping expedition, maybe even show him her purchases, but he did not want to talk; he merely ate and glowered. He was moving into one of those phases when he demonstrated his displeasure by speaking to her as little as possible. After dinner he returned directly to his study, leaving her sitting at the table.

At one time this would have distressed her terribly, but she was full of thoughts of her secret adventure. She remembered sitting on the bed in the studio and having her photograph taken. She remembered the way Mr. Auerbach had looked at her then. Leopold, despite his protestations of love, did not look at her that way.

That night she dreamed she was walking with Mr. Auerbach among the chiming clocks and the naked sculptures with their skins cool to the touch, the color of pale green grapes. She opened her mouth to confess that she was nothing but a confidence man, bent on stealing his money, but what came out instead was the most beautiful birdsong. Mr. Auerbach got up out of his wheelchair—his legs were healed—and then leaned in and kissed her. She kissed him back.

She sprang up and sat at the edge of her bed, uncertain where she was. It was completely dark, but it took a moment to realize that she was not sitting on that other bed, beneath the glass ceiling and the rolling clouds, having her picture taken. This was her room, the one she had lived in ever since returning to New York with Leopold. And yet the tingling in her lips seemed so real that she had to remind herself that she had not, in fact, done anything wrong.

The dream stayed with her the rest of the day. She had three private sittings at home, a consultation uptown, and then two hours of correspondence to dictate to Maisie, but through it all, the kiss lingered, a pressure in the pit of her stomach. She wondered if Mr. Auerbach might pay a call, and then became frightened and hoped that he would not. She would not be able to look at him if he did.

This made the scene at dinner that much more disconcerting. Leopold had arranged a surprise. The table was covered with a lace cloth and laid with their good china and the heavy monogrammed silver. "How lovely," she said. "But I thought you were angry at me."

Instead of answering, he pulled a magnum of champagne from the silver ice bucket and began to uncork it. "How are you, Verena? I feel we haven't had much time together in the last few days."

"I'm fine," she said.

"Busy day today, wasn't it? Good thing yesterday was so quiet." He poured her a glass and handed it to her. "What did you do yesterday?"

The champagne was sharp and electric. She looked at Leopold and felt guilty, though she knew it was absurd. She had done nothing wrong. "I went shopping," she told him.

He took a drink with exaggerated gusto. "Oh? What did you get?"

"A scarf, two pairs of gloves, and a new hat."

"Ah, the pleasures of money, eh, Verena?" His smile looked as if it had been carved on. "May I see?"

It was the look on his face—a look of such pleasure and pain—that made her realize he was only toying with her. He knew where she had been. "Did you follow me?" she asked him.

"Follow you? I didn't have to." He got up, walked over to the sideboard, and came back with a large envelope. "This came by messenger."

She took it in her hands and turned it over, a plain brown envelope, no indication of who sent it. No initials on the wax seal, which was broken. "You opened it," she said, barely able to hear herself over the disorder of her heart.

"I opened it."

She opened the flap, surprised to find that her fingers were trembling. What she found inside was herself: a photograph of her sitting very primly on the edge of a bed, a crudely painted backdrop behind.

There was also a note:

Dear Mrs. Swann,

It was a pleasure to meet with you earlier, and to give you a tour of the premises, including our photographic studio (normally not open to the public). I hope you found it informative and enjoyable.

Enclosed, please find a small souvenir of your visit. I hope that, on inspection, you will see the truth of my earlier remark—that your eyes are indeed very kind. The camera never lies.

Trust Me to be Your Most Obedient and Devoted Servant,

Augustus Auerbach

It was an odd note, to say the least: something between a business memorandum and a love letter. It should have made her angry, but she remembered the dream and felt her face grow warm. She looked over at Leopold, who seemed to be enjoying what he probably thought of as his trap. "You're as red as a tomato," he said to her.

"I went there to apologize," she said. "I wanted to make sure he was coming back."

"Do you think you may have ingratiated yourself a little too well?"

"The weepers always idealize me. It's part of the disease."

Leopold looked grave and lofty now. "What pains me most, Verena, is that you just don't understand, no matter what I do to show you."

"I'm sorry, I should have told you what I was doing."

"No, that's not what I mean." He drew a little jeweler's box from his coat pocket and pushed it toward her, like a gambler pushing his last stack of chips across the felt. He popped open the lid to reveal a shockingly large diamond ring. "This is what I mean."

She stared at it for a long time. "Leopold, you know I'm already married."

"Theodore is dead, Verena."

"He is disincarnate."

He spoke to the ceiling. "How can a man compete with the idea of a man?"

"He's not an idea. He's a spirit."

Leopold closed his eyes. Despite the grand beard, he looked like a little boy who had suffered some kind of schoolyard humiliation. She could see that his disappointment, intense as it was, had only so much to do with her, and that made it worse somehow. Her life was being siphoned off as an afterthought. "I can't stay here any longer," she said.

He waved away the suggestion.

She got to her feet and ran out, up to her room. Her chest was heaving. The powerful mechanism of grief was already working its way up from the diaphragm, into her throat and eyes. She got out a trunk, dragged it to her dressing room, and began piling in clothes—silks and satins, the rich booty of her years of success. It was soon full, but she did not have the heart to begin another. She had to leave now or she never would.

She tried pushing the trunk to the stairwell, but it got caught on the carpet. She went searching for Maisie and found her in her room, which was situated on the third floor, up above. Maisie was sitting in a chair, as if waiting for her to appear.

"I'm leaving," announced Verena, full of grand feeling. "He's driven me out."

Maisie seemed not at all surprised—but then she had probably heard most of it; sound traveled easily throughout the house. Maisie blinked and stood. It was this unflappable quality that made her such a good ghost. The weepers could grab at her hand or pull at her robes, but she never panicked. "Can I help you with something?" she asked.

"Tell me you will take care of him when I'm gone."

Maisie said nothing. Her face remained placid, with the usual hint of a smile and the intelligent, watchful eyes. No doubt Leopold would teach her everything she needed to know. She would make a good medium.

The rest happened quickly, in confusion. They got the trunk to the stairs and pushed it down; it clattered from step to step and crashed at the bottom. Maisie went outside to get a cab, and then came back for Verena, who climbed in and sat in the dark interior as the driver stowed the trunk. She was taken by surprise when the man asked where she was going. She had no friends and no relatives—other than Leopold—and if she moved into a hotel, the press would find out.

"Ma'am?"

"Fifth Avenue and Seventy-first Street."

15. THE MIDNIGHT VISITOR

Auerbach lay in bed, feeling panicked about the photograph he had sent to Mrs. Swann. He had meant nothing more than ordinary courtesy, a simple politeness between business associates. She had paid him a visit, and it was necessary to acknowledge that fact in some way, if only to note that she had asked to have her photograph taken and he had indeed taken it. But he realized now that sending the photograph, combined with the somewhat careless phrasing of the note, had accidentally pushed him into an area of potential misunderstanding. He did not want Mrs. Swann to think he had taken an improper interest in her.

The very thought was preposterous. He had never even intended to develop the photograph. After seeing her out the door, he had sat for a moment in the foyer, bewildered and unsure what to do next. Her presence seemed to linger behind, making him feel dazed and stupid but also restless.

The butler was thrown into a panic. "Shall I order the carriage for you, sir?" the man had asked, apparently assuming he wanted to go out.

"The carriage?" A part of him wished he could step out into the world as naturally as Mrs. Swann, as decisively as Miss Larue, but it was not so. "For godsakes, man, do you think Kleinfeldt goes for drives in the middle of the afternoon? He's in that dank little office of his, plotting my doom."

It was time to return to work, to the surety of contracts and invoices and correspondence. He wheeled himself back to his office, intending to salvage what he could of the day. Once he got there, however, he found himself no more able to concentrate than before. He sat at his desk, holding a pen and remembering his trip through the mansion with Mrs. Swann. She had caressed things with the tips of her fingers—a statue, a vase, a picture frame—as if spreading her touch throughout the house. Suddenly, he felt some new and undefined craving that he was powerless to fill. If only he could get up and run! He wanted to run through the house till he collapsed, utterly drained and emptied of all thought.

That was when he went back to the studio, retrieved the film, and took it to the darkroom. It had been years since he had been there, and the mix of sour chemical smells seemed to take him back to a time before the walls of the mansion enclosed him. He sat in the crepuscular atmosphere of the long, narrow room, watching the photographic paper float in its chemical bath, and remembered the way Mrs. Swann had looked at him from the bed. It was a look he could not define or explain but felt in his chest.

He did not actually think of sending her the photograph until he saw her eyes staring up at him out of the developing tray—just as he did not think of writing her a note until he addressed the envelope, and did not think of using the infernally problematic word "kindness" until he saw it on the page in black ink, written in his own hand. It was an avalanche of error he was seemingly powerless to stop.

Ever since sending it off, he had been overwhelmed with dread. Of all the reactions he could imagine her having, he thought scorn would be the easiest to bear. As a boy he had been chased, ridiculed, and banished to the darkroom. Miss Chiswick had toyed with his affections. After a lifetime of such painful lessons, he was finally immune to what people might think about him—secure in the knowledge that he was richer and more important than they.

But the thought of Mrs. Swann's scorn did not prevent him from also imagining the opposite possibility, that she might actually believe herself attached to him. If anything, this possibility was far worse, because he would then have to disentangle himself. There would be the mortifying scene, the crying—and he was never good with crying, as he knew from the photographic models. He would have to explain that it was all a mistake, that he had no such interest in her, that he could not allow himself to be distracted from his business affairs. She might accuse him of having trifled with her, and he would shrink in his chair and mumble apologies and offer her money.

Of course, there were men in circumstances at least superficially similar to his who had married. Look at Kleinfeldt: Kleinfeldt had that ugly clubfoot, and the big corrective shoe that he dragged behind him, with its six-inch sole and box toe. Yet even he was married. In the years before their business disagreement ended their relationship, Auerbach had endured many long evenings of horrifying domestic bliss chez Kleinfeldt. At dinner, Mrs. Kleinfeldt hovered over her husband, refilling his glass and cutting his food; afterward, she brought his slippers and loaded his pipe. Night after night, Auerbach watched with mingled pity and disgust, but there seemed no end to the sorry pageant. One evening, over sherry, Kleinfeldt told him in a confidential whisper that Mrs. Kleinfeldt did him the great favor of massaging his crippled foot with oil of cloves every night before bed—those were his actual words, *the great favor*. "To help the circulation," said the poor fool, his eyes bleary with sentiment. Auerbach could only look away, embarrassed by the man's weakness.

The business deal that severed their relationship was still years in the offing, but it had been, in a very real sense, struck in that moment—sitting by the fireplace in Kleinfeldt's smoking room, little glasses of sherry in their hands. Auerbach did not hold himself responsible. He had cheated his former partner, true, but the real cause of predation is always weakness. Kleinfeldt was to blame.

Auerbach would not suffer the same fate because of Mrs. Swann. He kicked off the sheets, sat up on his elbows and stared down at his legs—two undernourished limbs in blue silk pajama pants, the bare feet no larger than a child's. These were the things that had separated him out from the rest of confused, directionless humanity and saved him from a life of historical insignificance. These were the things that had given him purpose. If Mrs. Swann misinterpreted his completely innocent note to imply something he had not meant to imply, that was *her* mistake. It did not reflect on him, and he need not trouble himself to correct it. Nevertheless, he *would* correct it. Right away. Just to be sure. And so he got out of bed, into his wheelchair, and wheeled himself to his office, where he rang for Miss Parish—leaned on the buzzer till it seemed likely to break. He barely gave her time to stumble into her seat at the typewriting machine. "A letter, Miss Parish." He watched her fix a clean sheet into the roller, then compose her hands over the keys.

"Dear Mrs. Swann," he began. "In a lifetime of activity and achievement, there has been only one area of human enterprise I have avoided—the romantic. Of course, if I had wanted to marry, I could have, but my time and energy have been spent on building a photographic empire. Then too, my position in the world has prevented me from reaching down to the kind of woman who might consider taking a cripple for her husband. I apologize for being so forthright on this matter, but hope that you understand when I ask that all future relations be kept on a purely businesslike footing. Basis. Read back."

She did. "Give me that," he barked, and began tearing it to shreds.

Just then there was a knock at the office door and Mr. Grapes stuck his head in, looking sleepy. "I'm sorry to interrupt, Mr. A. There's somebody to see you—a Mrs. Swann."

Auerbach dropped the last bits of the letter.

"She seems upset."

"I'll talk to her." Wheeling down the hall, he prepared himself for an unpleasant scene. He imagined her standing in the vestibule, tearing the note he had sent into little pieces and laughing in his face. But when he finally reached her, she was standing by a large traveling trunk, shivering and pale, waiflike. "I'll wager that you didn't expect to see me twice in the same day," she said to him, trying to smile. It looked like she was about to burst into tears. "Much less with a trunk."

He started toward her but caught himself—no point in making the same mistake twice. "Are you all right?" he asked her.

"Leopold and I have had a disagreement. Our partnership is at an end."

This was excellent news. "I'll have a room made ready."

"I wasn't sure where else to go on such short notice. I'll leave tomorrow."

"You are most welcome here for as long as you like."

She said something in reply, but he was too intensely relieved to catch it. It was as if she had come just to tell him that nothing had changed between them: she did not hate him and did not want to marry him. She only wanted a room. It seemed miraculous, a kind of rescue. He wheeled over to the service buzzer on the wall and rang for help. Moments later a flock of little maids came running toward them, led by the butler.

This was the part Auerbach was good at. He ordered a room made ready; Mrs. Swann's trunk carried up and her clothes pressed and hung; hot chocolate prepared. He asked her if she had had dinner, and when she said she could not recall—staring out vaguely at the little crowd of maids—he ordered chicken soup and an omelet served on a tray in her room. There was light, bustle, the slapping of slippers—a pleasing commotion.

Later, he went with the little maid, Jane, to deliver Mrs. Swann's supper. Jane leaned back and rested the weight of the tray on the front of her hips, moving over the highly polished floor with a kind of slow skating motion. He eased the chair alongside. When they got to the room, she went in and Auerbach waited, politely facing away from the door while straining to hear as much as he could. He had never stopped to ask himself about the relationship between the Swanns, but he wondered now, and when Jane reemerged he accosted her. "Did she say what happened?" he asked. The girl seemed confused by the question. "I mean the reason why she's here."

"Oh. No, sir, she didn't say."

He thought for a moment. "You're her maid now, Jane. I'm assigning you to her. Keep your ears open and let me know what you hear."

He was far too tense to go back to sleep. Instead he wheeled from room to room, occasionally checking a window for any pinkness in the sky—till he rounded a corner and nearly drove into Mrs. Swann. They had both come to a sudden stop just a foot apart. "I'm so sorry," she blurted out.

"The fault is mine." He checked to see if his blanket was tucked in.

She was a beautiful wreck, her dark hair loose about her shoulders, flattened and twisted from the pillow. Her eyes were pouchy and glittery, her face pale. She wore a gray silk dressing gown, slippers on her feet, and her small frame seemed even more fragile than usual in the heavy marble hall. "I'm in your way," she said. "I should go back to my room."

"You stay, I'll go back." He reversed a foot or so, though the hall-way was a good ten feet wide.

"No, please don't. I was just feeling so—so agitated. I thought a walk might calm me."

"Can I get you anything?" he asked her. "A cup of hot milk?"

"I couldn't continue with Leopold anymore. Our views are too different."

Views on what? he wondered, and then before he knew it, the thought was taking form in words. "Were you and Mr. Swann ever— you'll forgive me—" He was shocked by what he was asking, and not even sure why he was asking it.

"No, no." She shook her head vigorously, horrified. "Nothing like that. Not ever a question."

"I apologize. I didn't mean to pry." But there was one more thing he needed to know. "You saw the photograph I sent you?"

"Yes, yes, I did."

"And read the note?" He winced when he said it.

She smiled reassuringly. "It's why I'm here."

He did not so much understand the words as feel them, like pebbles dropped one by one in his palm. He sat for a moment, working them through his fingers, then turned to look at the window. There was a streak of blue visible in the black sky above the garden wall. "This is my favorite moment of the day," he said.

"Mine too," she said.

He turned back to her. "Could I interest you in some breakfast, Mrs. Swann?"

16. CRITICAL THAT I SEE YOU

After breakfast, Verena returned to her room. She slept for a while but then woke abruptly, as if shaken awake. She sat up and looked at her surroundings for the first time: a bedroom the size of a train station, the furniture like foamy pink islands in a sea of red carpet, with floral curtains covering windows two stories tall. She was sure Mr. Auerbach had no hand in the decorating—had not even seen the room—but it carried a tincture of him, almost like a fragrance, that made her wistful and sad. She could feel his singularity in the world, his loneliness and pride. At breakfast, they had sat at a table the size of a river barge, a good seven feet wide. It would have made sense if he placed himself beside her, given the sheer breadth of the thing; she could see that the idea occurred to him too, but that he was too modest to act on it. And so he had gone over to the other side, and they had talked across the expanse of polished wood, while eating with silver the size and weight of blacksmith's tools. She sensed that he wanted to ask more about Leopold but was too circumspect to do so, and tried instead to comfort her. "Do not worry, Mrs. Swann. You have done such good for so many people. You have many friends to depend upon now. They will support you in whatever you choose to do."

"I'm nothing but an instrument to them, like the telegraph or telephone."

"I certainly don't see you that way."

She looked at him and felt the falsity of her position as a guest in his house. "What good have I done for you, except causing Miss Larue to leave?"

"You brought me my mother, after many years apart."

"But Mr. Auerbach—" She could not go on to tell him the rest: Leopold's research file; Maisie in her white toga and makeup; the way she herself had toyed with him at the beginning, insisting that he try to leave his chair, knowing that he would fall. She had not truly known him then.

He put down his cutlery. His eyes were shining; she suspected they were wet. "You showed me that life is continuous, that it does not end, that it goes on."

"But what does that mean?"

"I don't know, but I feel as if I'm willing to think about it. If you help me."

"I'm the one who needs help."

He smiled. "Perhaps we can be of mutual assistance, then."

She wanted to reach across the table, to take his hand in hers. "Thank you," she said.

But now, alone in a strange bed, with the morning light pouring in from the edges of the draperies, she ached for her house in Washington Square. It had been too full of Leopold and the business of mediumship to ever be a proper home, but her own room held things from her married life with Theodore that were vital to her: the mother-of-pearl hand mirror with matching brushes and combs; the silver nail scissors; the bronze filigree picture frame. It seemed like a terrible betrayal to have left them behind, even for a day.

Why had she fled in such disorder, without her most important things? And why had she come here, of all places, to be sheltered by a man she had harmed in so many ways? An unmarried man, furthermore. If Leopold found out she was staying here, he would be furious; and if the newspapers heard, there would be a scandal. Once dressed, she would have to leave and find a nice, quiet boardinghouse, near Washington Square if she could manage it. She had always wanted to sit a little in the park, if she had time, and now she would have time—a great deal of time to consider her future. But what would she do for money? She had only brought what was in her pocketbook. How would she get more? Half the money Leopold had was rightly hers, but how much was that? And would he give it to her? What if he refused? She did not want to continue working as a medium, and the only other thing she knew was hatmaking. What else could she possibly do?

There was one other thing, an idea so fragile that she had buried it away, as if to keep it from harm. Leopold had once suggested that they write a book about the spirit world—or rather that Theodore dictate the book, and Verena take it down in the trance state. They put the idea aside when her powers began to deteriorate, but she sometimes daydreamed about writing a book of her own, one that would tell the truth of her experience, in her own words. The thought filled her with a terrified fascination: words of her own, not Theodore's or Leopold's, not borrowed or stolen or forced upon her.

There was a knock at the door, and the maid entered carrying a letter on a little silver tray. Inside was a note saying only, *Critical that I see you.* There was no name, but the writing was clearly Leopold's: a large, round hand, utterly unlike Theodore's jagged peaks and valleys. At the bottom was the name and address of a café, followed by the word *noon.*

She had a moment of panic, as if she could feel his large, powerful arms grabbing hold of her, clamping her down. He was no doubt very pleased that he had guessed her whereabouts. He probably felt that her presence at the mansion confirmed all his suspicions, when the reality was simply that she had nowhere else to go. "Did you see who delivered this?" she asked the maid.

"A tall gentleman in a yellow coat, ma'am."

That could only be Leopold. "What time is it now?" she asked.

"Almost ten thirty, ma'am."

She bathed and then dressed as best she could, given the haphazard manner in which she had packed the night before: a dove gray dress with lace collar and cuffs; a dark blue velvet mantle; a hat with a single white ostrich plume. She covered the circles under her eyes with paint, powdered and rouged her cheeks. It was crucial that she look well because he would seize on any sign of weakness. He would try to convince her that she could not survive without him— or if that did not work, that *he* could not survive without *her*. He would expertly argue any number of points for which she would have no answer. If she tried to answer, she would become tangled up in his logic, trapped. She would have to be smarter than she had ever been before.

She walked out the gate, onto the avenue, and then down the street, the note with the address in her hand. Perhaps it was the clear blue sky, but she felt suddenly hopeful that Leopold would listen to her. She would tell him the truth: that she was too frail to continue as a spirit medium and that she could not marry him, either, because she was still married to Theodore. This formulation of the problem was wonderfully reassuring, as it left out all the perplexing things, like her hatred of the weepers, and her loneliness, and her feelings of friendship for Mr. Auerbach. She imagined Leopold's large, sensitive, wounded face as he listened, and felt a wave of almost nostalgic affection for him. And then she imagined him saying exactly those same things to her, as if they were *his* ideas and not hers. He was always able to explain things in such a compelling way that she immediately did them, even when she did not want to. She imagined him telling her exactly how to be free.

She entered the café and found him already waiting at a table. He rose when he saw her and pulled out her chair. He was in a yellow coat, as the little maid had said. She sat down and they talked for a while about trivia—the weather, the traffic—as if it were an ordinary conversation. She talked volubly but hardly listened, absorbed by the awareness that she had changed overnight—that the mere act of leaving Washington Square had changed her forever. She believed that Leopold, too, could sense the difference in her. His face was solemn, as if he finally understood the need to let her go. She could feel him struggling to find the words that would set her free. "I understand how you feel, Verena."

She smiled with relief. "I knew you would."

"Maybe I was a little sudden last night. But we don't need to decide all at once. We can go slowly."

This was not quite what she had expected. "Leopold, I can't be a spirit medium anymore."

"Your talent is God-given. You can't keep it hidden."

"Whatever it was is gone now. You know that."

"That's nonsense. Just the other day—" As if acknowledging the futility of the argument, he changed direction midsentence, his voice dropping to a whisper. "There are millions to be made, Verena. As soon as we lasso the pornographer." He mimicked throwing a rope.

"I won't do it."

"It's because of him, isn't it?"

The thought made her face grow hot and prickly. "That's absurd."

"Is it? Don't think I can't see what you're doing. You've stolen him from me. I found him, and now you get all the money and don't have to share."

She was so flabbergasted by this formulation that she sat in silence, unable to defend herself as Leopold continued. "I promised Theodore that I would take care of you," he said, "and I won't break that promise now. I am not going to let you do this to yourself. I am not going to let you do this to *me*, either, because I know that later you will regret it." His eyes were large, deep, beseeching. "That is why I am taking you to see a doctor."

"A doctor?"

"I've made an appointment. In fact, I have a carriage waiting. I've taken care of everything, as I always do." He pulled out his pocket watch. "Come, we don't want to be late." He left some money on the table, and then grasped her hand in his. She got up. The lack of sleep seemed to have caught up with her. She felt rubbery, could barely keep her eyes open, and yet at the same time she knew she was frightened.

He walked her out of the café and around the corner, where a large carriage indeed waited. It was not an ordinary hack but hired especially for the occasion, with four strong horses—she knew it meant they would be traveling some distance. He opened the door and half pushed her up. She paused on the step, startled to see two figures already inside, hulking men dressed entirely in hospital whites. One offered his hand; she took it, swinging into the empty seat opposite, and then made room for Leopold, who climbed in beside her. Before she could gather her skirts, the door was shut and the carriage moving. It was then that she understood the reality of what was happening. "I think I've changed my mind," she said. Her voice was a flutelike tremolo, irresolute and timid. "I've decided I don't want to go."

"It's for your own good, Verena."

"But I said I don't want to go." No, what she wanted, she realized, was to be back at the mansion with Mr. Auerbach, talking earnestly about the afterlife in that silly and touching cathedral of a dining hall, as the daylight brightened around them.

She needed to be stronger. "If you do not stop this carriage, I will jump," she said, reaching for the door. The man nearest put his hand over hers, and she drew back, shocked by the weight of it.

"Please don't make this more difficult than it has to be," said Leopold.

"What harm have I ever done you?" she asked him.

"You have hurt me in a hundred ways," he said, suddenly vehement. "But I have forgiven you everything. Now sit back and be quiet till we get there."

She understood the threat: if she tried to move, the men would hold her down, and she did not want that. She only wanted what was going to happen to happen as quickly as possible. She squeezed back into the corner, trying to make herself as small as her body would allow. She had already decided to accept the calomel drops or sleeping syrup that Leopold's doctor would offer her. Back in Mr. Auerbach's mansion in the evening, she would throw the medicines out. This time, he would sit beside her at the dinner table, and she would tell him about herself: what it felt like when a trance was coming on, the way it crept up her neck and into her mouth, and what it felt like when it would not come, the deadness in her chest, like a chunk of ice, stopping her breathing. Mr. Auerbach would listen with those large, beautiful eyes.

The window shades were down, but she knew they would have to be near the southern tip of the island by now. They began to climb a hill, or perhaps a ramp, and the clopping of the hooves on the cobblestones changed to the hollow drumbeat of wooden planks. Shadows appeared on the window shades: lines and crossbeams. "Why are we crossing the river?" she asked.

Leopold's eyes were glazed with thought. She could see that he had not been sleeping and felt a renewed sense of pity for him. His need was so desperate; if he did not devour her, she had no choice but to pity him. "The doctor is in Brooklyn," he said.

"Who is he?"

"Sit back and relax, Verena. I have it all taken care of."

The bridge came to an end and they rode on over cobblestone streets, crossed what seemed to be trolley tracks, heard the creak of a gate, and followed a curving gravel path. Then they stopped for good. The carriage swayed on its springs as the driver got down, and the enormous man on her right opened the door and followed. Leopold went next. He held out his hand for her and she obediently climbed out, blinking in the late-afternoon sunlight. The second man followed behind her.

They were at the entrance to a gigantic construction of dark red brick, reminiscent of a mill or factory. The front doors were of heavy wood, and the windows were all capped with black iron bars. The fact that the grounds were lovely—lawns, trees, topiary sculpture in the shape of animals—made it all the more forbidding. "What is this?" she asked Leopold, already knowing.

"A hospital," he answered.

"A madhouse," she said.

"A sanitarium. Everything is very scientific."

It seemed pointless—almost embarrassing—to protest so late in the course of events. The tide was already carrying her out to sea, and there was nothing she could do about it. "I didn't bring any of my things," she said.

"Maisie packed a trunk for you." He took her arm and moved her toward the doors, which were even now opening, and they walked through a deserted lobby toward yet another set of doors. Strange sounds drifted through the hush. It was hard to credit them as human voices, but after a moment she was certain that they were: wails of loneliness and betrayal, just clinging to the edge of audibility. She gripped Leopold's arm with all her might and pulled back, but he carried her along without effort, like a steamer pulling a skiff.

"Do you hear that?" she asked him.

"It's nothing," he said, eyes searching for the direction of the sounds. "The doctor is going to make you well again, and then we will pick up where we left off, exactly as before."

Her old life: she would have seized it greedily, madly, as if it were a lifeboat. "Let's go home right now. I'm feeling much better."

"No," he said sadly. "We can't. Not yet. Not till you understand the value of what I am offering you."

They had reached the doors. The two men from the carriage were on either side of her, poised as if to receive a package, and Leopold was prying her arms from his yellow sleeve. She was clearly meant to go through without him. "I never agreed to this," she said. "You have no right."

"But I do, Verena, as your only surviving male relative. I will visit as soon as the doctor allows." His eyes were full of tears. He planted a kiss on her forehead and tore away from her grip.

She would have run after him and begged his forgiveness, if the men were not holding her arms. Instead she started to wail, her own version of the whispery keening that laced itself through the building. They pulled her through the doors, down a corridor, into an office, and then placed her in a chair facing a small and very dapper man, who sat at a desk, reading a letter. She wiped at her nose and eyes, until the man looked up and removed his pince-nez. "Welcome, Mrs. Swann."

The soft white hair at the top of his head, the neat white imperial, and the blue eyes were all exactly the same as at the séance. "Dr. Mayhew," she gasped.

Dr. Mayhew put the pince-nez back on his nose and skimmed over the letter in front of him. "Mr. Swann tells me that you are not well. He mentions a whole list of symptoms—insomnia, nightmares, headaches, nervousness, lack of appetite, drunkenness, weeping without cause."

Shocking, cruel, unforgivable, it nevertheless made a kind of devilish sense: Leopold was adept at harnessing the contrary forces swirling around him. "I don't know what he means," she said. "I've never felt better. Not even a cold."

Dr. Mayhew put down the letter and made a church steeple of his fingers, clearly settling in for a long talk. "I was very impressed by your séance, Mrs. Swann. You are vastly superior to the competition—in another category entirely. I view it as a measure of your extraordinary sensitivity. And of your illness."

"I'm not ill."

"But of course you are. You aren't a simple fraud—a confidence man, so to speak. A simple fraud would indicate a moral disease, but not a mental one. You are different."

"I am compelled by the spirits to serve others."

"And yet much of what you do is clearly faked." He put up a hand to stop her protest. "I have been tutored by some of the very best, Mrs. Swann, by which I mean my patients."

"That is all Mr. Swann's area. I have nothing to do with that." She looked down at her lap, knotting her fingers together to keep her hands from shaking. "The trances used to come and now they don't. Or sometimes they do."

"If you do not believe your powers to be what they once were, why not retire? That is what singers and actresses do."

"This is my punishment for trying to do just that—I am kidnapped and brought here."

He made a puzzled face. "Your punishment is to see a doctor?"

"I told you I am not sick."

"What if I told you that I can cure your insomnia and your nightmares, that I can bring your suffering to an end?"

An end? It was what she had fled her home for in the middle of the night, leaving everything behind. But hearing it from Dr. Mayhew made the idea sound like an insult. "It's not that simple,

Doctor. There are those who depend on me to speak for them."

"You mean Captain Swann," he said. "You realize he is dead?"

Tears began leaking from her eyes. "Yet what *is* that?" After all these years she still was not sure. She knew that Theodore was gone, and she knew that he was still here. But she did not know how to reconcile those two facts, or what they meant when added together.

"That is the realm of religion, not medicine," said Dr. Mayhew, with a wave of his hand. "Have you ever heard the term *mediomania*, Mrs. Swann?" He did not pause for a response. "The name is modern but the phenomenon is ancient, stretching back to the Cumaean Sybil, no doubt. It stands for a type of insanity in which people believe that supernatural forces speak through them. It sometimes affects men but more frequently women, and is usually preceded by some kind of genito- or venerio-pathological history. In women this is usually a tipping of the womb in relation to the pelvis. Have you had children?"

"No."

"As I expected. Needless to say, we will have to begin with a full physical examination. If surgery is necessary, I will notify Mr. Swann." He gestured to one of the men standing beside her chair. "Mr. Spufford, please escort Mrs. Swann to the examination room."

17. WAITING FOR MRS. SWANN

Though he had been up all night, Auerbach left breakfast feeling not the least bit tired. He had stumbled on a new and intensely interesting project: making Mrs. Swann happy. He was not exactly sure why it felt so vitally important, or what he stood to gain from it, but he liked the way it made his lungs fill with air and his thoughts speed like electricity down a wire. And Mrs. Swann was so clearly in need of his ministrations. A woman of her qualities should not be weeping over scrambled eggs.

He believed that he had already made some progress, encouraging her to feel at home in his home, making it clear that he was available if she chose to confide, that he would do his utmost to help in any way possible. She had seemed to appreciate the attention, drying her eyes, blowing her nose, even smiling. But there was much more to do.

He began by summoning the cook. Auerbach's usual luncheon of clear broth and fruit compote would not do for a guest. "I understand, sir," said the cook. "Something similar to what we do for the gentlemen of the Clean Living League."

"No, most definitely not like that." The Clean Living League liked everything soaked in rum and lit on fire. "Mrs. Swann has been entertained by the crowned heads of Europe. Her tastes are highly refined."

After much discussion, they agreed on a luncheon of caviar, smoked salmon, a leg of lamb, two wines, and champagne. Dinner would be built around lobster tails, followed by pheasant in a cranberry glaze and a soufflé. Breakfast the following morning would be kippers, creamed eggs in a pastry shell, and lamb chops. Then they would meet again and plan out the rest of the week.

By the time the menu was settled, Auerbach had begun to worry about the hours between meals. Mrs. Swann had enjoyed the tour of the house, and there were still two wings left to see—and maybe the gardens, though he would detour around the grotto and the gate, as he wanted nothing melancholy interjecting itself. But he wanted to be able to tell her something true this time, and so he called for Miss Parish next.

When she arrived, Miss Parish was in a dress of pale blue, her hair neatly coiffed. She did not look like herself at all. "It's odd seeing you in something other than a dressing gown," he said.

"I could say the same of you, Mr. A."

"I guess you could, but there is no time for it. I want you to take me on a tour of the house."

She looked amused. "*Your* house."

"I don't know a thing about it, and I suspect you do. Am I right?"

"I keep my eyes open."

He headed toward the doorway, signaling for her to follow. "I'm not sure why, but I suspect you of knowing all sorts of things."

He was right; she *did* know things: the titles of the paintings, the strange and distant countries from which the rugs came, the specialized purpose of each room. As she talked, they passed from place to place until they came to a large and airy chamber filled with light. An entire wall of glass doors looked out onto the garden, and great bowls of flowers sat on each of the little tables spread about. "This was Miss Larue's favorite room," she said, sounding nostalgic and sad. "She loved the flowers."

"Will there be many mementoes of Miss Larue on this tour?"

His tone of voice had been unintentionally harsh. Miss Parish stood at attention, her eyes wide with alarm. "No, sir."

"Can you tell me where she is?"

"She hasn't contacted me."

"Then let's stick to the business at hand."

They resumed their tour, though Auerbach found it difficult to pay attention. He had every right to be angry with Jane Larue for leaving, and yet he could not overcome an inexplicable sense of failure, as if the fault were his and not hers. "Do you hold me to blame?" he asked suddenly.

Miss Parish understood immediately; their thoughts had clearly been circling the same subject. "For her leaving? It was time for her to leave."

"I meant, for the baby's death."

"Only God decides such things, Mr. A."

It did not feel that simple to him. "*She* blames me."

"If so, that's her mistake."

This did not make him feel any better. He had tried to make Miss Larue a happy employee and had failed. How could he possibly succeed with Mrs. Swann, who was not even an employee—and for whom happiness seemed to be a much more complex proposition? Would she expect him to be charming? To tell witty stories and make her laugh? To understand the sadness at the center of her heart? He was not equipped to do those things; he did not know how.

Then again, he did not have the option of despair; luncheon was only a half hour away. "Miss Parish," he asked, "where is the library?" He frequently sent Mr. Grapes there for research materials. Perhaps they could find something about happiness as well.

"Just down the hall, Mr. A."

"Take me there."

The library was tall and octagonal, three stories of bookshelves leading up to a glass dome, through which the light poured down. The smell was of polished wood, leather, and paper, and the silence was of a very particular kind, different from the rest of the house— the silence of arrested motion. It was as if those thousands of books were birds, and a signal would send them into flight.

"I need to ask your help in locating a volume," he told her. He had nothing specific in mind; indeed, hardly knew what he was looking for. "Something practical. Something on the art of conversation."

Miss Parish went over to the card catalogue and searched diligently, but there was nothing on the subject—nothing in the entire library other than photography manuals and erotica, the tools of his trade. Just then the clock began to chime noon. "I'm afraid I have to go," he told her, wheeling toward the door. It was important that he get to the dining room before Mrs. Swann in order to inspect the table settings. They had been something of a problem at breakfast, with the two of them on either side of a vast plain of polished wood. "We will continue later."

"I'll keep looking, Mr. A."

He arrived in the dining room a little out of breath. The place settings were on either side of one corner, and he could see right away that the effect was just what he wanted: they would be close enough to hear each other, but not side by side, which brought the danger of accidentally touching.

He fussed a bit with the settings, fluffing a napkin, nudging a wine glass closer to the plate. He thought he saw a water spot on one of the knives; inspecting it more closely he caught a bit of his own reflection: a slice of cheek, a pouchy eye. He changed the angle, trying to look at his teeth and then his hair. He had used a little more hair tonic than usual to get rid of the waviness.

It was a moment before he noticed the butler standing behind him. "Would you like me to serve the soup now, sir?"

"We're waiting for Mrs. Swann."

"I'm sorry, sir, but I just spoke to Jane, and it seems that Mrs. Swann may have stepped out."

"Stepped out?" He felt something very tall inside him topple.

"Sometime after eleven, sir."

"Well, what time is she expected back?"

"She gave no word, sir. Jane says she received a note and left quickly."

A note. Only Leopold Swann could have known she was here. They were no doubt patching up their differences over lunch. She would be coming back this afternoon to collect her bags and return to Washington Square.

"Shall I serve the caviar, sir?"

He glanced down at the boutonniere in his lapel, a red bud from a vase in his room, and felt intensely foolish. "No need. I'll take a bowl of broth in the office."

He got to the office and slammed the door shut, then removed the boutonniere and threw it in the trash basket. The bud sat atop the crumpled papers, like evidence of a crime; he reached into the basket and stuffed it deeper.

It was just as well that she was leaving, he told himself; she had been there for only half a day, and his desk was already piled high with correspondence and photographs to review. He would be laboring through the night to catch up. What had he been thinking? Friendship, love, marriage, children, the consolations of domestic life and the pleasures of society—everything that made life sweet for ordinary humanity—these things were not for *him*.

There was a knock on the door. He assumed it was his broth, but it turned out to be the little maid, Jane, with a letter on a silver tray. No doubt it was from *that woman*. "I'm a little busy now," he told Jane. "Leave it on the desk and I'll get to it later." As soon as the door clicked shut, he tore open the envelope.

Dear Mr. Auerbach:

I know that you are aware of the unusual difficulty of the spirit medium's profession, and that you have seen how close to complete nervous exhaustion Verena has come these last few days. As you know, it makes her very emotional—an unfortunate byproduct of her sensitive personality. I therefore hope you will be able to forgive her intrusion last night. She is back at home, resting, and should be strong enough to resume her duties in the next month or so. We will contact you when she is ready.

As one last favor, could I possibly impose on you to have her trunk packed and sent to us here? It would be much appreciated.

Thanking you for your kindness and consideration,
As always, your humble servant,

Leopold Swann

So she had been ill—nervous exhaustion—and he, Auerbach, was a feverish mistake. He put the note in his pocket and went to the room Mrs. Swann had been using. Everything was still just as she had left it. He wheeled himself to the night table and looked at the things forgotten there: a tortoise-shell comb, a long silver hat pin, a cashmere shawl. He picked up the comb. It felt warm, as if it still stored the heat of her hand.

He put the comb down and wheeled into the dressing room, an octagonal space surrounded by mirrored panels that looked like silvery lakes. He opened one panel and found her dresses hanging in a row. Half buried in shadow, they looked like spirits come to tell him the truth about his purpose on this planet. Yet they were silent.

18. THE SILENCE IS THE ROAR OF THE STORM

Verena Swann walked down the hall, next to the large man in white. "Did I hear him call you Spufford?" she asked him. She wanted desperately to gain an ally.

"Yes, ma'am." He did not turn to look at her.

"Where are you taking me, Mr. Spufford?"

"Examination room, ma'am."

"You know I'm being held against my will, don't you?"

A flicker went over his large, fleshy face. "This is the room, ma'am."

He opened a door and ushered her into a chamber with vaulted windows and white tile walls—less like a doctor's office than a scientific laboratory. Her eyes went directly to the examination table that stood in the middle of the floor. It was clearly designed for the unwilling, with wide canvas straps and complicated metal stirrups for the feet. "Is he going to hurt me, Mr. Spufford?"

"I'm sorry, ma'am, I'm not really supposed to talk to you. It's the regulations."

"You will just let this happen?" It was the wrong thing to say; he looked at his feet and shuffled nervously. She realized that she could not afford to alienate him. "I'm sorry," she said. "I know you are just doing your job."

"The doctor will be here in a minute, ma'am."

She looked about for some means of escape: a door, an open window. She saw a pair of human skeletons suspended in the corner—male and female, judging by the difference in their builds. She noticed a display case full of skulls, and a shelf with glass jars containing what were clearly bodily organs—pinkish gray bags. She averted her eyes, and that was when she noticed the babies. They floated curled in jars, eyes closed as if dreaming. One had no top to its head, like an eggcup; another was covered in fine hair. Oddities, miscarriages, waiting forever to be born.

Her breath was ripped out of her like the stuffing from a doll. She leaned on the examination table, and Mr. Spufford steadied her from behind. "It's better if you don't carry on too much. Otherwise the doctor gets very strict." His voice was gentle, but seemed to come from far away, another world.

The door opened, and Dr. Mayhew came in, looking businesslike and rushed. "What, still dressed? Mr. Spufford, that won't do at all."

"I'm sorry, sir," said Mr. Spufford. "The lady isn't feeling well."

"Of course not, that's why she's here. Mrs. Swann, I must ask you to take off all your clothes, at once. Or do you want Mr. Spufford to help you?"

That was the last thing she wanted, and so she began by removing her hat, and then her gloves. Mr. Spufford did indeed help with the buttons at the back of her dress—very gingerly, at arm's length—picking up and carefully folding each item as she removed it, and then placing it in a box. It did not feel like undressing— indeed, had no relationship to that most ordinary, daily activity. She finally stood in her corset and petticoats, shivering.

"I'm sorry, Mrs. Swann, but I need you to remove the last of your things," said Dr. Mayhew. "Modesty is not a virtue here."

Mr. Spufford helped with the laces to her corset, and then in one dreamlike moment she was standing before them, naked. For some reason she thought of Jane Larue, perhaps because nakedness was her business, and she had nevertheless survived.

"Lie down on the table, please," said Dr. Mayhew.

Mr. Spufford gave her his hand. She climbed up and lay down, trembling as they worked over her, buckling the straps. "Is this necessary?" she asked.

"A precaution," said Dr. Mayhew. With the last of the straps tightened, he began running his dry, clean hands over her body, poking and prodding, tapping and pushing. While working, he made a strange sort of small talk. "Are you familiar with the work of Swedenborg, Mrs. Swann?"

"No."

"Really? I'm surprised. It is the foundation of modern Spiritualism." He gave a painful push to her stomach.

"I'm not much of a scholar," she told him, colluding in the illusion of a normal medical visit.

"And yet your husband knows his work."

"They meet often on the spirit plane."

"I see." He put a cold stethoscope to her chest and listened for a moment. "Swedenborg believed that heaven and hell are emanations of the individual's thoughts. When they die, good people make a heaven for themselves with their good thoughts, and bad people make a hell for themselves with their bad thoughts." He moved the stethoscope to the other side. "It's just poetry, of course, but as an alienist I am in a position to recognize the essential correctness of the underlying intuition. What are lunatics but poor people beset by bad thoughts? And yet the world becomes a living hell for them." He stuffed the stethoscope in the pocket of his coat, moved down to the foot of the table, and began unbuckling the strap that held her ankles. "The question, of course, is what *makes* the thoughts—that is what we are trying to answer. Perhaps it is a particular shape or size to some portion of the cranium, or perhaps it is a diseased uterus." He unbuckled the strap that held her knees.

She was too distracted to follow what he was saying. It sounded like a list of threats in a foreign language. "Are you letting me go?" she asked.

"I'm putting your feet in the stirrups."

He placed first one foot and then the other in a stirrup, belting them tightly at the ankle. The stirrups were attached to jointed arms, which he arranged in such a way as to hold her legs apart, tightening a series of screws to keep them in position. With her shoulders strapped to the table, she could not see much more than her legs dangling in the air—with only Mayhew's head and neck visible between them. She turned her head to see Mr. Spufford standing off to one side, his eyes closed.

For some reason she thought of the photographs in Leopold's file on Mr. Auerbach. In one of them Jane Larue had lain on a bed in just this position, showing herself to a man.

"I'll try to make this as easy as possible, Mrs. Swann," said Dr. Mayhew.

The examination hurt, and she cried out, but the straps held her in place. After they were removed, Mr. Spufford helped her off the table and into a white cotton robe and slippers, the inmate uniform. He then escorted her—half carried her—to a small, bare room, her cell, where he placed her gently upon the bed. She curled in a ball for some stretch of time—she may even have slept—till the door opened once again. She sat up.

It was Dr. Mayhew. "I hope you are settling in," he said, lingering by the open door. There was no place for him to sit—the bed was the only piece of furniture.

"What did you find?" She was terrified that he had found an excuse to butcher her and put her womb in a jar.

"I'll write to Mr. Swann in the morning."

"I have a right to know."

"But you *don't*, actually." He gave her a look of irritation, and then caught himself; in a moment, his usual benign expression had returned. "Have you noticed the eye, Mrs. Swann?" He pointed to a polished globe of crystal, maybe three inches across, sunk into the wall above her bed. It did indeed look much like an eye. "I'm very proud of this device. It allows me to look into each and every room in the sanitarium at the same time. Nothing happens in this place that I do not see."

"That's absurd," she said.

"No, it is simply fact. Good behavior will be noted and rewarded. Bad behavior will be punished." He gave a bow and then left.

She heard the heavy door lock, ran over and tried the handle, then looked back at the eye in the wall; she could feel its gaze—*his* gaze—on her skin. She knew it was impossible and yet could not rid herself of the sensation. She stared into the glass, trying to make out whatever was behind it, but the convex surface glinted like the membrane of a blind eye.

She looked around. The windows were narrow rectangles toward the ceiling; they offered light but no view. She fought off her self-consciousness and stood on the bed, hoping to see out, but was not tall enough.

She longed for the outside world with a hunger that seemed to pull her apart. Every bit of the life she had once despised now felt unbearably precious: the muffled cries of children from the street; the warmth of the sun through the window; the soft weight of a book in her hand. Is that the way Theodore had felt in his tent, with the polar winds screaming outside? Had he longed for the ordinary, boring world—the world of which she had been a part?

There had been a time, not long ago, when she had wanted to know everything Theodore had suffered on his last march to the Pole. She could not rest until she incorporated it into her body, like a medieval penitent reenacting the martyrdom of a saint. Cold like fire. The weight of the sledge. The black fingers and toes of frostbite. Gangrene. The bloody mouth of scurvy. Snow blindness. A hunger so deep and pure it resembled music. She wanted it all, even if it killed her, and tried to get aboard the first of the rescue missions that left for the Arctic. Leopold had slung her over his shoulder and carried her back down the gangway to the dock. She was needed for six weeks of trance lectures in New England.

Denied her chance, she had walked through the snowbound streets of New York without a coat, testing the limits of endurance. She stood at the very southernmost tip of the island, the Battery, where the winds flailed fists at the granite city—arms spread, mouth open, sleet lashing at her face as she looked out to sea. There were times when she staggered home in tears, and other times when she forgot the pain and felt like an open window, the elements rushing through to an empty house, to a barren field.

Over the years, she had asked the disincarnate Theodore to tell her the truth of what had happened, to spare her nothing, to release her. But on this subject alone he fell into a cagey silence. She took his refusal as a form of accusation: *you were not there.*

She sat back down on the bed, knees to her chest. Theodore's fate seemed to foreshadow her own. If he could not survive, what hope was there for her? She had nothing like his determination, his will. She had always depended on others. It was Theodore who had saved her from the millinery store, and Leopold who had saved her from the despair of obsessive mourning. But Theodore could do nothing now, and Leopold would not; she doubted he understood how dangerous Mayhew truly was. Mr. Auerbach was her only chance, but there was no way to get him a message...Unless Spufford would carry one. But Spufford seemed such a timid soul; he would never do it. She did not even know if she would see him again.

She felt drained, an empty flask. Her thoughts began to drift, and then she felt the familiar pressure at the back of her neck. She had no pen, no paper, but it did not seem to matter; the writing was there in her mind, as if she had read it before, and now remembered.

We spent eight days unable to leave the tent before the weather cleared and I gave the order to turn around. I had to: we were already on half rations, and it was three hundred miles to the nearest supply depot. But I was not disappointed really, though I had to go through the motions with the others. No, I found myself excited. We threw away whatever we could not carry: the geologic specimens, the scientific instruments, the charts and logs—all that had made it a real expedition and not just a boys' adventure. And I emptied my mind too, of everything extraneous to the job of walking. It was so interesting, Verena, to see what's left when you only keep what you need. The thoughts dwindled down to a handful, incredibly precious—that perfume you wore, you remember which—

Lilac.

Yes, a clean, powdery smell. The house we were renting.

On Eighteenth Street.

You remember the brass knocker on the door, the curious—

Yes, shaped like a clamshell.

With the green residue of polish caught in the ridges. I clung to these things, little bits of the past hidden away in my memory. They told me who I was. And then three hundred miles more and I threw those away too, threw them to the wind and they were gone. I didn't need them after all. I knew who I was.

You were my husband, she said.

I will tell you what I was: I was everything that was not the whiteness. I was my opposition, my resistance. The snow looked wonderfully inviting, Verena. Just one more step, I would tell myself, then you can lie down and rest. It doesn't matter if you never get up again. That one step will count. You will have done your job. No one can say otherwise.

The act of walking seemed strangely complicated. The snow was up to our knees. It stretched ahead as far as I could see, a pristine white surface carved by the wind. Loose powder rose like smoke. To take that one step I would have to extricate my foot from the snow, push it forward, and then plunge it back down. It was just too much to ask. Only the promise of rest could make me go through all that again. To lie down seemed so wonderfully simple, and the implications no longer so terribly ominous. But if I did lie down, I did not want a big fuss—to be lectured, to be laid on top of the sledge—a useless gesture, and one we could no longer afford. Everyone already understood that. No, I imagined them removing my harness. I imagined watching the sledge move on without me, imagined it disappearing into the whirling snow. I imagined the snow covering me over, slowly at first, then more quickly, gaining speed till I was white, white, white.

But lying down was not so simple, either. In order to lie down I first had to take that one step. That was the bargain I had made with myself. So I lifted my leg and then threw my weight forward against the harness, a kind of drunkard's lurch, kicking through the snow. And having done all that, having taken that one step, the very last blessed step of my life, I would then make myself do it all over again. That was the trick I used. Just one more step, one more step, and then you can lie down and rest. It doesn't matter if you never get up again. I went the last hundred miles that way.

She felt him hesitate, pause, recede, and then return, as if he had decided to tell something he had not originally intended to.

On the way back we left Boyle in the snow. He was in bad shape. We all knew he wouldn't make it, so the next time he fell down we just kept going. No one said anything, it was just understood that we wouldn't look back.

He knew the risks.

Oh, yes, if it had only been that clean. The thing is, he actually caught up with us that night, when we were making camp, came in crawling on his hands and knees. In the tent the three of us huddled together for warmth with the man we had left to freeze on the ice, and when I woke, he was dead. The first to go.

Jackson was the next to go. He limped alongside the sledge, unable to pull. It was just Portus and me in the harness now. At night in the tent, Jackson took off his boots and rubbed his feet with ice, trying to get the circulation back. They were black up to the ankles, and the smell was terrible, rank and fishy. Portus and I huddled together at the other end of the tent. "What do you think?" I whispered. I could not take my eyes off Jackson. His every gesture, his every move was fascinating. It was something about knowing that he would soon be dead, like Boyle, and something more—that he had the power to take us with him just by trying to stay alive.

But why?

There wasn't enough food, Verena. We had rations for five days, but the supply depot was nine or ten away, and he was slowing us down. He knew it too—he had turned around and left Boyle lying in the snow, just like the rest of us. "I don't see how he's gotten this far," said Portus.

"Sheer willpower," I told him.

"We can't carry him."

"He knows that. He knows what he has to do." Just a few feet away, pretending not to hear, Jackson bent over his feet, rubbing them over and over with the ice, as if he could bring them back to life. But when I woke the next morning, he was already up, pulling on his boots. "What are you doing?" I asked him. "It's not light yet." But of course I knew.

"Going out for a stroll," was all he said, then undid the tent flap and left.

Where did he go?

God knows. Nowhere. Everywhere. We didn't look for him because we couldn't afford to find him.

With Jackson gone the equation changed. Both Portus and I grasped the logic: now that it was only the two of us, we had enough food for another nine days, and since the supply depot was only ten days away, assuming the weather held up, we actually had a chance. And we almost made it. Portus died overnight, just two days' march from the depot. I left him there and continued on alone for another day. That night the weather failed. I waited another two days alone in that tent, unable to leave. The silence was the roar of the storm. For the first time I understood what it was to be alone with your own devouring self. I had murdered those men so I could reach this point, and now all I wanted was to grasp that clam-shaped door knocker, and knock, and be allowed to enter. I did not want to linger by myself. I took off my snowsuit and felt the cold reach into me. You remember that first day we met?

At the arcade.

And the funny little electromagnetic contraption?

For a penny. We both put a finger in.

And couldn't pull apart, no matter how hard we tried.

I didn't want to.

That's how it felt to die.

By morning, when the sun began to lighten the room, she was sure that she did not want to die. She wanted to see the sky again. She wanted to walk down Broadway and see the people rushing to and fro. She wanted to talk to Mr. Auerbach about the weather or his house full of curios, or something else equally inconsequential— just to pass the words back and forth. She wanted to have a child.

And for that she would need paper and pen.

The door opened, and Mr. Spufford entered, huge and deferential, the biggest small man in the world. "Sorry to disturb you, ma'am." He kept his eyes on the floor, as if she were still naked.

"Not at all, Mr. Spufford. I hope you are well." She intended to cultivate him; she had years of experience with the weepers to draw upon.

"Please come with me, ma'am."

She put on her slippers and followed him down the hall, amazed that she had noticed nothing the day before. This wing of the asylum was clearly cylindrical: the corridor was curved, with cell doors on one side and windows on the other. She could see the grounds through the window bars—a rich green lawn and some trees. Though she did not remember climbing stairs, they were two or three floors above the ground.

They came to a door, and entered the adjoining wing, walking down a long, straight corridor. "Can I ask where we are going?"

"Another examination," he said, and then before she could panic, quickly added, "They'll just measure your head with the calipers. It doesn't hurt."

"Will he be there?"

"It's one of the assistants usually."

"Thank you," she said, feeling greatly relieved.

They walked on, and she observed the complexity of his expression, a number of different kinds of misery layered on top of each other. "What is the matter, Mr. Spufford?"

"The matter?"

"Is it something at home?" She reached out and put a sympathetic hand on his forearm, just as she always did with the weepers—feeling her way through their emotional dark.

He seemed shocked and a little frightened. "Can you tell?"

"I am something of an expert on troubles. You can confide in me."

She held her breath, watching that large, timid face on the verge of a human moment, but her luck did not hold: another attendant appeared, walking briskly toward them. Spufford pulled away.

The examination room was the same as before, with its bones and poor lost babies. Their true purpose, she realized, was to imply that she too was now a specimen, to be studied and jarred. But she did not have to submit to that judgment. She kept her eyes from the shelves, and looked instead at the man who would be doing the measuring. He looked back at her with a mild and curious expression, as if she were already a skull. Beside him, on the examination table, were a set of calipers, neatly arranged from small to large on a cloth. Next to them sat an open ledger, and next to the ledger some loose sheets of paper and a trio of sharpened pencils. She glanced at these and quickly looked away, feeling the yearning in her hands.

The man sat her in a chair, and then, without a word, proceeded to measure the topography of her skull: not just width, height, and length of the whole, but the breadth of her forehead, the length of her nose, and a dozen other aspects. In each case, he painstakingly adjusted the calipers, read the dial, and then inscribed the information in the ledger. Occasionally, he stopped to make some arithmetical calculations on a piece of paper with one of the pencils.

She waited for him to finish, feeling the proximity of those sheets of paper, those pencils, hungering for them; and then suddenly the man told Spufford he had forgotten something, and left the room. She knew she had to act. "What odd instruments," she said to Mr. Spufford. "Do you know how they work?"

"Please, ma'am, they're not to be touched."

She took the largest—the size and bulk of garden shears—and dropped it on the floor. "I'm so sorry, Mr. Spufford. Let me get it." Bending, she made sure to take the corner of the cloth with her, pulling the rest down as well. There was a general clatter and skittering under the table.

He chased after them, lumbering on hands and knees, and she

took the chance to slip a sheet of paper and a pencil down the neck of her hospital dress. It was not the most agile trick; she thought he might have seen her. But if so, he chose to pretend that he had not. She joined him on the floor, and together they collected the calipers and lined them up once again by size on the cloth.

A minute later, the man was back with a tape measure. He wrapped it around her head, then around her neck, and noted the figures. When he was done, he packed his instruments into a leather case and inserted paper and remaining pencils into the ledger. She sat very still, terrified that he would notice the missing things, but he left without a word.

"Let's go," said Mr. Spufford, unusually curt.

So he *had* seen. She smiled as brightly as she could, hoping that he would decide to let the matter rest. "You were right, Mr. Spufford, that was painless."

He did not respond to her overture, merely opened the door and ushered her out into the hall.

"I'm sorry to have dropped those things," she said. "Forgive me, please." Reluctant or not, he was her only ally; she would need him to carry the message, if she ever managed to write it. "And thank you again for your many kindnesses."

He nodded, his large, candid face overcome with worry. He seemed frightened of confronting her, and yet frightened of remaining silent—of what Dr. Mayhew would do to him. "Mrs. Swann," he began.

"You will be rewarded, Mr. Spufford."

"Mrs. Swann," he repeated, seemingly trying to calculate the relative pain of each choice.

"I'm still not well from yesterday. Is there somewhere I could freshen up?"

He led her to a water closet, apparently resigned to what was going to happen. She stepped inside and closed the door, then pulled out paper and pencil. The eye in her cell made it impossible to write there, but it looked as if Dr. Mayhew's vision did not yet extend to the toilet. She sat on the commode, placed the paper on her knee, and immediately began to scribble:

Dear Mr. Auerbach—

I have had a falling-out with Leopold, a complete rupture, and he has had me placed forcibly under the care of the mad doctor, Dr. Mayhew—you may have seen him at one of our sittings. I am locked in his private sanitarium, under constant observation. There is a peephole in the wall, among other outrages. I am persecuted for spurning Leopold's indecent advances.

Mr. Auerbach, I do not mean to presume on our friendship. May I even call it a friendship? I think—pray—that I can. Over the last few weeks I have certainly come to think of you as something more than a client, and now you are the only one I can turn to for help at this most dangerous moment. I am a widow and an orphan—I have no living relatives other than Leopold. Dr. Mayhew hates me for my gift and is determined to find me insane. The treatment, the torture, I am receiving here will shortly make me so, and then he will have his excuse to cut me open.

Yours in distress,

Verena Swann

She folded it in thirds, scribbled Mr. Auerbach's address on the front, and then folded it a number of times further, till it fit neatly in her palm. Then she opened the door and stepped back into the hall, smiling for Mr. Spufford.

19. MEET JOHN SMITH

Spufford sat at his desk. It was nearly midnight, but he could not sleep. Open before him was the letter that the new patient, Mrs. Swann, had asked him to deliver for her. It was much the same sort of note that patients always tried to smuggle out, about being perfectly sane, and the victim of a mistake. What was different was that the addressee was not a spouse, attorney, congressman, or figure from the Bible. The addressee was Mr. Augustus Auerbach.

Spufford knew this name from the signature at the bottom of the monthly "Letter from the President" that prefaced each new catalogue he bought. He knew it also from the two letters he had received in answer to his own recent missives, written over the pseudonym he used on his post office box: John Smith. Mr. Auerbach had replied personally both times. One of the great figures of the age had taken a personal interest in Josiah Spufford's plight.

Spufford's problems had begun when his wife accosted him about the dairyman's bill. "I'll pay it tomorrow when I get home," he had told her. Her response was to pull out a small package wrapped in an old cloth, and then to remove the cloth to reveal the box of stereographs inside: Tiny Tina, Queen of the Midgets. He had remembered leaving it in the left-hand drawer of his desk.

"What is that?" he asked, playing dumb.

Instead of answering, she began flipping through the cards, holding them by their edges with a disdain that cut him to the heart. He glanced at the small figures, doubled side by side on each card, so vulnerable in their nakedness.

"Somebody gave them to me," he said. "I didn't know what to do with them, so I just stuffed them in the back of the drawer. That's all."

She stared at him till he was finished, then pulled out another, much larger bundle and untied the rag. He recognized the contents of the hollow tree in the backyard: seven packets of stereographs.

"I can explain," he said, thankful she had not found the secret drawer.

"I'm sure you can. But I don't want to hear."

When he got home the next day, he found a note saying she had moved to her mother's with the child. He made the obligatory trip to retrieve her, was turned away, and did not try again. Within days he had established a routine that was almost monastically severe. Returning from work, he went straight to his study, closed the door, propped the wastepaper basket against it, and unlocked the secret drawer. His life away from the stereoscope withered to nothing. He slept on a bed without sheets, ate bread and cheese, left the apartment only for work and the post office.

At first everything was perfect. The silence in the apartment matched the calm within him. But by the end of the month he had started to weaken; it was as if the intensity of his devotion were too much for him. His eyes stung from overuse. When he closed his lids, it was as if Tiny Tina, Miss Melba, and Carmen the Carmelite Nun had exploded in his skull, flinging limbs everywhere. The silence in the house and the awful noise in his head began to sound the same. Unable to fall asleep, he would pick up his stereoscope, but it no longer felt like a free and happy choice. The figures in the photographs had lost their electrical charge, without losing any of their magnetic power. He was bound to them, but they felt like fellow prisoners now.

The very first letter he sent to Mr. Auerbach was about why he had to burn his photographic collection. Of course, he wrote it in the hope that telling Mr. Auerbach would instill the resolve he needed to actually carry the plan out. He had been circling the idea for weeks and could not bring himself to stuff them in the furnace.

In the stillness of the closet he called his study, he used to listen to his little boy moving about the house, banging the furniture with what sounded like a wooden spoon. It was a sound full of longing, and it made him wish that he did not have his stereoscope or the secret compartment in his desk, that he could be outside with his little boy and completely happy. At the next moment, it made him wish the reverse: that his little boy would stop calling to him, that he was free of this distraction from the important, truly vital work of looking at pictures of naked ladies.

There are great, dangerous forces at work in the world, he thought, and we can only close our eyes and hope—hope that they are not us.

He remembered a moment right before the end, when his little boy was running up and down the long hallway in that peculiar headlong way of his, with his belly out as if running down hill. The boy had stopped as if tired, and Spufford had bent to pick him up. But at the very moment his hands were about to close about the little chest, the boy had shrugged them off—expertly, as if that were the point of his waiting—and shot off in the other direction. "Catch me!" he squealed.

He had tried to explain all this in his letter to Mr. Auerbach; the result was an avalanche of words some eighteen pages long. Two days later he had received this in reply:

Dear Mr. John Smith:

Thank you for your communication of April 30, 1896. My guess is that you are unfamiliar with the standards of decorum prevalent in the business world today, but the first and foremost tenet is brevity.

Burn if you must, but you will only have to buy more.

Thanking You for Your Continued Patronage,

Augustus Auerbach
President and Sole Proprietor

The thought that he would only have to buy more made him so frightened that he promptly ordered everything in the new catalogue, including a special edition goodbye to Miss Melba that cost a staggering seven dollars, money he had been saving for the rent. He then sat down to write a reply—a brief reply of twenty-one pages that, over the course of a week, he slowly and painfully pared down to three short paragraphs:

Dear Mr. Auerbach:

You are right, it would have been a terrible thing to burn my collection, like cutting my own throat. Miss Melba and the others are my friends. When I am lonely they keep me company. I watch their busy and exciting lives, so full of pleasure and adventure, and feel a little of the fire that warms them—just a little, but enough to keep me from freezing to death.

Though I am six feet tall and can lift a keg of beer in each arm, something feels broken inside me, and my job in the madhouse only makes it worse. The lunatics want me to feel sorry for them and help them, but that is a line I must not cross. And with Miss Melba there is a line that I *cannot* cross, no matter how hard I try.

I miss my wife and son, though I know that I lost them because I did not deserve them. If you have a suggestion, I would listen.

Yours Sincerely,

John Smith

The answer came two days later:

Dear Mr. John Smith:

Thank you for your admirably brief communication of May 5, 1896. Burning your collection of Rive Gauche photographic products would have been an obvious act of scapegoating. Refraining from doing so is a laudable step toward personal responsibility.

There is no denying that natural selection is a very harsh master. We can console ourselves that, while indifferent, it is also fair. I am glad that Rive Gauche products have eased your way during these difficult times.

Thanking You for Your Continued Patronage,

Augustus Auerbach
President and Sole Proprietor

It was while he was waiting for this second reply that Mrs. Swann was admitted to the sanitarium. He took her to and from her examinations, and sat with her at meals. Of course, he knew that she was the wife of the great explorer, and a famous figure in her own right. She had an aura of glamour about her. Her manners and speech were refined. And so it was hard to resist her offers of conversation, especially because he had so little contact with anyone now that his wife and child were gone. "What is the matter, Mr. Spufford?" she had asked him.

"The matter?"

"Is it something at home?" She had reached out and put a sympathetic hand on his forearm.

"Can you tell?"

That was already much too much. Regulations strictly forbade any conversation between patients and minders. He kept to the other side of the hall as they walked. But when she came out of the water closet, she looked at him with a frightened, beseeching expression. "Can I trust you to help me, Mr. Spufford?" she whispered.

He did not say what he should have said, which was "It is time for hydrotherapy, Mrs. Swann." He said nothing at all, and in response she stuffed a letter into his hand. This had happened to him a number of times before. Regulations required that he pass all unauthorized patient communications to Dr. Mayhew.

"The address is on the front," she whispered.

He looked down at the paper in his hand: it was the piece he had seen her steal in the examination room, folded up into something the size of a silver dollar. He unfolded it just enough to read the address, and then read it again, to make sure he was not mistaken. "Not *that* Augustus Auerbach?" he asked.

She gave him an earnest look. "He will reward you handsomely, Mr. Spufford."

"You know him?"

"We are friends."

And so Spufford found himself doing the unimaginable, which was stuffing the letter in his pocket and carrying it out with him when he left the sanitarium that evening. Helping a patient communicate with the outside was grounds for immediate dismissal, but he told himself there was no harm, because he had no intention of actually delivering the letter. He just wanted to read it, and to do that with any safety, he would have to take it home.

On entering his apartment, Spufford did not wait to sit down or remove his coat before he pulled out the letter and began reading. If he were to carry it to Mr. Auerbach, he would instantly win the gratitude of one of the most important men in America. Of course, actually doing so was completely out of the question, as it would endanger his job at the sanitarium. And there were other barriers too: he would have to make the trip to Manhattan, and then uptown to the address on the back of the letter. The streetcars would cost money. He would have to rap on Mr. Auerbach's heavy oaken door and explain his errand to a hostile functionary who might well slam the door in his face. And though tomorrow happened to be his day off, the trip would require a great deal of time away from his collection—just when he was planning to review stereographs from the previous year's summer catalogue.

And yet...

Spufford went into his desk drawer, pulled out the two letters from Mr. Auerbach, laid them next to the letter from Mrs. Swann, and immediately understood that he should tell his wife. If she knew the size of what was happening, she would not only beg to come back, but would accept whatever terms he offered her.

But when he got to his mother-in-law's, his wife stood in the half-open door, barring his way. "I don't want you upsetting the child," she explained.

"How would I upset him?" he asked, hurt by the remark, even as he instantly accepted its truth.

The happiest moments of Spufford's life had been spent sitting on a bench in the park, watching the little boy play with his toys. From four or five yards away it was like looking at a picture, and while it lasted, Spufford could rest. His son was safe and he, Spufford, was doing no harm to anyone, failing no one, not even himself. For a second, suspended in that delicate balance, he could feel that there was goodness hidden at the core of the world. But those moments never lasted long. The boy would come running over—he would be crying; there was a problem that could not be solved—and the picture would disappear. The world would resume hurtling forward, dragging its wake of loss and confusion behind.

He had no choice but to tell her standing in the doorway. "I am in correspondence with Augustus Auerbach," he said. "He's a millionaire, one of the greatest men in the country, and he's taken a personal interest in me—my development, my future."

"Do you owe him money?" she asked.

"Of course not. He thinks I have great natural talent."

"Is he going to give you a job?"

Why hadn't he thought of that? "I'm taking care of a confidential matter for him right now." He held up Mrs. Swann's note. "A matter of the utmost secrecy. I'm delivering it as soon as I leave here."

"Shouldn't you get going, then?" she asked.

He could see that she had begun, ever so slightly, to doubt her doubt, but he was not sure how to press his advantage. He reached into his vest pocket, thinking that a glance at his watch might make a suitable end, then remembered it was gone; he had pawned it just the other day. So he turned and went down the stairs.

She had not believed him, and yet she had not treated him quite as badly as she might have, either. If he hurried directly home, he would still have the day to devote to his stereographs. Waiting for the streetcar, however, he pulled out the letters and remembered his boast—his threat. He walked across the street to the other stop, the one that would take him into Manhattan.

The foolishness of the undertaking did not strike him till he arrived at Mr. Auerbach's iron gate and pulled the bell chain. A little man came out, leathery and silent, and led him over a gravel path that crunched beneath his boots. Spufford wished he had been turned away; there would still have been time for some stereographs. He almost turned around and fled, but they entered a door and walked through a marble corridor decorated with glossy dark portraits, columns, and busts. Finally he was in a gigantic office, before a great solid lake of a desk, and at the other shore sat a man. Spufford stood with his cap in his hand, resisting the temptation to fall to his knees.

He had expected Augustus Auerbach to have white hair and a great white beard, but he was in fact the opposite: dark-haired and clean-shaven. Nevertheless, there was something ancient and wise about him: his capacious eyes seemed to see all the pain in Spufford's heart. Spufford had been afraid that nothing would come out of his mouth, but now that the moment was here, he found it strangely easy to talk. There was so much to tell, a lifetime of woe. "Of course, you don't recognize me," he began. "My name is John Smith."

"*You?*" asked Auerbach. The man was enormous—at least six and a half feet tall—but soft-looking, as if made from biscuit dough. "*You* are John Smith?"

Smith bowed. "At your service, sir."

Auerbach could do nothing but stare. He had devoted his life to understanding John Smith, much as a naturalist might spend his career studying a particular species of moth or beetle. The difference was that, unlike the entomologist who crawls through the weeds to observe an insect in its habitat, Auerbach tracked John Smith by way of his shadow. The monthly sales figures and the strange, irrational letters that waited on his desk each night were all he needed or wanted to know of his quarry. Anything more risked confusion, distraction, entanglement. "How did you get in here?" he asked.

"I'm not sure. It's almost as if I'm dreaming."

If so, it was best to wake him—wake them both—right away. Auerbach pressed the buzzer on his desk to call for Mr. Grapes. "I should tell you right away that we do not extend credit," he said. "It's company policy."

Smith looked mortified at the thought. "I would never dare to ask, sir. No, never in a thousand years." He began nervously wringing his cloth cap between his hands. "My only wish is to thank you. Your encouragement has meant more to me than anything else in the world—especially now, with my wife gone."

Auerbach was not surprised by the missing wife. He knew from two decades of letters that the wife was always missing. Yet he could feel an odd sort of sympathy for the man. He had spent much time rereading Leopold Swann's note, trying to puzzle out its hidden meanings. Twice he had ordered his carriage readied for a trip to Washington Square, only to cancel at the last moment.

The door opened and Mr. Grapes stuck his head in. "Did you call, Mr. A.?"

He had intended to have Smith ushered out, but now thought he might stay a little longer. "False alarm, Mr. Grapes. I apologize." He waited till the door was closed to return to his conversation. "Why did your wife leave you, Mr. Smith?"

"I don't know. Money, maybe."

Auerbach thought this likely enough, the lack of money being an indication of a more general inability to master the complexities of life. But then he himself had plenty of money, and Mrs. Swann had left him—though that was *not* what happened, he reminded himself. They were not married, not even romantically involved; there was never any thought of that. "Do you miss her?" he asked.

"I am too busy planning my future."

"Very sensible," said Auerbach, impressed with this answer—not at all what he would have expected from John Smith. "The key is to find useful work. You must lose yourself in your work." It was what he intended for himself.

"I was hoping you could help with that, Mr. Auerbach." Smith began nervously pulling at the cap in his hands. "You see, it isn't my idea, but my wife thinks you should give me a job." He laughed with embarrassment, eyes averted to the floor.

Auerbach was disappointed by this turn in the conversation, as he had not quite finished his lecture on the emotional benefits of hard work. He gave an elaborate and theatrical sigh of regret, which is how he always prefaced a refusal of any kind. "I only wish it were possible, Mr. Smith."

"But you seemed to say in your letters—you indicated that I have certain special talents."

Auerbach shook his head. The idea of special or unique qualities was contrary to the very nature of John Smith, and to his place in the great chain of being, which was at the bottom, deep within the great mulch pit. "I'm sorry, Mr. Smith. Customers cannot become employees. The two are completely different species." He pressed the buzzer to summon Mr. Grapes again. "I hope you understand."

Smith's struggle was evident on his face: the eyes confused, the mouth fixed in a frightened smile. "But look," he said, reaching into his overcoat and bringing out a pair of letters. "These are the letters you wrote me."

Auerbach pointed to the pile of mail heaped two feet high on his desk. "Do you see that stack there? I get that much every night of the week. And do you know where it comes from? It comes from *you*."

"Me?" A blink, and then another.

Auerbach grabbed a handful of letters from the pile and began reading signatures. "John Smith, John Smith, John Smith, John Smith. I don't know why it's never Cooper or Williams or Harrison, but it never is. That is one of the enduring mysteries of this business."

It took a moment for Smith to put it all together, but only a moment. His eyes seemed to expand and fill with a black light, like the sky before a storm. "There are others?" he asked.

"Thousands."

The tears, when they came, were violent, outrageous, florid. Auerbach gripped the handrests of his chair, stunned by the force he had precipitated—the power of grief. Luckily, Mr. Grapes was at the door. "Mr. Grapes," said Auerbach, "will you please give Mr. Smith a set of stereographs on his way out, compliments of Rive Gauche." It was like yelling through a gale.

Grapes stood watching from the door with his usual immutable calm. "This way, Mr. Smith." He held out a handkerchief.

Smith dutifully turned to leave, but then turned back to address Auerbach. "Let me go," he pleaded. "Please just let me go." He seemed genuinely afraid of being detained.

"Nobody's holding you here, Mr. Smith. Quite the contrary."

"I can't think, I can't breathe."

"I have nothing to do with that."

Smith seemed to remember the letters in his hands. He threw them on the floor, and then reached into his pocket and retrieved a third, which he shoved at Auerbach. "Here, take this, it's from *her*. Take it and let me go. That's all I ask in return."

"Her?" But of course Auerbach knew—what other *her* was there? He took the letter in hand and began to read. *I have had a falling–out with Leopold, a complete rupture, and he has had me placed forcibly under the care of the mad doctor, Dr. Mayhew—*

It was like lighting a lamp and seeing to the very back of the room, all the mysterious corners. It explained her disappearance, and her brother-in-law's cryptic note and many other things—everything, really, though he could not stop right now to piece it all together. "Where did you get this?" he asked.

"I was going to tell you," Smith stammered. He looked frightened by the vehemence in Auerbach's voice. "I meant to."

"But where did you *get* it?"

"She gave it to me," he said, wiping his eyes. "I work there."

Auerbach saw at once that he would have to go and get her. He told Grapes to order the carriage and then turned to Mr. Smith. He would need this ridiculous, self-pitying fool, if only to guide him to the sanitarium. "You wanted a job, Mr. Smith—here is your chance. Help me recover Mrs. Swann and I'll give you a job."

Auerbach reached into one of his desk drawers, pulled out a thick roll of bills, and placed it in his coat pocket. He was frightened, and hoped it did not show. He would have to go *out there*, into the chaos beyond the mansion, and cross the East River by way of the Brooklyn Bridge, something he had never done before—had never even seen except in stereographs. He would have to buy off the mad doctor. Hardest of all, somehow, he would have to look Mrs. Swann in the eye, and in so doing, admit all the things she made him feel— no, he would have to actually *feel them*. A small part of him wanted to shut the door of his office and pretend he had never received her note. But that part of him was quickly overruled. He had no choice; a force he had never known before was pulling him toward her. He had to race to keep up or risk being dragged.

20. WE ARE HERE FOR MRS. SWANN

Auerbach's carriage crept down Fifth Avenue, through a hideous tangle of traffic. After twenty minutes and little progress, he grabbed the speaking tube that connected him to the coachman up top. "Can't we go any faster?" He was tormented by the idea of Mrs. Swann alone in that place, surrounded by violent lunatics and the malevolent Dr. Mayhew. Indeed, he felt so desperate that he actually lifted a corner of the window curtain, peering with horror at the chaos of coaches, wagons, and streetcars, all battling for space. "This will take hours," he said to Smith. "And in the meantime, she's locked in that madhouse."

"The danger is worse than you know," said Smith. "Terrible things happen there."

Auerbach reached into his pocket and brought out her letter. "What did she mean about Mayhew cutting her open?"

"He believes that certain kinds of madness are connected to problems with the female anatomy."

Suddenly the heavy immobility of the carriage was intolerable:

the heat, the lack of air. Auerbach flung open the curtains, slid the window up, and thrust his head outside. Instantly his top hat was gone, his face blanketed with dust. He pulled out a handkerchief to clear the grime from his eyes and peered down the avenue, trying to identify an opening. There was shouting, lots of shouting, and the ringing of metal wheels on cobblestone. Wagons and carriages were everywhere, tangled around streetcars, pressing through crowds of pedestrians, and the side streets looked just as bad. In any case, he had never traveled them and didn't know what traps or pitfalls they might present.

Something stung his cheek—a pebble. He pulled in his head, slammed the window shut, and grabbed the speaking horn. "A hundred dollars if you find a shortcut," he yelled up to the coachman, breathing hard. "No, two hundred."

They took a sudden turn to the right, headed down a side street, rode up on the sidewalk for a stretch, the carriage leaning precariously and bouncing on its springs, then turned left and began moving downtown again, at a much better rate. Auerbach wiped at his cheek with the handkerchief and saw a thin streak of blood. "When she came to me, I did not understand the danger she was in."

"You can't blame yourself, Mr. Auerbach."

"I don't." But the thought had lodged like a burr. He should have assigned Mr. Grapes to watch her. Instead, he had wheeled about the mansion, ordering hot chocolate and looking for books on the art of conversation.

"Is she a *particular* friend?" asked Smith.

That question, again. "She needs help. Shouldn't I help her if I can?"

What if he had been able to run beneath his mother and catch her when she fell? The world would have spun on its head. He would have grown up to become an ordinary man, like the men he could see outside the carriage window, walking down the street in overcoats and bowlers, so comfortable in their skins.

Smith had begun biting his nails, as if he had only now remembered that this was a rescue mission. "It is very good of you to give me this chance to prove myself."

"You will acquit yourself well, Mr. Smith." There was some truth to that: the noisy regularity of Smith's breathing was comforting, like the snoring of an old dog.

Smith brightened. "If I were to be completely honest with you, the job I've always dreamed about is appearing in the pictures. That's the job I've always secretly wanted."

"You mean a photographic model?" The idea was absurd, but Auerbach could not worry about that now. "Certainly, that can be arranged."

"Oh, no, you've misunderstood me, Mr. Auerbach. I don't want to get undressed. I just want to *be* there, in the pictures."

"In the pictures?"

"Yes, in the pictures, but sitting to the side, or standing by the mantel, someplace unobtrusive."

He wants to watch himself *watching*, thought Auerbach. It was like the final stage of some terrible nervous illness, where the victim combs his hair day and night until there is no more hair left to comb. "If that's what you want, Mr. Smith, it will be your reward."

"Thank you," said Smith, smiling for the first time that morning. "Everybody seems so happy in your pictures. Nothing bad ever happens. Nobody ever gets angry or yells."

Is that all they wanted—for nothing bad to happen? It seemed to explain something essential about John Smith, but Auerbach could not decide exactly what, as his mind kept drifting back to Mrs. Swann. Was she all right? Did she know that he was coming? Did she trust him to save her?

They rode in silence until the entrance to the Brooklyn Bridge came into view, far larger and more muscular than he had ever imagined. It would be his first time on any bridge whatsoever. He pulled shut the curtains and then grabbed hold of the hand rest. "You take the bridge often, Mr. Smith?"

"I live in Brooklyn."

"Could I ask you to close your curtains, please?"

It helped to blot out the view, but there was no way to eliminate the hollow clopping of the horse's hooves on the wooden planks of the roadway, or the feeling of rising into the air on something as delicate as a wish.

They came out on a broad avenue. Auerbach opened his curtains again, the better to observe progress. He knew Brooklyn only as a series of statistics recorded in his ledgers: 26,218 catalogues mailed each month, resulting in average monthly sales of approximately four thousand packs of stereographs—a number which, in one of those geographic quirks he always noted, usually doubled in February (by contrast, Singapore saw its annual surge during the rainy season, in June). But now that he was here, Brooklyn looked surprisingly similar to New York: long rows of dusty brownstones, covered in garish and pushy signs advertising everything from sausage to candles. The difference was that the buildings thinned out quickly; the signs dwindled; and soon there were weedy lots interspersed among the houses; large gardens; front yards with chickens scratching around. The carriage picked up speed.

"We're very close to the sanitarium," said Smith. This was clearly true because he had started to shift and fidget. He looked over at Auerbach. "I won't have to see Dr. Mayhew, will I?"

"Not if you don't want to."

"He treated me like I was a trained ape, fit for nothing but to turn the crank in the observatory. I hope you destroy him." He seemed to ruminate on all the various wrongs he had suffered at Mayhew's hands. "I don't think you can get her out secretly. The doors are all locked. You will have to break her out."

"I'm going to *buy* her out, Mr. Smith." Auerbach held up the roll of bills from his pocket, and watched Smith's face fall.

"You are too easy on him," said Smith.

"It is the most efficient way to handle matters of this kind." *Matters of any kind* was what he meant. Money made the models strip off their clothes, made the Clean Living League look the other way as shiploads of stereographs sailed out of the harbor.

They came up on the black iron fence that surrounded the sanitarium; a moment later, they were driving through the front gate and up the long gravel path that cut through the grounds. Smith pulled his curtains closed and sank down low in his seat. "Courage," said Auerbach. "This is the final test." His heart was banging like a barker's drum.

"I'm not brave like you," said Smith.

"You don't have to be."

They drew up at what seemed to be the main building, a big red brick pile composed of odd and clashing shapes, half factory, half castle. The coachman helped him down into his chair and then, with the help of the footman, carried him up the stairs to the large front door of the sanitarium. Auerbach tucked in his lap rug and wheeled himself inside.

Just minutes later, Auerbach sat in his wheelchair in front of Dr. Mayhew's desk, watching the doctor peruse his calling card. The best thing, he knew, was to treat this like any other negotiation, as if it were a percentage of sales at stake, instead of Mrs. Swann. But maintaining an air of unconcern was costing him dearly; beneath his blanket, his feet twitched. He wanted to grab Mayhew by the neck and force him to tell where he kept her.

"Oh, yes, now I remember," said Dr. Mayhew. "Mr. Auerbach,

the *photographer*." He gave the word special emphasis, as if Auerbach were producing dirty postcards for a penny apiece out of a filthy room on Orchard Street—and trying to hide the fact.

"I own a photographic *company*," said Auerbach. "We have sales in the tens of millions."

"And no more fainting spells, I hope? As a doctor, I can tell you that the Spiritualist game is far too exciting for a man of your constitution."

Auerbach's foot jumped beneath his blanket, but he managed a smile. "I might as well get right to the point, Dr. Mayhew. I have been delegated by a group of concerned individuals to see into the matter of Mrs. Swann."

"A group of concerned individuals?" asked Mayhew, smiling broadly to indicate that he was less than convinced.

"We want to arrange her release."

"You have no standing, I'm afraid. Only a blood relation can do that."

"Nevertheless." Auerbach produced the roll of bills from his coat pocket and held it aloft between two fingers. "You will release Mrs. Swann to me, and I will compensate you for the time and effort you have spent on her behalf." He began peeling off hundred-dollar bills and placing them on the desk in a neat pile. "Two thousand dollars. One thousand for each day she spent in your care."

Dr. Mayhew looked at the money with exaggerated contempt. "Let me make sure I understand you," he said. "You are offering me money to release a patient committed to my care by her family. Is that correct?"

"She's not mad."

"She speaks to dead people, Mr. Auerbach."

Was that so strange, thought Auerbach, if they had something to say? "Here's another thousand," he said, counting out the bills and placing them with the others.

Dr. Mayhew drew himself up, ready to speechify. "There are other people at risk here, sir, innocent people who need to be protected. Mrs. Swann will seduce them into believing things that are not true, things that will end up undermining their sense of reality. I have a responsibility to those people as well."

"All right then, another two thousand," said Auerbach. "You can add a whole new wing to the hospital." He placed the last of the roll on the desk.

Dr. Mayhew got up without even looking at the money. "You misunderstand me, sir—misunderstand me completely. Follow me and you will see."

Auerbach left the money sitting where it was, to continue its work as a challenge and a temptation, and then followed Dr. Mayhew out of the office. They traveled together down a hallway that smelled faintly of ammonia, past shut doors and empty stairwells, devoid of human traffic. And yet Auerbach could sense lives hidden away behind the walls. He heard a faint cry carried from some other part of the building, barely more than a squeak, immediately stifled. And then they passed through a set of double doors and into a curious round atrium that was both narrow and tall. It felt as if he were at the bottom of an empty grain silo, with a plug of sky stoppering the top. A lone chair sat in the middle of the floor, attached to ropes which traveled upward.

"This is the observation room," said the doctor. "From that seat I am able to look in on any and all of my patients." He picked up a large brass rod by the side of the chair and held it out to Auerbach. "All I have to do is just point this telescope to the spy hole." Auerbach could see that there were rings of these portholes at each floor.

"And they do not know you are watching," said Auerbach, beginning to suspect that Dr. Mayhew was not all that different from John Smith.

"They cannot know if I am watching, and therefore must always suspect." Standing right where he was, Mayhew extended the telescope till it reached one of the portholes in the lowest row, and put it to his eye. "This one, for example. She knows that I am out here, but she does not yet know what that means." He offered the telescope to Auerbach, who dutifully gazed inside.

He saw a little white cell that looked more like the inside of a sack, as the walls and floor were clearly padded. A woman stood naked in the middle of the floor, her clothes piled by her feet. She had her hands to her ears and was screaming—silently screaming—while staring into the very porthole through which he was looking. Her eyes seemed to lock on his, though he knew this was an illusion. He watched her throat quiver, her stringy muscles tense. Her body was all sinew and bone. She looked like she would burst the tiny closet with her nonexistent voice, with the sheer tension of her body.

Auerbach took the telescope from his eye, shaken. "Shouldn't you send somebody in?"

Dr. Mayhew looked at him with a professional's disdain for misguided sympathy. "She will have to scream herself out, I'm afraid." He pointed to another porthole immediately to the left. "Take a look at that one there, please."

Auerbach hesitated, dreading what he might see. The entire building was a stereoscope, but instead of stereographic views, it contained actual people—frightened, angry, suffering. "I think I've seen enough," he said.

"I think you will change your mind."

Auerbach lifted the telescope. The chamber was a little different, in that it was unpadded. He saw a woman lying on a bed—tied to it, rather. Looking more closely, he could make out the canvas straps that wrapped around her arms and under the bed frame. The woman was weeping so piteously that it took a while before he realized it was Mrs. Swann. He dropped the telescope and it clattered on the marble floor. "You've made your point," he said to the doctor. "I can give you ten thousand."

Dr. Mayhew wore an interested look, as if he had finally come across the reaction he had been seeking. "I will be frank with you, Mr. Auerbach. She is priceless to me. I have been studying Spiritualists for ten years now, but have never had a specimen of Mrs. Swann's originality or notoriety. Her cure will establish once and for all the great public utility of our branch of medicine."

"Let me at least speak to her, so she knows I was here."

"She is not allowed visitors."

"I am not used to being denied, Doctor." Indeed, his legs twisted beneath his lap rug with the unfamiliar sensation.

"I am *helping* her," said the doctor, with the peevishness of the chronically misunderstood. "Can you say that about *your* customers, Mr. Auerbach?"

"I don't have to. I am a businessman." Selling was its own justification, an act as primal and holy as Jane Larue giving her breast to her baby. It needed no defense.

But Mayhew did not seem to understand that. "One day soon, after we have cured all the Spiritualists, we will start on the pornographers."

Auerbach was rattled in spite of himself. He started for the observatory door, intending to go and find Mrs. Swann, but his path was blocked by an attendant in a white uniform—a man the size of Smith, if not larger. "Out of my way," said Auerbach, banging on his handrests as if the man were a cat he could scare off. "You heard me. Step aside." By then, a second attendant had arrived, cupping Auerbach's roll of cash in one gigantic palm. And someone else had the handles of his wheelchair and was wheeling him out. "Let go," he said.

It was Dr. Mayhew. He leaned down and spoke into Auerbach's ear. "They will escort you to your carriage, Mr. Auerbach. But let me warn you, the next time you come here I will put you in the cell next to hers." He stood up and addressed the attendants. "Give him his money on the way out."

Auerbach's carriage rolled over the gravel driveway and out the front gate. Smith slouched low in his seat, attempting to hide. He tried to say something, but Auerbach silenced him with a twitch of the eyebrow. The image he had seen through Mayhew's telescope—Mrs. Swann alone in her cell, weeping in silence—filled him with rage. Not since childhood, when he watched his mother fall, had he felt so helpless, so humiliated. He grabbed the speaking tube, and in the most level voice he could manage, gave the coachman his directions. "Take us to the Second Precinct," he told him, meaning the dirty brick building near City Hall that Inspector Wolfscheim used as his base of operations. The secretary of the Clean Living League was an expert on the use of force in resolving human differences.

As they reversed their journey, back to Manhattan, Auerbach fidgeted with the roll of cash. Did Dr. Mayhew really believe he could win so easily? He was going to get a lesson in how to treat a great industrialist. Auerbach would take what was rightfully his— Mrs. Swann—and raze the rest to the ground.

At the precinct, he had Smith carry him upstairs in his wheelchair. They found Inspector Wolfscheim on the third floor, in a little room that seemed dedicated to the aesthetic of force. The floorboards were splintery, the paint on the walls peeling in large, moist strips of green. The inspector sat at a desk that looked like it had been beaten with a baseball bat; there were dents and gouges all along the edges. But a clean green baize blotter covered the top, and the inspector himself sat solemnly in his bulky woolen overcoat, untouched by his surroundings. He seemed unsurprised to see

Auerbach, though they had never before met outside of the mansion. "Welcome, Mr. Auerbach. What can I do for you today?"

Under ordinary circumstances Auerbach would have hesitated; it was not good business to owe the Clean Living League. But now he felt only relief. Inspector Wolfscheim looked like he was carved of granite. He would be Auerbach's battering ram, his sledgehammer. "There is somebody I want to remove from a madhouse, Inspector."

"Of course," said Wolfscheim, as if this were the most ordinary of problems. "A model has gone insane."

"A business associate," said Auerbach, not sure what to call Mrs. Swann, but knowing that *model* would not do. "And the person in question is not insane. The person in question—" it seemed too late to say "she" now that he had taken such a detour— "is the victim of a family dispute."

"And the family does not want to see her leave," said the inspector, as if confirming the usual turn of events. "Have you tried to buy her out?"

"The doctor is a lunatic."

Inspector Wolfscheim nodded, as if this too sometimes happened. "And if you don't mind me asking, what exactly is *your* interest in the matter?"

"Financial."

Wolfscheim smiled wistfully. "We are old friends, Mr. Auerbach. You can be forthright with me."

It had never occurred to Auerbach that he was being anything other than candid, but just saying her name was so very difficult. "The person in question is Mrs. Verena Swann," he said finally, hearing his heart begin to echo in his ears. "You may be familiar with her from the newspapers."

"You want her out, that's all I need to know."

"I don't care how you do it, as long as it's done today."

Wolfscheim seemed to think about this. "You are a civilized

man, Mr. Auerbach. You take feelings and turn them into pictures. But my job is to cause pain." He leaned forward and the springs in his leather chair creaked. "In the service of order, of course. But, either way, it is very messy."

"Messy is acceptable," said Auerbach, "as long as she is freed."

"Very well, then." Wolfscheim pulled out a drawer and removed a delicate crystal decanter and two matching glasses. The set looked utterly out of place on his battered desk, like a bride and two bridesmaids in a waterfront tavern. He poured whiskey into the glasses and gave one to Auerbach. "I should warn you that things get complicated when you descend from the world of the mind into a world that's all bone and muscle." He had a thoughtful look on his muscular face. "You can go back, but a little bit will stick to you afterward."

"Let it stick," said Auerbach. He lifted the whiskey to his lips and drank it down in a single gulp. "There, the bargain is sealed."

Wolfscheim opened another drawer and pulled out a printed writ. "Let us go see the judge." He meant Judge Montcrief, vice president of the Clean Living League. "He will give us his signature."

"It's a waste of time," said Auerbach. "We must hurry."

"Force is not the same as lawlessness," said the inspector.

The judge was no longer in his chambers, so they took the carriage to his house on Twelfth Street, only to find that he was not there, either. Inspector Wolfscheim sent a man around to the various saloons, and the rest of them waited in the front parlor, sipping coffee provided by the judge's wife. Auerbach sat glowering, his eyes on the grandfather clock. It was six-fifteen; the entire day had been spent fruitlessly. "My God, where is he? What is he doing?" The image of Mrs. Swann strapped to the bed so filled his mind that it felt as if he too were strapped down, unable to breathe.

"Patience, Mr. Auerbach," said Wolfscheim. He had gotten pen and ink from Mrs. Montcrief and was filling in the blanks on the legal document he had brought for the judge. Mr. Smith sat beside him, drawing a map of the sanitarium with great concentration.

It was almost eight when Montcrief finally arrived, staggeringly drunk and carrying a pot of beer. "My God," he exclaimed, peering at Auerbach as if through a keyhole. "Is that Augustus Auerbach? What is he doing here?"

"You are drunk," said Auerbach, feeling as if he wanted to slam the pot on the judge's head.

"Obviously."

"You have cost us two hours."

Inspector Wolfscheim stepped between them, relieving the judge of his beer pot, and then steering him to a seat on one of the couches, before a low table. "We need your signature on a little piece of paper, Judge, and then we will leave you to your dinner." Wolfscheim placed the document before him and inserted the pen into his hand. Through some judicial habit, Montcrief began skimming through the pages, his head wobbling. "Where have I seen that name before? Swann, Swann...One of your actresses?" he asked Auerbach.

"Absolutely not."

"And yet it seems like an awful lot of trouble to go through." The next moment, Montcrief's face had reformed itself into an extraordinary leer, worthy of a stage villain in one of the plays Auerbach's mother used to perform in. "Why, of course, that's it! The millionaire monk is no better than the rest of us!"

Auerbach's face flushed. "That's none of your business," he growled.

"Don't be so touchy, old man. I was just having a little fun."

"Sign the order or I'll tell Mrs. Montcrief all about the Clean Living League dinners."

That was enough. The judge glanced around the room—searching for his wife, perhaps—and then signed the bottom of the document with a great, unsteady flourish. Auerbach ripped it from his hand. "There. Let's go."

After that it was back onto the street, where a storm was taking shape. He had been too distracted to notice before, but now the transformation was unmistakable. The air was wet and electric, and the wind whipped around in confused circles. Overhead, great black clouds massed in the sky, seeking each other out, trying to fit together like the pieces of a jigsaw puzzle. Pedestrians bent into the wind and held their hats, anxious to reach shelter before the rain began.

Auerbach and his party returned to the precinct to collect Inspector Wolfscheim's men, and then set out for Brooklyn in a line of three carriages. By this time they were the only vehicles on the road. The sky was black in a way that had nothing to do with night; it made Auerbach wish he had the courage to ask Wolfscheim to close the curtains so he did not have to see. And it did not help matters that they were on the bridge when the thunder began: great resounding booms that made the horses skitter on the wooden roadway. The rain came soon after: heavy sheets, slapping the top of the carriage from one direction and then the other, blurring the window.

Wolfscheim seemed unconcerned. "We might as well discuss tonight's strategy, Mr. Auerbach. I will take a small party upstairs to get Mrs. Swann. You will stay downstairs with the rest of the men to break things. When I have her, we will leave."

"She doesn't know you," said Auerbach. "It's best if I get her."

"There will be doors and stairs."

"Mr. Smith can carry me."

Wolfscheim took on a resigned look—the professional who must humor the amateur. "Very well then, you will go upstairs and I will break things."

"And what about the other inmates?" asked Auerbach. "Can we let them go too?"

"What could you possibly do with them?"

It was an obvious point. They could not pose, or develop photographs, or do any of the things he needed people to do. They were out of luck.

It was still pouring when they reached the iron gates of the sanitarium. Two men with bolt cutters jumped out of one of the carriages behind, broke the lock, and opened the gates. Auerbach stuck his head out the carriage window to watch this little demonstration of the efficacy of force—enjoying it immensely, even as the water poured over him. His carriage proceeded up the gravel path, which sizzled in the rain.

At the doors to the building, Wolfscheim's men used a sledgehammer, and a few moments later, Auerbach found himself once again in the lobby of Dr. Mayhew's sanitarium. It was unlit, and the thunderstorm was reaching its peak, with flashes of lightning followed by huge booming thunderclaps seemingly right overhead. Perhaps for that reason, the place was full of the screams of the afflicted. After each boom the wailing stopped, and then started up again, louder than ever.

The policemen lit kerosene lanterns, which gave a ghostly glow to the lobby: a dozen or so men standing around Auerbach's chair, frozen by the cries that came in from beyond the inner doors. Only Wolfscheim seemed unaffected, examining the map that Smith had drawn. "Through there, Mr. Smith?" he asked, pointing to the doors.

A flash of lightning, and then the boom of thunder. "Yes, sir," said Smith, looking cowed.

And then a set of inner doors opened, and Dr. Mayhew came forward carrying a large candelabra. "What is this?" he cried. "What are you doing here?" He rushed halfway across the lobby, candles trailing smoke, to examine the front doors, and then came back to look at the policemen. "This is a hospital," he said. "What are you doing here?"

"We are here for Mrs. Swann," said Auerbach.

Dr. Mayhew turned to face him. "The patient is ill, Mr. Auerbach. She needs treatment. I thought you understood that."

It felt wonderful, not having to pull out money, or offer compliments or reasons—to bargain in any way. He wanted Mrs. Swann, and he would get her. "Inspector Wolfscheim has the order for her release."

"Indeed, I do," said Wolfscheim, holding the paper out to Mayhew.

The doctor quickly perused its contents. "I've never seen an order like this. It makes no sense at all."

"Let me explain it to you," said Wolfscheim, who signaled Auerbach and the others to go ahead.

Auerbach left the inspector and the largest part of his contingent behind, and passed through the inner doors with three patrolmen, one of whom was armed with a sledgehammer and chisel. Along the way he found Mr. Smith—who had been lurking in a corner, trying to hide from Dr. Mayhew. When they came to the staircase, Mr. Smith grabbed hold of the wheelchair and Auerbach felt himself begin to rise. Floating upward, he listened to the growing altercation in the lobby: first the sounds of glass and masonry breaking, and then Dr. Mayhew's piercing cry. The inmates recognized the doctor's voice between thunderclaps and screamed even louder than before. A great wave of sound rushed down the stairwell to crash over Auerbach as he rose.

Smith led them down the curving corridor. The doors were all exactly alike: a slot at the bottom for inserting a food tray, a heavy lock, a peephole about two-thirds of the way up. Auerbach could hear the inmates beat fists against the doors, a dull thudding tattoo beneath the shouting, punctuated by thunderclaps.

When they came to her door, Auerbach had them lift his chair so he could glance through the peephole. He expected to see her still tied to the bed, but she was sitting on the cot in an attitude of imminent departure, despite wearing nothing but a plain blue robe and a pair of carpet slippers. He had the officer with the sledgehammer break open the door. It was an immensely satisfying thing to hear the metallic bite of the chisel—once, twice—and watch the lock fall through. Smith pulled open the door and Auerbach wheeled himself into the little room. "Good evening, Mrs. Swann."

"Good evening, Mr. Auerbach." She stood up with exaggerated composure, her hands clasped in front of her. "My husband sent you, didn't he? He told me he did." She looked drained, exhausted.

"I like to think it was my idea."

"He's not against you anymore," she said.

"I didn't know he ever was."

She became very earnest. "Forgive him, Mr. Auerbach. There is so much he still wants to do, and it's just not possible, and so it makes him very jealous sometimes."

"I understand." She wavered and he took her arm. "I'm here to take you home."

"I can't go home." She stumbled a few steps to one side, and he reined her in. "Leopold is the one who put me in here."

"I mean to *my* home. You will be safe with me."

"Yes, maybe that's best." She leaned against the arm of his wheelchair.

"Come, let's go," he said. He took her hand in his and they moved out into the corridor, Mr. Smith pushing the chair, one of the patrolmen guiding her on the other side. The hallway still rang with the calls of the incarcerated—all the people who would not be leaving with them.

At the stairway, Mr. Smith lifted Auerbach into the air once again, but she would not let go of Auerbach's hand. She held one finger like a child holds a string to a balloon.

21. NOBODY LISTENS TO THE TRUTH

There was no way to know what had happened to Mrs. Swann in the sanitarium, as she would not—or could not—say. More than anything else, she seemed to be suffering from exhaustion. In the carriage, on the way back to Manhattan, she mentioned the eye in the wall—Mayhew's peephole—and then babies in jars, but within a few minutes she was asleep, her head against Auerbach's chest. It was an odd moment; no one had ever used him as a pillow before. He held his arm up in the air, unsure about the etiquette of the situation, whether it was permissible to drape it around her shoulder. In the meantime, there was the weight of her body on his, and the scent of her hair in his nose, and his arm beginning to ache—and so he finally placed it around her shoulder, drawing her in tight. That seemed to trigger something: his first intimation that he had lived a life of loneliness was that he did not feel lonely anymore.

Back at the mansion, he carried that feeling with him as if it were one of the old glass photographic plates he had used as an apprentice, the kind that shattered with a sudden movement. He helped Mrs. Swann into bed and then went to the office to write a note to Mr. Grapes:

> Mr. Grapes, Please be advised that our newest male model, Mr. John Smith, will report for work in the studio at seven in the morning. Use him in addition to our regular cast, but with the following limitations: he must be fully dressed, and he must be placed in the background only. He does not want to *do* anything, other than watch the proceedings, but I sense that he is extremely good at that. Think of him as a sort of memento mori. I will be engaged in a personal matter much of the day and unavailable for consultation. I entrust the studio to you.

It was the first time he had ever left the studio in Mr. Grapes's hands, and he folded the note with a sense of its momentousness. Mr. Grapes was taking photographs; Mr. Smith, a customer, was working in the studio. Everything was changing and there was no telling the outcome.

He gave the note to the little maid, Jane, to deliver to Mr. Grapes's room, and then returned to the guestroom where Mrs. Swann was sleeping. At first he sat in the corridor outside, feeling that it would be improper to enter; then he entered, reasoning that she might have taken ill. He found her in a troubled sleep, murmuring things he could not understand and tossing her head on the pillow. After some hesitation, he put his hand on her forehead and she calmed. He took his hand back and watched her engaged in a new and better sleep, for which he took silent credit. It was not that hard, taking care of someone. He settled back in his wheelchair, gazing at the slight rise in the heavy quilts, the sliver of face beneath a mass of hair. At some point he must have fallen asleep as well, because it was midmorning when he awoke, judging from the seam of whiteness at the edge of the curtains. Someone was knocking at the door—and then Jane padded in bearing a silver tray with a visiting card. Silently, Auerbach took it in his hand:

LEOPOLD I. SWANN

SPIRIT PHOTOGRAPHER

"THE UNTHINKABLE MADE VISIBLE"

Auerbach had assumed that Swann would seek to retaliate, but from a distance, perhaps through some kind of blackmail scheme— yes, money would be his most likely medium of revenge. But he had never imagined a personal visit. It was so brazen, so completely shameless; it suggested someone who would stop at nothing. "Where is he?" he whispered.

"The salon off the foyer, sir."

For years, the only people Auerbach ever dealt with in person were naked, and he was beginning to realize what a great advantage that had given him. Naked people listened and did what they were told. But Leopold Swann was six feet four inches of impudence and cunning, encased in a frock coat. He had legs like tree trunks, a heavy black beard, and a voice that was silvery and dark.

That was why he had chosen to come: to use his height and broad shoulders against the cripple in the wheelchair—to draw a visual contrast for Mrs. Swann. Auerbach glanced over at her, still asleep beneath the covers. It was better to deal with him now than risk his coming around later, when she was awake and could see the difference between the two men. "I'll go with you," he whispered to Jane, and then followed her out to the salon.

If Swann was intimidated by the splendor of the mansion, he did not show it. He stood in the middle of the room as if staking it out for his own, his legs planted far apart in their gray, striped pants, his big shoulders thrown back, and his hands clasped behind his back. "Mr. Auerbach," he said. "I am here to clear up our little misunderstanding."

"Has there been one?" asked Auerbach.

Swann's look seemed to say that it was only natural for a cripple to imagine himself a knight rescuing a damsel—natural and forgivable. "She is so brilliant and so beautiful, so utterly beguiling," he said. "You would have to know her as intimately as I do to see the problem beneath it all." It was an obvious pose: one aficionado of womanhood speaking confidentially to another about the vulnerabilities of the male heart.

"You imprisoned her in order to force her to marry you."

"That is pure delusion, the product of her sickness."

"You kidnapped her from my home." Auerbach's voice quavered. He remembered the shock of finding her gone, the place setting empty at the table.

"I admit to that," said Swann, thrusting out his chest and raising his chin. "But there was no other way. I promised my brother that I would protect her, and I will keep that promise for the rest of my life."

"Mayhew was going to cut her open—butcher her—all for some kind of medical experiment."

That did it: Swann grew like a balloon filling with air. "That is a lie! A lie! A damn lie! You think of her as a saint or a martyr, but the truth is different. What you don't know is that I have used up my life in her service. It was necessary that I do something to save us both from the abyss."

It was impressive, a man of that size and voice yelling like that, waving his arms as if addressing a crowd. Auerbach recoiled, and yet he could not really tell whether the outburst was calculated or genuine. In any case, he held his ground. "Well, then, you're saved—free to go. I will take responsibility for her from now on."

"Do you expect me to simply sign her over to you, like a package?" Swann gave a bitter, sarcastic laugh, a stage laugh. "I demand to see her right away. I am going to take her home."

"She is asleep," said Auerbach. The confrontation had veered in exactly the wrong direction. He knew he could not allow Swann to see her.

"Wake her then," said Swann. "Bring her out here and ask her what she wants to do. I know how she will answer."

"I won't let you bully her."

Swann's muscular chest swelled, and he pointed a thick finger at Auerbach. "I will go to the police, the newspapers. Oh, they will have great fun with this." He swept his hand in the air as if mapping out the newspaper headline: *Merchant of Perversion Kidnaps Widow of National Hero*. Church groups will picket outside your gate. The police will seize your shipments. Miss Larue will sell her story to one of the weeklies. Even the Clean Living League will be unable to help you." Again the laugh, booming this time.

Auerbach waited till it had passed. "I will not give in to blackmail," he said, very quietly. He had of course considered the various forms of ruin available to a businessman in his field; there was nothing that Swann could add. But he was tired of paying and paying, simply to exist.

It was then that he noticed the figure in the doorway: Mrs. Swann, wrapped in a red silk dressing gown that he recognized from the studio, her long hair loose about her shoulders. She came forward into the open, looking from one man to the other, and then turned to her brother-in-law. "Please do not threaten him, Leopold."

Swann moved forward as if to embrace her, his arms open. "Verena, thank God you're all right. He hasn't hurt you, has he?" Auerbach watched from his chair, helpless to stop him.

"Do not touch me," she said, darting behind a sofa.

Swann stopped where he was, surprised and clearly hurt. "Verena, don't do that. I was only trying to help you. Mayhew told me it was necessary."

She kept her hands braced on the sofa back, ready to run. "Please don't make it worse, Leopold. Go home."

"I don't know what he's told you about me, but it isn't true. He's twisted your mind against me. He is just using you."

"I want you to leave."

"Not without you."

She seemed so fragile, so pained—it was not at all clear that she would be able to stand her ground. Yet she came out from behind the couch, tightening the neck of her dressing gown. "I cannot go with you, Leopold. Mr. Auerbach has asked me to marry him, and I have accepted." She walked over to Auerbach and placed her hands on his shoulders, as if posing for an engagement photograph.

Auerbach sat, stunned. A current seemed to radiate out from her fingertips and down his spine, and it did not matter to him that all three of them knew her announcement to be a fiction.

"That's absurd," said Swann, looking utterly disdainful. "I won't allow it."

"You will have to, because I am pregnant."

"This is in poor taste, Verena."

Mrs. Swann turned and planted a long kiss on Auerbach's mouth. It was difficult to register all of it as it happened: the force of her lips against his, the taste of her mouth, the heat of her face. And then she drew back, looking into his eyes. "Tell him the truth, dear," she said.

"Yes," said Auerbach, finding it hard to form the words. He had never kissed anyone before. "It is true. She is pregnant. We are getting married."

Auerbach could see that Swann did not completely believe this, but that it did not matter: he obviously understood that something essential had shifted and she would not be going with him. His face had lost all expression, as if his haughty, mocking intelligence had receded into some interior part of his being. He looked around the salon, for the first time noticing the splendor of its furnishings. When he spoke again it was with the self-possession of a man who has decided to throw everything away. "If you mean to take her off my hands, it is only fitting that you know the truth," he said. "She is a fraud. An incorrigible, relentless, unredeemable fraud."

That word, *fraud*, landed like a blow from a stick; Auerbach winced with the impact. Mrs. Swann dropped her hands from his shoulders and stumbled to a sofa. They looked at each other for a moment, shamefaced—as if deceiving and being deceived were equally humiliating—and then turned away, overwhelmed.

"But you forget that I've seen her," Auerbach said to Swann, meaning his mother's spirit. In fact, all he could remember was the *effect* of seeing her, like opening one's eyes to purest scrubbed sunlight after years of darkness.

"What you saw was Maisie in a sheet," said Swann.

And yet that moment had given him the strength to ride through a storm to save Mrs. Swann. He looked over at her where she sat, hanging her head. His mistake, he realized, was letting the conversation go on too long, into places it should not have gone. He pulled out his pocket watch and went through the motions of checking the hour. "I am afraid my fiancée and I must get ready for another appointment now. I must ask you to leave."

"Very well, then, believe what you like," said Swann, with something like his earlier disdain. He straightened his cuffs and tugged on the lapels of his black frock coat, preparing for his grand exit. "You will see. It is not that she is ever false—just that she is never true."

It was a long time until Auerbach turned to look at Mrs. Swann. She was sitting in the exact same position on the sofa, hands by her sides. "Do you want me to leave?" she asked.

The dressing gown had fallen open to show two pink knees, touching in their vulnerability. A part of him *did* want her to leave— it would be so much simpler—but that was the part of himself he had grown used to resisting. "His motives are obvious. Pay no attention."

"How can you *not* pay attention?" she asked.

"Because I know what is necessary." That head on his chest, those hands on his shoulders, his mother's voice, returned to him after thirty years.

"But you will always be thinking about it," she said. "I don't want charity from you."

"Shouldn't you try to deny it, then?" he asked.

"Would you believe me if I did?"

"I would if it were true."

She looked up at the ceiling, as if the story were written there. "At the beginning it was true. It was just as if I'd gotten a letter from him. I'd read the words over and over again, and feel—less frightened."

This was more familiar territory to him than true or false; his business experience prepared him to recognize a need. "I can make you safe," he said, and a picture came into his mind: Mrs. Swann wrapped in his arms, protected. "I can at least try."

She came over then and took his face in her hands—a feeling for which he had no equivalent in his adult life. It was as if he were a boy again, and his mother inspecting him with that mixture of gratitude and amazement he had once taken for granted—his due as her child.

"You were never supposed to make me feel this way," she said, and then leaned toward him, closer and closer until she filled his vision.

He had seen it a hundred times a day for twenty years: the slight

turn of the face to avoid the nose; the eyelids closing; the lips parting. But this was completely different: her lips, her tongue, the crash
of her breath in his ear, and the rhythmic slamming of his own
breath, like the waves against the pilings at South Ferry.

A little later, in his bedroom, he lay in bed under the mink coverlet,
and watched as she let her dressing gown drop to the floor. She was
surprisingly thin, all nervous muscle, rib cage, and hip bone—the
bare architecture of womanhood. He compared her to Jane Larue
and the other photographic models—voluptuous, hothouse flowers. And yet Mrs. Swann seemed to fill the room as if nothing else
were there. It was the way she held herself, with a great, burning self-
consciousness. Miss Larue had been that way at the beginning too.

"Do you like what you see, Augustus?" she asked.

It was the first time she had used his given name—the first time
anyone had, since his mother died. He drew the coverlet tight
around his chin. "Yes, I do, Verena." In truth, he hardly knew what
he was looking at; it was an entirely different order of nakedness
than he was used to: not something happening for the camera—
something happening to *him*.

"You must be used to such beautiful women," she said.

The question made him think of Jane Larue once more, and
what he felt this time was regret. He had pampered and indulged
her, but only in the way a racehorse is indulged, as a reward for running. "I am always completely detached at work," he said, feeling
that there was no adequate way to explain all that had happened, the
mistakes he had made. "It's like I'm not even there."

He realized that this did not make much sense. The important
difference was this: if she were Jane Larue, he would give her
detailed instructions: how to stand, how to sit, how to bend. She

would do whatever he said, giving form to what was in his mind, and the moment would be preserved in stereographs for others to hunger over.

"Would you like to touch me?" asked Verena.

His mouth went dry. "Yes," he said, studying the sheer fact of her: the way her breasts pointed outward; the deep wells of her collarbone; the small scar on her arm; the dark mole to one side of her belly button. Each detail seemed exactly right in its *herness*, its irreducible truth. He felt an impulse to reach out and touch that mole, to run his fingers over the fine hairs that ran from belly button to pubic area, but he hesitated, uncertain what the ultimate result of so extreme a gesture might be. "You are more beautiful than any of them," he told her.

She smiled wistfully, as if she did not believe him. "I can lie down beside you, if you like."

"Yes," he said, gripping the mink coverlet tight in his fists.

"You won't need that." She pulled it from his grasp, drawing it down till his legs lay sprawled out in front of him, clothed in their striped pants and calfskin boots—the legs of a little boy. She looked them over, but registered no surprise, no alarm. Instead she busied herself removing his clothing: coat, vest, necktie, suspenders, cuffs, collar, shirtfront, and undershirt.

He gave himself over to her, rolling to one side or the other to help, and it was not till his eyes welled with tears that he realized he was afraid. He thought of the thousands of nights he had been too frightened to sleep—too frightened to do anything other than dictate letters to men who were themselves too frightened to look up from their stereoscopes. He had somehow taken himself out of the stream of events that make up life. This was, in a sense, the first real thing that had happened to him in years. "Are you sure about this?" he asked her.

"Aren't you?"

He was not sure of anything anymore, but he kept silent and watched her finish the rest: pants, garters, socks, and then underwear. He looked down at his naked legs, and then up at her, searching her face for any sign of incipient revulsion. It seemed better that he say it first. "They must disgust you," he said.

"Of course not."

Her face was so carefully at ease, he could only assume she was acting. "You can tell the truth," he said.

"Nobody listens to the truth." She climbed on the bed and then lay down beside him, her face just inches from his. "Kiss me," she said.

He brought his lips to hers, which opened in response—as if the world itself were opening, drawing him inward. If only he could completely devour her, and in the process be completely devoured, the mystery would be solved and he could rest forever. But no end was truly possible. The more deeply he kissed, the more she pressed against him, until finally he felt her reach between his legs. It was a strangely proprietary gesture, as if his hunger were now hers.

"Here, let me," she said, pushing him to his back. She crawled on top of him and then reached down and placed him inside her. He felt caught, fused. How strange, he thought, making a business of something for years and never truly understanding. But in the next instant the thought was slipping beyond his grasp, carried away in a stream of sensation: eye, hair, lips, chin, breasts, the up-and-down motion of her body like the rise and fall of waves.

"What if we have a child?" he asked—and then immediately thought of Augie Larue. The sweet, sad voice from the séances remained utterly convincing to him, regardless of Verena's disclaimers. What they were doing now only proved it, somehow.

"Could you love me?" she asked, out of breath.

He felt the shape of the idea, not with his mind but his hands—his hands that grasped her thighs, that felt the totality of her contained in his grip. "Yes," he told her.

"Ah," she cried, moving faster.

"And what about you?" he asked. "Could you?"

She kissed him long and hard.

He reached inside himself, groping for the words with which to tell her all the necessary things: that the sweat on her shoulders glistened in the late-afternoon light; that he had never imagined this moment; that life has a shapeliness no less real because we cannot comprehend it. But when he finally opened his mouth to speak, the full contents of his mind came pouring forth as a long deep moan.

22. LEOPOLD SWANN MAKES SENSE OF THE PAST

Leopold Swann hurried down Fifth Avenue as if he were on his way to a pressing engagement, though in fact he had no engagement—indeed, hardly knew where he was going. Instead of the sidewalk and shade trees and limestone mansions, he saw Verena kissing Auerbach. He recalled the many months he had yearned for just such a kiss, and the many times it had been denied to him; he recounted each of her excuses and evasions. A swelling began in his chest, a compound of sorrow and anger and burning-hot humiliation.

Was he not twice the man that Auerbach was—ten times the man? He could lift great barbells, charm irritable widows, make spirit photographs so convincing that even the most suspicious would break down in tears. He had greatness in him—he could feel it inside, striving to get out. But life never gave him a chance to use his talents, and so he was nothing. Less than nothing! A rich man like Auerbach could stretch out his hand and steal Verena away on the merest whim, and there was nothing he could do about it. Nothing!

All his life, he had encountered nothing but roadblocks and barriers. The year Theodore went on his first Arctic expedition, Leopold bought an old carnival and took it down the Mississippi in a paddle wheeler, stopping to perform in the small river towns along the way. If Theodore was going to be the next Franklin, he reasoned, then he, Leopold, would be the next Barnum—a far greater thing. But the boat took on water, and the troupe came down with dysentery and finally disbanded in Arkansas, with just two dollars left in the exchequer. He made it back to New York in time for Theodore's victory parade.

Was that his fault? Could he control the weather? Could he keep an old boat from leaking? He had labored like a man possessed, tending the animals, doctoring his hapless performers, working the bilge pumps and stoking the boiler when the crew fell ill, sleeping only an hour a night. But nothing he did mattered; the end was preordained—because he was who he was, the *other* Swann.

And so it continued through the years, each attempt foiled by bad luck and other people, their incompetence, stupidity, and lack of faith—until Theodore was lost and Verena became available, and he found an opening for them in the Spiritualist game. For the first time things worked out as he envisioned them. Verena took direction. The weepers swarmed around him, pulling at his elbow, vying for the chance to empty their wallets. Suddenly he was respected, sought after, desired, *loved*—just like Theodore had been loved.

And that was when she chose to destroy it all.

You temptress, you seductress, you whore! It was I who did the research, who gave you the information you needed to make your ghosts real! It was I who cultivated the weepers, the newspaper editors, the psychic investigators, the rich and influential. I slaved for you in the shadows, so that you might shine in public.

He walked on, oblivious to the passing hours and the changing scenery, till he noticed that they were lighting the streetlamps. He had made it all the way downtown: Union Square was up ahead, with its theaters, music halls, placards and billboards, electric lights and noise. Another block and the sidewalk grew crowded; the press of bodies made him realize how tired he was—exhausted, near toppling. But he would not—*could* not—go home. The town house was full of her, drenched with her presence: her perfume, her dresses, her books, all the things he had given her. He was afraid to go back.

He stopped in front of one of the vaudeville houses, and without even glancing at the placard, bought a ticket, climbing the stairs up to the balcony. Onstage, a juggler was in the midst of his act, tossing flaming swords from one hand to the other and high into the air—faster and faster till they seemed to blur into one great loop of flame. But Leopold barely paid attention. His mind wandered to the time Theodore had first introduced him to Verena outside a little tea shop. She was small and dark, and still very, very young, her face half-hidden beneath a hat as big as a barge—one of her mother's creations. It was not till she removed it in the shop that he understood his brother's infatuation. She had eyes of such startling intelligence—eyes that saw right away what you wanted.

And so she became another thing of his brother's that he coveted.

A burst of applause drew his attention back to the stage. The juggler took his bows and was immediately replaced by a troop of toy poodles—little dogs with their sleek woolen bodies and frothy heads. Leopold watched with a bitter sort of amusement. Had not Verena also seemed like a little poodle? Eager to please, quick to snap, in need of care. He watched as the dogs began their performance, leaping through hoops and over sticks, climbing ladders, diving off ledges, crossing paths in midair—a chain of acrobatic cause and effect. They seemed to know exactly what to do. Their trainer, a woman in dancer's tights and a gauzy tulle skirt, merely lifted her baton and off they went, like thoughts.

There had been moments just like that with Verena—moments

of perfect accord, when a significant glance from him, or a press of the foot, or a squeeze of the hand would launch her into the most thrilling acts of spirit ventriloquism he had ever witnessed. Someone would spring up from the table and yell, "Aunt Clara!" or "Cousin Jeb!" and the others would twist into postures of fear and awe and the deepest, truest satisfaction. At such times there was no Verena, no Leopold—only one perfect person in perfect command of the world.

Leopold sat forward in his seat now, interested in spite of himself. For their finale, the dogs wore human dress and sat at a table laid out with silver and crystal. Their trainer raised her baton, and they passed serving dishes to one another, ladled soup into bowls. Leopold followed one dog in particular, a little gray poodle in a frilly white gown. She bent her head to her tablemate on the left, then to her tablemate on the right, and then wagged her head up and down. *All I wanted to do was help her achieve her true potential*, thought Leopold. *It would have saved us both*. He stared at the dog trainer, who stood serenely to one side, and felt so envious he could have murdered her.

He spent the next few days burning Verena's things in the fireplace—beginning with letters, notebooks, photographs, and then moving on to hats and dresses. Maisie hid in her room upstairs, coming out only to make him meals he did not eat. He canceled all sittings, not sure how to explain Verena's defection, not even sure that he wanted to. Why should he make excuses for her? He inclined toward giving up the spirit game altogether and starting something new. That was what he had always done in the past, when a line of work failed to meet expectations. He thought of opening a kinetoparlor or perhaps going on Wall Street, but in truth his future felt blank.

The fire went all day and much of the night, till he finally passed out on the buffalo skin spread in front of the hearth, poker still in hand. The house filled with a permanent haze; everything smelled of smoke. Maisie stopped coming out of her room altogether, even for meals. But Leopold began running out of things that would burn, and soon the fire was cold and he was furiously boxing up the inflammables: jewelry, shoes, mirrors, brushes, and combs. The fact that they were so outlandishly expensive only increased his satisfaction. He took them out—more than a dozen boxes in all—and left them on the corner.

The next day he dressed and went out, testing the world again, like a man with a hangover, sensitive to light and noise. He walked around Washington Square, and then the adjoining streets, pretending to window-shop while thinking about the possibilities before him. If he wanted to stay in the spirit game, there was always Maisie. She knew a great deal already; it would not take much to train her to fill Verena's role. She would be pliant, easy to work with. There would be none of Verena's histrionics, her nervous difficulties. And he sensed she had a personal interest in him that would give him useful leverage, a means to control and shape her. But Maisie did not have Verena's extraordinary talents, and would never be as good a medium. Leopold could not bear the idea that his life after Verena would be anything less brilliant than his life with her.

He stopped in at a bookseller's, more for the quiet of the shop than for the books, and spent twenty minutes or so wandering up and down the narrow aisles, running a gloved finger over the spines, until one of the volumes happened to catch his attention. It was Pinchbeck's *The Expositor; or, Many Mysteries Unraveled*—a classic treatise on the arts of magic and deception. He pulled it out and began leafing through it, browsing from magic tricks to mind-reading acts to the training of "learned" animals—which reminded him of the toy poodles he had seen the week before, performing in such perfect unison, as in a lovely dream. Perhaps for that reason he bought it, thinking it might provide some distraction.

It did not work, of course. Each time he sat down with it, his thoughts drifted back to Verena. He kept asking himself why—why Verena had betrayed him. Was it really the power of Auerbach's money, or was it something he, Leopold, had done, a mistake of some kind? Perhaps sending her to Mayhew's asylum had been a misstep, though what choice did he have? By that point only the most extreme remedies had any chance of working. She had already destroyed the bond of trust between them.

When he did finally begin to read—late at night, a bottle of whiskey by his side—what he discovered was a revelation. Far more than a manual on how to train animals, what Pinchbeck offered was a book of practical philosophy on the nature of love. It started from the principle that the hidden wish of all animals is a state of selfless devotion, and that it is by granting this wish that the animal trainer gains power over the animal. It went on to show how this power could then be used to make animals perform extraordinary feats—dancing, acrobatics, even arithmetic—to the point that they seemed almost to pass from the bestial realm to the human.

Selfless devotion! Verena had seemed selfless to him too, till the other side of her had begun to show. She clung to his shirtfront and hung on his every word, asked only to become whatever he most wanted her to be—and then hated him for it. Was that not the real reason for her betrayal? Not Auerbach's money, not Mayhew's madhouse. She hated Leopold for granting her wish. And so the betrayal had always been there, hidden in the devotion.

He rose and looked out the window, where the city was rematerializing in the blue of dawn. He would never allow another woman to fool him like that.

23. AUERBACH MAKES SENSE OF HIS DREAM

Auerbach awoke in the dark, breathing heavily, a cry of sorrow lodged in his throat. He had dreamed that he was in the studio, taking photographs of Jane Larue. She was dressed in the white satin gown that his mother had worn in *God's Newest Angel,* and she held baby Augie in her arms. "Quick, before he knows he's gone!" she whispered, but Auerbach was equipped with the glass plates he had used during his apprenticeship, thirty years before, and they required time to prepare and change. In the next moment, Verena was beside him, pulling on one end of the plate he held in his hand. "Don't look," she said, and he saw an image of his mother floating on the glass, looking as she had when she sang him to sleep. He smashed the plate on the floor, and then that shattering became the destruction of the studio itself, glass showering down around him.

He sat up and looked over at Verena, who slept on, breathing deeply. He was aware of an absurd little spark of resentment, as if the woman curled beneath the sheets were the same woman in the dream. He reached down and found his pajamas on the floor, dressed in the dark, then climbed into his wheelchair and arranged the lap rug over his legs.

Out in the hallway, he felt as if a magic spell was wearing off, and he was becoming himself again. He had not been to the office in days, and the implications, the consequences, were suddenly clear to him. The correspondence must be piled to the ceiling. Mr. Gupta was probably in arrears again, and what about the catalogue? He had no idea what Mr. Grapes had been doing in the studio, whether it would cohere as it should—whether Mr. Grapes was even *going* to the studio and producing photographs.

What if there were no photographs? Would Verena continue to sleep beside a cripple with no gigantic oil paintings on the walls, no golden cutlery on the dining table? She might think so, but he knew better. To keep her, he would have to give her diamonds for each spoke on his wheelchair, emeralds for each stunted toe on his feet.

He wheeled down the hall into the office, a little frightened of the thousands of pages that would be piled on every flat surface in the room. How would he get through them all? He reminded himself that he had survived worse dangers. There was the time he had gotten the croup and missed two days of work. He had come in on the third day wrapped in a bearskin coat with hot water bottles in the pockets, and still shivering…But what he saw when he turned on the incandescent lamp was so unexpected that it made his breath stop.

The room was clean of paper. There was not even a stray envelope to be seen. He wheeled over the carpet, passed his hand over the polished surface of the desk and the soft leather of the couch, as if his fingers might convince him of the fact. Where were the contracts and invoices, the letters of entreaty and woe, the business proposals with their lies and tricks? He remembered the dream, and the sorrow that came wrapped inside like a caramel, sticky and sweet. Was this the end of Rive Gauche? Not a storm of glass, but this deep silence?

He rang for Miss Parish, and called to her even before she had time to clear the doorway. "Where is it? There should be stacks of it, and it's gone."

She was dressed in her quilted housecoat and slippers, and she looked at him with sleepy confusion. "I'm sorry, Mr. A. I wasn't expecting you back quite yet. Mrs. Swann had mentioned that you were having a champagne supper and—" She stopped, seeming to realize she had said too much.

How did they even know each other? thought Auerbach. How did everyone in the mansion know each other when he knew no one? "The correspondence, Miss Parish. Why isn't it here?"

She nodded, took a deep breath, then turned and opened one of the file cabinets, speaking very rapidly as she searched. "I knew you wouldn't want to fall behind, and after so many nights of taking dictation, I felt that I had a general sense of what you might want to say." She turned back to him, a thick folder in her hands. "But of course I kept copies of everything." She laid the file on the desk in front of him and then stepped back quickly, as if from an open fire.

He stared at the manila cover. "You've been answering my mail," he said, barely above a whisper.

"Only out of necessity, sir."

He opened the file slowly, forcing his eyes over the pages inside: *Dear Mr. Gupta… In regard to the current arrears…compelled to take immediate legal action…As always, warmest regards to Mrs. Gupta… Dear Mr. Chang… As to our discussion of openings in the China market… At a reasonable and fair discount…* He struggled to make sense of what he read, as if translating from a foreign language. The phrases were apt, he realized, the sentences succinct—just the sort he would have composed—and yet they tore at his heart like sharp stones. At the bottom of each letter were the words *Miss Annabelle Parish on behalf of Mr. Augustus Auerbach, President and Sole Proprietor.*

"How could you?" he asked.

Miss Parish looked stricken. "I thought you would be glad."

"Did you have any idea of the complexity of these decisions, the subtlety of the phrasing they required?"

"I knew I could never equal your genius, but something had to be done. They were waiting for an answer."

He closed the file and pushed it aside, and then turned to gaze out the window at the garden, which was silvery in the moonlight, a stereograph that moved and breathed in the wind. He had been replaced by the typewriter and it didn't even matter. He was no longer completely himself, the president and sole proprietor of Rive Gauche, the man who was going to revolutionize an industry, and it was Verena's fault, just as in the dream. "She wants to change me," he said finally. "She doesn't approve of the business."

Miss Parish walked over to the typewriting machine and turned her chair to face him. "Are you sure of that, Mr. A.?"

"It's not anything she says, it's the flicker that passes over her face whenever I tell her I have to go to the office."

"Have you thought of trying something else, then?"

The idea struck him as absurd—maddeningly absurd—and yet he realized that he had, in a sense, already considered it. Just two days before, Verena had taken him on a brief excursion to the docks, and for the first time ever he had seen the barges that carried his photographs up the Hudson: squat creatures that hunkered low in the water, filled with wooden packing crates. A steamship was just then pulling a line of them out into the middle of the river, smoke from its chimney trailing like a woman's feather boa, and Auerbach had watched it go, wondering what it would be like to steer such a craft, to witness the red brick walls and copper roofs of the city slipping away.

But there were so many things he needed to learn first. "She wants to talk, and I'm not used to talking," he said to Miss Parish, smoothing out the blanket that covered his legs. "Dictation is another matter, of course."

"You are a superb dictator, Mr. A."

"She's always asking what I think and feel, and she seems to expect me to ask her the same."

Miss Parish nodded. "That would be hard if you are not used to it."

"And it is strange having so much idle time. Little things become excessively important. We were in the garden and there was a kind of tulip by the fountain, yellow and red with streaks of purple at the bottom."

"Yes, I know which ones you mean."

He had sat beside Verena, gazing at the tulips for what felt like a century, trying to hide his fright. What do you do with the sort of beauty that cannot be catalogued, packaged, and sold? How do you keep it from devouring you? "It can be taxing, Miss Parish. Sometimes I just wish for the old days when life was simple."

"I'm not sure the old days were ever so simple."

And so he thought that he might as well ask the question that had been circling his thoughts these last few minutes. "Have you heard anything from Miss Larue?"

"She leads a Spiritualist circle in San Francisco."

He imagined her standing on a dock much like the one he had just visited, looking out not at the barges and the river, but at the endless expanse of the Pacific, with that gentle, innocent face the camera so loved. "Have you ever wanted to change the past, Miss Parish?"

"Isn't that what the present is for?"

He thought of his dream, the image of his mother on the glass plate, and Verena telling him not to look. He had spent his entire life averting his eyes from the past, and therefore was ruled by it, sleepwalking through the present—the present, in which the real Verena slept even now in his bedroom. "I must go," he said, full of a new kind of urgency.

"Regards to Mrs. Swann," said Miss Parish.

But there was one more stop he needed to make. He wheeled himself out and down the long corridor that led to the studio, then passed through the entrance. Moonlight silvered the floor. The glass was up above, unbroken but invisible; beyond it, stars spread like sparks from an explosion. He wheeled toward the stage set, recalling how in the dream Verena had tried to pull the plate from his hand. He remembered now that he had not let go. No, he had held on, and smashed the plate down a moment later, with a big arc of his hands. It was *he* who had destroyed the studio. That was the meaning of the dream—or at least, out of all the possible meanings, that was the one he would choose.

He turned his wheelchair and headed out, back into the hall, back to his room, and got into bed beside Verena. She grasped him without opening her eyes, and he felt his body melt into hers. Her voice was dark and breathy. "Where have you been?" she asked him.

"Nowhere, my darling. Go back to sleep."

24. LEOPOLD SWANN AND MADAME BRUNUS

There was no clear moment when Leopold decided to train a performing animal. He simply began visiting the various exotic animal dealers in the city, looking over pythons, cockatoos, hawks, vultures, ferrets, and iguanas—even a seal with the face of a tragedienne. But when he came across the small brown she-bear cub, he knew he had found the animal he would train. The bear cub was like a child transmogrified into something dangerous, with sharp little teeth and a blunt wet nose, and paws that were almost the wish for hands.

Leopold built a den for the bear cub in the cellar, and let it travel up the stairs and into the parlor as it chose. It slunk out on all fours that very first evening, head down, shoulder bones working one at a time beneath its loose coat of fur. The click of its toenails was light and strangely musical. It breathed with great concentration, its mouth open and loose black lips drooping like a band of India rubber, its babyish canines exposed to the air. It took the piece of meat Leopold offered and began to chew. Leopold stroked its back. "I am going to teach you some tricks," he told it. "Some very simple tricks. When you do them right, you will be rewarded. And when you do them wrong, you will be punished."

Leopold had always known that his primary asset in life was his voice. Whether he was selling life after death or a cure for cancer, it had fired the desire of his audience. Verena too had felt its power. But he had never known anyone to listen like the bear listened, its nose in the air and black lips open, saliva falling in strings. It mattered not at all whether Swann read the paper or recited a nursery rhyme—it pulled the sound deep within itself like cigarette smoke. Leopold's voice was its religion and its music.

He began introducing the bear to the large alphabet cards that would be the learned-animal act's most important stage properties. He arranged them in a semicircle on the floor of the parlor and led the bear to first one and then another, holding out a piece of sausage as a reward. Crawling on all fours, he demonstrated how to pick the cards up and hold them in the mouth without dropping them. The bear quickly mastered the technique. Soon, Leopold could simply point to the card he wanted it to lift, and eventually, he found that Pinchbeck had been right:

> Intimacy will make speech and even gesture superfluous; you may relinquish them by degrees. Once that is done, the animal will appear to read your very thoughts. The way in which you stand will arise naturally from your anxiety and will determine the card to your pupil. Nothing else is needed.

Based on this wordless communion, Leopold taught the bear to spell—or rather, to simulate the act of spelling, picking up the alphabet cards he wanted it to pick up, yet with an air of independence and purpose. On the same principle, he taught it to do arithmetical calculations, using a set of numbered cards. He would read out the problem, the bear would pause as if calculating, and then pick up the card bearing the correct answer. From there it was a short step to factual questions of the sort that could be answered with a simple yes or no—these two words imprinted on cards for that purpose. All of these tricks depended on the same basic precept given by Pinchbeck: "Nothing can be done but its master must first know what he wants. Once its master knows, the animal will be ruled by his unspoken wishes."

Thinking it over, he decided to present the bear as a mind-reading act. It was a simple adjustment to make: Leopold already knew the basic techniques required of a mind reader—how to ask leading questions, how to read faces for hot and cold, true and false. As long as he himself could figure out the correct answer, the bear was assured of picking the right cards.

He began using Maisie in their practice sessions. Unflappable Maisie, who had rattled furniture, impersonated spirits, and otherwise helped at the séances, nevertheless had trouble with the bear. She stiffened as it approached and looked terrified. "Don't be ridiculous," Leopold scolded. "It's perfectly safe."

"It doesn't like me," said Maisie, her eyes fixed on the bear.

"That's because it knows you're afraid."

Maisie nodded at the logic of this. "I'm afraid because it wants to hurt me."

"Nonsense. This bear loves people." Leopold placed one hand atop Maisie's head, and the other on his own brow, and then called out, "Madame Brunus, tell us the woman's name!"

The bear sidled up close, clearly enjoying Maisie's discomfort. Hot meaty breath and a sharp nervous smell: the impression was not of an animal so much as a person gone terribly wrong. It held its wet nose just inches from her stomach, drawing short noisy sips of air, like an asthmatic. Its wet tongue lolled between its canines. Then, almost reluctantly, it moved off toward the semicircle of alphabet cards, its black nails clicking on the wooden floor. There was a preening feminine self-consciousness about its movements, as if it were aware of Leopold's gaze. It leaned over the oversized cards, staring nearsightedly with first one eye then the other. Finally it chose the M, lifting it in its mouth and carrying it over to Leopold's feet, to be followed in turn by the other letters, A, I, S, I, E.

"You see?" asked Leopold. "Just like Pinchbeck says. The bear has lived with us here like a normal human child. She knows nothing else. I am her master. I feed her. I am everything to her."

"It likes you too much," said Maisie.

Leopold laughed. "There's no such thing as too much! I am her father and her husband. She watches me like a farmer watches the sky. She cannot really spell, but she can read my face, my hands, the way I stand. I am her holy book, and—" he began to coo—"she is my sweet little girl." He popped a plug of sausage into the bear's mouth, and then rubbed vigorously behind its ear. The bear's mouth snapped shut and emitted a low obscene moan.

It was not hard getting a booking at one of the top houses on Union Square: traditionally, circus bears did nothing but the simplest of tricks, dancing and balancing on top of a medicine ball. They wore a muzzle and were led on a leash. But Leopold's bear was *learned*: it could communicate, display scholarship on most any subject, and most important, it could read minds. They were given the featured slot and top billing on the program.

Backstage in his dressing room, Leopold straightened his tie in the mirror and adjusted his top hat. He remembered how he had had to wrestle the sherry bottle away from Verena before séances, and how he had had to talk her through her deep-breathing exercises. Now he wondered if she had been doing him an inadvertent service. As long as she was terrified, he did not have to be. He could busy himself with taking care of her—with despising her, actually. But now that he was the only one around, he seemed to have inherited her role as the frightened one.

He found it odd that he was thinking about Verena, since he had all but forgotten her ever since he bought the bear. There had been the late-night walks past the Auerbach mansion, of course, but those were something different, a kind of lash he used to intensify his dedication to the austerities of animal showmanship. There was no longer any need for that kind of motivational trickery. In just a few minutes he would be escorting the bear onstage, and then everything in his life would change forever. He would be a public figure in his own right, free of any need for Verena or Theodore or the spirits, or even the bear, for that matter. What he had achieved with this bear would be reproducible with any other bear—that was the beauty of the thing. The creature was just a tool. The skill, the knowledge, the vital force were all his own.

It was time; he led the bear from the dressing room to their place in the wings. There was a short wait for their cue, and then they were through the curtain. The footlights made it impossible to see the audience, but he could feel its presence just beyond the edge of visibility, as shapeless and powerful as the ocean at night, murmuring, rustling, whispering, breathing. He put the bear through its paces, forgetting for moments at a time that Verena might conceivably be out there in the audience, watching. The spelling earned polite applause; the mathematics and geography a little more. His request for a volunteer brought a little girl up from her seat to stand beside him. He whispered in her ear and bent down so she could whisper back in his. He placed one hand atop her head, pressed the other to his brow, and called out, "Madame Brunus, tell us the child's name!"

The bear wore a blue satin cape imprinted with star and crescent moon, eyeball and pyramid. Leopold had brushed silver dust into its thick brown coat, and the dust shone in the light, making Madame Brunus look like a creature from another planet. It circled the alphabet cards laid out on the floor of the stage till it came to the R, then picked the card up and carried it over to the little girl, who hung it on the board Leopold kept alongside. Next, in quick succession, Madame Brunus brought an O, S, and E. "Is your name Rose, child?" asked Leopold. He held the little girl aloft in his arms so the audience could hear her shy assent.

Almost immediately, audience members were vying to ask questions about the future. The questions would come out of the darkness and Leopold would repeat them for the bear. "Will the gentleman get a promotion at work?" "Will the young lady marry her beau?" Madame Brunus would gaze into an enormous crystal ball—lit from within—and then choose one of the three cards laid out before her: YES, NO, and BEWARE. Each answer met with great applause, and at the end of the show the audience pounded the floor with its feet, demanding more.

Leopold stood next to the bear, taking elaborate bows. "They love us!" he whispered into its ear, hoarse with excitement, and then broke off to bow again, grinning as if he had just won the entire world with a single roll of the dice. "The stupid fools! They see magic, a miracle, but what is a miracle? Anything where the mechanism is not explained. But there is always a mechanism. Always."

The clapping intensified. He began blowing kisses to the audience, the bear doing likewise beside him, as it had been taught—one ungainly paw rising to its snout and then out and away. Leopold's thoughts raced. He had been a fool to admire Verena, as gullible as the audience shouting its questions to the bear. Verena was an illusion, just like Madame Brunus. She was a set of attitudes and gestures, a way of wearing a dress, a perfume, a manner of talking—all of which, taken together, created a certain intoxicating effect he knew as Verena. That's all she was, *an effect*, just as light from an incandescent lamp is an effect.

"The world is like a gigantic machine, with interlocking wheels and gears, one fitting inside the other," he told the bear, still blowing kisses this way and that. "You are forced by your very nature to love me, and I allow you to do so. I twitch the corners of my mouth, you pick a card, and the audience is amazed. Verena is just the same. Her choices are only the appearance of choices. She is a slave, and doesn't even know it."

It seemed like the applause would never end, but slowly it began to die away. They took one last bow together, and then the curtain closed.

25. THE WATER BY THE BRIDGE

Auerbach and Verena sat side by side in a paddleboat carved in the shape of a swan. It was Verena who did the peddling, sending them on a slow journey over the glassy surface of the lake in Central Park, which was the color of a brown bottle of beer. The weather was hot, the proximity to water headachey. Dragonflies dipped down to touch the murk, then swooped away. Other boats—shaped like swans, ducks, frogs—moved to the left and right. The occupants were mostly children in sailor suits and summer dresses, or courting couples—the men in straw boaters, the women holding parasols.

Verena was holding a parasol with pink fringes, and Auerbach was wearing a straw boater, but they were far older than the other couples and he, for one, felt a little self-conscious. In the last few weeks they had been everywhere, it seemed: the Museum of Natural History, the Museum of Art, a stroll down Fifth Avenue, even a restaurant. It was a lot to assimilate in such a short time.

He was getting better at being outside, he thought, though he was not sure he would ever truly get used to it. The too-muchness of it could be hard, even when riding on a paddleboat: the sunshine on the brown water; the tall grass waving at the shoreline; the breeze that seemed to carry the summer heat. He looked down at the outline of Verena's legs beneath the folds of her white cotton dress, and then at the blanket covering his own.

There were times he yearned for the clean simplicity of his old life, when he thought he knew who he was and why. Verena had introduced him to such longing, such need; because of her, simple answers no longer sufficed.

He reached into his coat pocket and put his hand on the little box containing the engagement ring. He had been carrying the box around for two days, trying to find the right moment, not sure what that moment might be.

Verena had given up pedaling and was now looking up at the clouds, a vague smile on her lips. "Are you getting tired?" he asked her.

"Just content to drift." It was true: she had been growing languid and dreamy over the last couple of days.

"I thought they had rowboats," said Auerbach. "If they had rowboats, I could have rowed us." He was still worried about being the invalid—there was no getting over that fear.

"The exercise is good for me," she told him. Indeed, she looked much healthier than she had only a few months before. She had gained weight, her limbs were thicker, her face fuller. When they undressed for bed at night, he no longer saw her ribs or the bumps of her spine.

It was still extraordinary to him, her presence in his bed. As they settled down to sleep, he gripped her from behind, feeling her shoulder blades against his chest, cupping her breasts in his hands. On those nights when he could not sleep, he no longer left for the office. Instead, he sat up and watched the deep concentration on her face, the slow in and out of her breathing. It seemed marvelous that there was this other way of being in the world, *her* way, and that if he could not ever truly know it or emulate it, he could at least reach out and touch it.

He stuck his hand in his pocket and grasped the box. "How is your book coming along?" he asked.

"I don't know. I'm afraid to read it." She laughed, as if this did not particularly bother her.

"You seem to be making progress." It was one of the benefits of traveling around on pneumatic tires that he could wheel himself into the doorway of her study without alerting her and watch her as she wrote. She sat at a delicate, feminine desk, a great ledger open before her. Sometimes she scribbled in a fury, her head down low over the paper, dipping her pen in the inkwell with surprising violence, little droplets of ink flying over her sleeves. Other times, she sat immobile, eyes up toward the ceiling, the pen forgotten in her hand.

"Oh, yes, the pages add up," she said. "But it's hard. I have to worry about what to say, and how to say it, and what it means. It was so easy when the spirits did it for me."

"But then you were limited to what they wanted to say."

"That's what made it easy."

And that was the reason her dreaminess worried him: he feared she might be snatched away from him by the spirits or by the past— by whatever was not their life together. "Am I in it?" he asked.

"You appear at the end." She looked toward shore, where couples strolled down the path by the water. "It's Theodore's birthday today."

Auerbach felt a pang, the twinge he felt whenever the name was mentioned. He released the box from his grip. This was not the day to ask her. "I'm sorry, I had no idea."

"We don't know when he died, exactly, so I've always used his birthday as a time to remember him."

"I wouldn't have suggested coming."

"I'm *glad* we came." She took his hand in hers. "I have a new life, with you, and I never believed that would be possible. This is the perfect way to mark the occasion."

He lifted her fingers to his lips and kissed them. "Do you want to do something else? Visit the grave?" It was a mistake to fight the first husband, he realized. It was better to embrace him.

"No, I want to ride around the lake with you." Verena began pedaling again, steering the boat to a more private stretch of water, near the little footbridge.

She had been meaning to tell Augustus about her condition for a couple of days now, but had not found the right moment. When she thought about it calmly, she knew there was nothing to worry about. He would be happy—happy in that frightened, mystified way of his. And yet she remained nervous. She wanted the baby more than anything she had ever wanted. She could feel it even now, she believed, a kind of gentle bubbling deep inside her.

"Verena," said Auerbach, as if broaching something difficult. "Do you still communicate with him?"

"With Theodore?" She stopped pedaling once again and turned as best she could in the small boat, to face him. "You know I don't do that anymore." In fact, this was not completely true. There had been one time, one time only, after she began to suspect that she was pregnant.

It had happened to her while she was working on her book. She had unlocked her desk and pulled out the large leather volume, just like the notebooks in which she used to take dictation from spirits. She opened the covers and ran her hand over the pages, still not used to seeing her own handwriting instead of Theodore's. It seemed incredible that these words were telling *her* story, from when she was a little girl, sick in bed, all the way to the present moment: a grown woman, a widow, finally pregnant with child.

She turned to the place at which she had left off, a passage describing her first meeting with Theodore, at the arcade: how they had stuck their fingers in the little electromagnetic generator, and the peppery tingling had seized control of their bodies, making it impossible to release hands. "I can't let go," she had said, laughing with the helpless pleasure of it.

"Good," said Theodore. "Because I don't want you to."

It had proved difficult to continue from there, and she had sat for what seemed like hours, the pen jiggling in her fingers. Eventually she felt that sleepy drift that was so familiar to her, followed by the pressure at the back of her neck, as if somebody were pinching her there. She dipped the pen in the inkwell, and it started to move over the paper.

It's a boy, it wrote, *with perfectly normal legs, and you will name him Theodore. And don't say you're sorry. I know you're sorry. This is a death sentence for me, of course, though I guess it was inevitable that some day you would be seduced away by another man, one with arms to hold you, and lips to speak.*

Not true, she said, understanding that of course it was true. We can still communicate. Any time you need me.

And will you *need me?*

I need you now.

You have him.

She felt his sadness, then, an overwhelming thing that seemed to rise up and fill her till she shook and gasped. It was as if he finally understood that life could not include the dead. And just when she thought she would drown in that sorrow, she remembered Augustus and the baby in her womb—a vein of such sweetness that she began to laugh through her tears.

That was the last time; she knew they would never speak again. And now she was in a little paddleboat, on a little artificial lake, beneath a clear blue summer sky, and Augustus was beside her. "I don't want to be anywhere but here, with you," she said.

He took her hand and kissed it again. "Thank you."

She began pedaling once more, directing them to the cool, shadowed privacy of the water by the bridge. She would tell him there.

EPILOGUE

Augustus Auerbach guided his wheelchair to the far end of the gilt ballroom, where the walking harness he had devised hung from its ceiling track, a tangle of straps and buckles. He slipped the contraption over his black cutaway, fastened himself in, and then pulled up on the hoist line with his powerful arms, swinging free of his chair. He bounced for a moment because of the carriage spring that connected the harness to the ceiling track, and then began letting out rope, till his patent leather boots made contact with the floor. The room was silent except for his breathing.

In another part of the house, Verena Auerbach sat at her desk, writing in a notebook the story of how she learned to talk to the dead. The child in her stomach kicked and she dropped the pen, splattering ink on the green felt blotter.

At that very moment, in a theater downtown, Leopold Swann stood onstage beside Madame Brunus, listening to the applause that filled the hall. He grasped the bear's paw in his hand, and together they took a deep bow.

Back in the ballroom, Augustus Auerbach began sliding his feet in a sort of abbreviated skating motion, moving across the floor as if it were a frozen lake. His plan was to gather speed until he had enough momentum to lift his foot and step, and it worked out better than he had expected: one step became two, three, four. With each he got a little more bounce from the spring at the top of the harness, until he was actually leaving the ground. He went faster, taking long, exaggerated leaps, his arms outstretched for balance, his coattails flapping behind him. He flew through a room of gold, on winds of electric light.

ACKNOWLEDGMENTS

Thank you to my publisher, David Poindexter, to my wonderfully sensitive editor, Kate Nitze, and to my supremely patient agent, Geri Thoma. Thank you to my readers: Jennie Litt, Timothy Bush, Margaret Mittelbach, Dana Sachs, Sarah Messer, Rebecca Lee, Nina de Gramont, David Gessner, and Clyde Edgerton (he of the lethal serve and the incisive line edit). Many thanks to Professor William D. Moore of the University of North Carolina at Wilmington, who guided me so nimbly through the history of esoteric thought, and also to my family: Frances, David, Perrin, Sean, Vassilios, Norma, and Victoria. Blessings on Jonah and Maia for opening my eyes and teaching me how lovely the dawn is. And a deeply humble thank-you to my wife, Karen Bender, who read every draft and listened to every muttering with the all-encompassing insight of love.

C.B.
2/08

M.G.
11/08

ML

3/0